A
MODEL
of
DEVOTION

A
MODEL
of
DEVOTION

MARY
CONNEALY

BETHANYHOUSE

a division of Baker Publishing Group
Minneapolis, Minnesota

© 2022 by Mary Connealy

Published by Bethany House Publishers
11400 Hampshire Avenue South
Minneapolis, Minnesota 55438
www.bethanyhouse.com

Bethany House Publishers is a division of
Baker Publishing Group, Grand Rapids, Michigan

Printed in the United States of America

Library of Congress Cataloging-in-Publication Data
Names: Connealy, Mary, author.
Title: A model of devotion / Mary Connealy.
Description: Minneapolis, Minnesota : Bethany House, a division of Baker
    Publishing Group, [2022] | Series: The lumber baron's daughters ; 3
Identifiers: LCCN 2022017361 | ISBN 9780764239601 (paperback) | ISBN
    9780764240805 (casebound) | ISBN 9781493439027 (ebook)
Subjects: LCGFT: Novels.
Classification: LCC PS3603.O544 M63 2022 | DDC 813/.6—dc23/eng/20220414
LC record available at https://lccn.loc.gov/2022017361

Scripture quotations are from the King James Version of the Bible.

This is a work of historical reconstruction; the appearances of certain historical figures are therefore inevitable. All other characters, however, are products of the author's imagination, and any resemblance to actual persons, living or dead, is coincidental.

Cover design by LOOK Design Studio
Cover photography by Aimee Christenson

Author is represented by the Natasha Kern Literary Agency.

Baker Publishing Group publications use paper produced from sustainable forestry practices and post-consumer waste whenever possible.

22 23 24 25 26 27 28   7 6 5 4 3 2 1

To Josie, Wendy, Shelly, and Katy

It was easy to imagine how smart,
well-educated women would think and act
because you grew up into brilliant women
in front of my eyes.

ONE

MARCH 1873
SAN FRANCISCO, CALIFORNIA

J ILLY STILES ALWAYS CAME BACK to the mansion on Nob Hill.

She was alone, and that never happened. Two sisters. A very attentive mama. Servants.

When had she ever been alone in her life?

Right now.

In the black hour before dawn, walking through the upstairs hallway with a burning candle, she approached the servants' stairway. Narrow and dark, winding tightly down to the kitchen just as fear wound tightly in her chest.

There were lanterns set in the wall sconces. At night, they were usually turned low, but now they were snuffed out. No lantern light, no bustling servants. No sisters, the mainstays of her life.

Only the circle of light from her flickering candle. She approached the top of the staircase in her white flannel nightgown. She shouldn't be out of her room dressed like this.

Where was her robe? Why hadn't she dressed before coming on this errand?

And what was her errand? She couldn't remember. Searching perhaps. Searching for Laura and Michelle.

They were lost. That was it. Her sisters were lost to her. Leaving her alone. Leaving her defenseless.

A shadow that shouldn't have been there cast itself on the wall ahead of her. She turned to look into the eyes of Edgar Beaumont, her stepfather.

He grabbed her and laughed as he dragged her into his bedroom. With a shriek of terror, she dropped the candle, and it rolled across the floor toward his bed. The lamps were slightly turned up in there, yet everything was murky, haunting. But not dim enough that she could fail to see the cruelty in Edgar's eyes. Feel the brutal grip of his hand.

The bedspread caught fire from the candle. Edgar ignored the growing flames.

He closed the door behind her with a loud slam and shoved her against it, pressing her to the door with the length of his body.

"You've flirted with me for the last time, Red." His voice dripped with something. She didn't quite recognize the tone, but it was a threat. She braced herself for something terrible to happen. The flames grew and crackled, she smelled smoke. She tried to shout a warning, but her voice wouldn't work.

"A woman who teases asks for this." Edgar laughed.

Jilly felt his hot breath blasting straight into her face. His breath was the fire, the smoke. She felt it burn her lungs. Turn her heart to ash.

"Your green eyes excite me. And everyone knows red hair

and green eyes hide a temptress. That's what you are, Jillian. A temptress."

Shaking her head, Jilly forced her throat to work. "No."

"Yes, beautiful tease." He grabbed her upper arms, shaking her violently. Her head whipped back and smacked into the hard oak door with a sharp thud. She felt the flames spreading around her, catching her nightgown on fire.

"You know this is what you've wanted." Edgar's fingers dug into her arms. She'd be bruised tomorrow. Bruised and burned.

The thud of her head continued until it was a knock at the door. The flames crept up her gown and spread to the door behind her. They caught on the bed, along the floor, spreading until the room burned all around.

In a house that was empty, except for her and Edgar, the thud penetrated her fear as if someone were really knocking.

Edgar's lips curved into a sadistic smile. "If you tell your precious mama this happened, I'll tell her you came to me. You are in *my* room in the night, after all. I'll tell her you threw yourself at me. She'll hate you for it. Moreover, if she doesn't hate you, if she takes your side . . ." Edgar leaned so close their lips could have touched. For a sickening moment, she was afraid he'd kiss her. Instead, he whispered, "I'll kill her and make you watch. Then I'll kill your sisters one after the other. And I'll do it right in front of your eyes."

The knocking grew louder.

"You know I'll do it, don't you, pretty tease? Keep your mouth shut." He tossed her aside.

She landed hard on the floor as he went out. The fire was

all around, crackling and snapping. Laughing at her as she realized she had no way to escape.

The knocking came again.

Jilly's eyes flickered wide when she saw the door swing open.

Laura poked her head in.

In an instant, Jilly realized the room was flooded with morning light.

No Edgar. No fire. No house on Nob Hill. Only her terror followed her into wakefulness. She was lying on the floor in her nightgown. Her heart was pounding, but she wasn't going to burn. Not today.

She was facing the door to her own room in the mountain mansion, not Edgar's room in the house on Nob Hill.

Edgar was gone. Long gone. Maybe forever, though she couldn't quite believe it.

"I heard you call out. I knocked, then there was a loud thud. You must've fallen out of bed." Laura rushed to her side and reached down for her. Jilly cringed away, then stopped herself.

But Laura saw, and the knowledge was in her eyes. "Bad dream again?"

Both of Jilly's sisters knew she was afraid. Knew she had nightmares. They had slept in the same room, after all. But they didn't know what caused them. They'd asked many times, but the words were frozen inside her. Keeping them there might be the difference between life and death for Mama. The difference for her sisters, too.

As Jilly got to her feet, the dream hung on, pressing out what was real.

Safety. Her sister. Bright daylight. Those were real.

Still, she was haunted by the dream. Always the dream. What had happened between her and Edgar hadn't been exactly like that. But the terror, the feeling that the world was burning down around her, the guilt for luring him away from his love for Mama. She carried it all.

Laura reached down a hand. Jilly, in control of herself this time, took Laura's hand and got to her feet.

Laura was the one Jilly had always protected. She'd probably pushed her around plenty, too, but she loved her little sister, and the big sister helping the little one was the natural order of things.

Now Laura was married to Parson Caleb Tillman and helping Jilly. Things were upside down.

"When are you going to tell me about your dreams?" Laura frowned, love in her gaze. "It might help to talk about it."

Jilly thought not. It would only make things worse.

Shaking off the remnants of the nightmare, Jilly checked the bedside clock and saw it was eight o'clock already. "Why'd you let me sleep so late?"

This was a big day, and she'd been waiting too long for it to arrive. She had a train track to build.

"There was no hurry to get up. When you sleep late, it usually means you've had a bad night."

"It was a fine night until I fell out of bed." Jilly's smile was meant to ease Laura's worry, but Laura's brow remained furrowed.

Jilly moved to her closet and pulled out clothes to get dressed for the day. She was wearing her usual white flannel nightgown, just like in the dream. Long sleeves, skirt brushing her bare toes. Collar buttoned up to her throat. Nothing teasing or tempting about it.

She stepped into her changing room and shed her night-gown, then pulled on her clothes. She dressed for comfort, not style, and that was always much faster.

"I wish you would've gotten me sooner. You know we start construction of the trestle today."

"The first load of lumber is heading for the gorge. It's slow going even on the trail you built. You can get dressed, eat breakfast, saddle your horse, and be there before they get the logs unloaded. You're not going to be one minute late. Nick's been out with the men since sunrise working on the railroad bed. He just came in to tell us they're finished with the stretch to the gorge and ready for iron railings."

She'd purchased the timber from Stiles Lumber, and she had hired extra men with extensive railroad construction experience. Massive steel girders for the railroad tracks were on order from California Ironworks and should be here any day.

Today was lumber. Mule teams were hauling it to the bottom of the gorge, where they'd build the base for the trestle. She'd charted a course that ran the tracks as low as she could over the gorges and riverbanks. One low-slung stretch of the tracks needed a bridge with a section that turned for the big boats that passed down the river.

It was thrilling to create blueprints, order material, and hire men. She couldn't control her excitement.

This was what she wanted for her life.

The nightmare faded, and the fear along with it.

She regretted every moment she'd slept past sunrise.

TWO

NICK RYDER STRODE AWAY from the railbed he'd spent weeks working on. It wasn't the job he'd signed on for, but somehow he'd ended up in charge—not counting Jilly—of building a rail line down a mountain. A train track sturdy enough to haul tons of tree trunks.

He walked back to the Stiles mansion through towering trees, down a flat stretch of ground wide enough for a train to pass, as it someday would if they could get this thing built.

Working on the railbed was a huge undertaking. Woods cleared, land leveled, rocks blasted. Jilly poking her nose in all the time, laying out the route they forged. Talking with him and the men about the maps she'd drawn in detail. Referring to the beautiful model she'd built for the biggest venture: a railroad bridge.

Her urgency almost pulsed off her. Nick knew they needed this train track built in one lumber season. And there was labor to be done every day of the summer to achieve that. The cost was staggering. Nick had seen the figures. The potential for profit was also huge, but they needed to start making that profit as soon as possible or Stiles Lumber, for all its impressive wealth, might not survive the expenditure.

Nick didn't mind Jilly being the boss. Every time she came near, the men sucked in their stomachs, stood a little straighter, flexed their arm muscles . . . usually with some effort to be subtle.

Because, as smart as she was—she was smart enough to humble a college professor—and hardworking as she was— she worked hard enough to humble a lumberjack—on top of all that, Jilly was beautiful.

Nick thought all the Stiles sisters were so pretty it wasn't really fair, as if God had been overly generous to this one family.

But redheaded, green-eyed Jilly topped them all. She made his heart want to speed up and stop at the same time. And that couldn't be good for him.

Her lively eyes could assess their progress, then she would use her surveying tools to change the route by inches, and order a finished section smoothed out or slanted at a slightly different degree. And she did all this without ruffling feathers. Not only would the men take it from her because she was the boss, the founder's daughter, and smarter than all of them combined, but also because she tended to smile at them when they eagerly agreed she was right.

And there wasn't much any man here wouldn't do to earn a smile from Jilly Stiles.

Nick cooperated completely, but he liked to think he had better control than the rest of the men. And to that end, he didn't follow her orders like an eager puppy. Oh, he followed her orders, because he knew she was smarter than him, too. But he kept the eager-puppy thing well under control.

Mostly.

For now, the railroad bed to the first gorge was hours away from being completed. He'd left a crew to finish up—save for the iron rails that had yet to arrive, nearly a week overdue.

They had cut a steep slope out of the heart of the dense forest to reach the bottom of the first valley. It was a wretched and difficult trail, but it was done at last, and today the trestle building would begin.

One wagon filled with steel bolts and cut wooden braces had already started down. Teams of mules hauled those heavy wagons down, then slowly, painstakingly, picked up logs that had been cut to clear the trail and dragged the timber to the place where Jilly planned to build a trestle.

This railroad track down a mountain was the biggest thing Nick had ever been involved in. In fact, building just the road to work alongside the railroad track was massive enough.

He, who'd worked at a bunch of jobs in his twenty-five years, was surprised how much he enjoyed this.

He ended each day eager for the next and eager for a well-earned deep sleep, unbroken by the bad dreams that had chased him through the years. Dreams of hungry children, an always round-bellied ma with another child on the way.

An angry pa.

And being cast out when all he could feel was fear.

But those were old dreams. That time was long past.

Now he was a friend to a family full of lovely, brilliant women. And keeping up with them as best he could was a challenge he enjoyed every day.

THREE

JILLY MADE SHORT WORK of getting up and going, still braiding her hair as she left the room. She had friends with maids who did their hair, helped them dress.

Not Jilly. And not her sisters, either. Oh, they had a lady's maid back in San Francisco, but they always left the servants behind to stay and tend the town house.

It was a very small crew who came out to the mountain-top mansion. And they'd brought even fewer of them this year.

Sarah, Mama's loyal maid of many years, had come. She couldn't be dissuaded. Besides Sarah, they had two porters to help with the heavy cleaning and lifting, the cook, and two young women who helped her get the meals and worked as maids. Jilly had spoken very quietly to the cook about steering clear of Edgar if he came back, and those young ladies were always together or at the cook's side.

That was the extent of the mansion staff, and if the place was a bit dustier than usual, Jilly thought it was a fair enough trade-off for the women's safety, with Edgar revealed to be of an unsavory character.

Though with Edgar gone for the last six months, they could have brought more servants, but things were working decently for now. And Mama was always afraid he'd come back. Mama and everyone else.

Jilly jogged down the stairs and reached the office about ten minutes after she woke up.

Mama was there with Nick. He was a sweaty mess. His dark hair had a crimp where his Stetson had been. He'd given up his cowboy boots since he'd left Zane Hart's employ to work for the Stiles family. Now he wore the heavier, wide-toed boots of a lumberjack.

He'd been working since dawn. Late March in the high mountains northeast of Sacramento was cool, and there was still snow in shadowed deep places, but it didn't stop the work, and Nick had been working hard, while Jilly had been sleeping.

Nick was being trained to run Stiles Lumber. He worked under the direction of their longtime foreman, Tom Harmon, whom they all called Old Tom. Or had been, before Jilly swiped him from working as a lumberjack to help her build the railroad.

Nick was nearly a member of the family. He'd found out Mama's new husband was abusive to her and a danger to the sisters, and rode faster than lightning to stand between Mama and Edgar. When Nick informed Old Tom of Mama's plight, Tom had also become a staunch defender. He would step in as bodyguard if needed, but that job mainly fell to Nick.

Nick glanced up as Jilly entered the office, and she noticed his two different-colored eyes, one bright blue, one bright green. They seemed to hold an intensity beyond what the different colors should make. He had the most distinct case of heterochromia Jilly had ever seen—not that she'd actually seen another case in person, only in the books she'd studied.

With Nick and Mama was Laura's husband, Caleb. Parson Tillman to the men who worked for Stiles Lumber. He sat in a chair near the window that looked out over the lumber camp, reading his Bible. Either preparing for the Wednesday prayer service or Sunday's sermon or just reading for the love of it.

Beside him stood a large table bearing a model of the bridge Jilly had planned. She had worked on it all winter while they were in San Francisco and transported it up here. The details thrilled her. She tripped a latch and turned the center of the bridge one hundred eighty degrees. When she turned the model into a real bridge, it would be an accomplishment that she could always look on with pride.

Proof that a woman could do anything she set her mind to.

Papa's dream brought to life.

For a fleeting moment, she was struck by the concern that her pride was too much. Too self-centered. Too rooted in wanting to live out her father's dream when maybe she should have dreams of her own.

She should pray about it. Ask God for forgiveness for the deep pride she felt.

Before she could, she thought of how much work she had to do today and decided now wasn't the time to ask for humility. She was risking a fortune on this. But she could do it.

She could get this train track built and carrying logs down the mountain in one season.

Jilly had calculated the lost income from diverting her lumberjacks from logging, which meant fewer logs to market, and paying the men to build rather than log. She had the money figured out closely, but she kept in mind a saying her father was fond of repeating, "No matter how carefully you do your figuring, a project usually takes twice as long and costs twice as much as you expect." Papa had always said one working season was all he intended to spend. And she had to prove she was as capable as Papa.

Jilly was trying not to run up a huge bill, and she was pushing hard to have this track finished before the winter closed down their work. They had to begin to recoup the ruinously expensive project.

The model built over the winter was part of Jilly's goal of being ready when the snow let loose of the highlands. Now she was ready to build and not everything was in order.

She straightened the swinging center of the model bridge and asked Mama, "Have you had word from the ironworks?"

"We can begin the foundation work for the first gorge today," Mama said from where she sat at Papa's huge oak desk. "Once we get the rail in place to the first gorge, we can carry lumber and steel out on a train car to finish the top section of the trestle and lay tracks across it."

Jilly knew all this. A flash of annoyance snapped her temper. "So, no, the rails didn't come."

"California Ironworks is usually so dependable." Mama frowned down at the paper in front of her. Jilly didn't have to ask to know it was all financial figures.

California Ironworks had written in response to Jilly's purchase order. She knew they were running double shifts to meet the booming San Francisco need for iron. Some delays were understandable, but the Stiles family had a seat on the board of California Ironworks. And she'd made this order well in advance so they would have plenty of time to meet the deadline. They had a right to expect better than this. But even so, the rails hadn't come.

Irritated but still with plenty to do, Jilly knew it would get here as fast as it could.

"We've got the roadbed smoothed all the way to the top of the first gorge," Nick said, "and the trail to the bottom of it is finished. The men are hauling the timbers, braces, and bolts down right now. I've got your horse caught and waiting to be saddled. We can ride out and begin the trestle as soon as you're ready."

There were four spans to build: three trestles over gorges and one bridge over a river that had a fair amount of boat traffic. And they needed to blast two holes through the mountain and had another blasting job that would cut into the side of the mountain. All of it needed to be done, and rails weren't necessary for the bases of the bridge and trestles. Still, she was just so eager to lay the first stretch of track. Once the bed was down and the railing started, it'd go fast. The track-laying crew would be to the trestle before she got it finished. Unless she really hurried. And she intended to.

"I'm ready now. Let's go."

"Jilly, eat some breakfast first." Mama never quit being a mother, even with her children fully grown. "You've got a long day of hard work, and it will be hours before lunch is brought out to the gorge. Go eat. We left breakfast out for you."

Michelle, the oldest, was twenty-two, and since she lived a distance away, she never had to take orders from Mama. It tweaked Jilly's temper, but then most things did. Mama was right. Jilly darted toward the breakfast room. There were biscuits, bacon, and a platter of eggs being kept warm on a chafing dish, along with toast, milk, and coffee.

She realized she was famished and scooped up big servings.

Sitting at the table, she reflected on everything that had brought her to today. An odd fact of her strangely functioning brain was that she had a vast and vivid memory of almost everything she'd ever seen or done. Some called it a photographic memory, but the correct term was *eidetic*, and she preferred to be correct. Anyway, she didn't remember life like a photograph. Photographs were dark and murky. Jilly's memory was sharp. She remembered pages from books she'd read. Word-for-word conversations she'd had all the way back to early childhood, almost from the time she was able to talk.

Though she'd often made good use of it, her memory quirk was honestly a burden at times. She remembered the bad along with the good, and she certainly remembered all that had passed between her and Edgar. She remembered it during the day, and it followed her into the night and haunted her dreams—although the dreams liked to twist things around.

She ate fast before the family could wander in and try to make breakfast fun when she only wanted it to be over, then rushed out to find Nick and head for the base of that gorge.

Caleb and Laura were coming later, too. But Mama wanted to finish her bookkeeping, and no one ever left Mama home alone. Nor Laura, and especially not Jilly, who was not yet in possession of that great goal: a husband.

Not as long as Edgar was out there. And not as long as Edgar had not repaid the money he took from Royce Carlisle for Jilly's hand in marriage.

With a shudder, Jilly remembered Carlisle, that horrid little man, would want a lot more than her hand.

Carlisle owned the largest bank in northern California. He was reputed to be an absolutely ruthless and cold-blooded man who enjoyed kicking people out of their homes and businesses.

Laura had seen him with Edgar and the other two men Edgar had arranged their marriages with. Carlisle was the leader. The other three, equally wealthy, let Carlisle control everything.

Which made Jilly wary of him beyond just knowing he was a loathsome man whose meek wife had died under mysterious circumstances.

Jilly couldn't stand the idea of getting married or letting any man close to her. But Carlisle . . . the very thought nearly made her run screaming.

She regained her self-control as she poked her head into the office. Everyone was diligently working, including Laura who was writing something, possibly a letter to Michelle.

"I'm ready to go."

Mama looked up with a half-amused shake of her head. "Jilly, you know better than to bolt down your food."

"I ate faster than a starving draft horse, Mama. No doubt

23

I'll soon be foundered. But until then, I'm ready to get to work."

Laura set her pen aside. "Your first trestle."

With a delicate shiver of excitement, Jilly nodded and smiled.

"How long will it take?" Laura asked.

"Two weeks of working long days plus weather delays. I have it all scheduled. By then the steel will be here, and the tracks will reach the gorge. Then they'll build on my trestle and level the next railbed while I work on the next span."

"When do you build the big one?" Caleb was paying attention now. "The bridge across the river?"

"I'm leaving that until last. We'll be a seasoned building crew by then."

Jilly knew it wasn't a truly vast stretch, not like some bridges, but it was big enough. Her eyes slid to the model, and she felt another rush of excitement. She was planning a swing bridge. It served the same purpose as a drawbridge, but instead of the middle of the bridge separating and rising, it would turn on a center pylon so the boats could get past. She'd have to reroute the river, put in the pylon, and turn the river back to flow under the bridge.

It would prevent having to build a bridge high enough for boat traffic to pass under, which on the land she was working would have become a very long and complicated structure. Instead, she'd build it low and make it pivot. She couldn't wait.

"I'm glad we have the trestle and other simpler structures to make sure we've learned how to support the beams." Her eyes went to Laura. "And you know I'm counting on you to blast the tunnels and such. There is no practical way to go around."

Laura took a quick glance at Caleb, then looked back at Jilly. With studied casualness, she said, "Let me know when it's time."

Laura loved setting off blasts. While they were still hiding from Edgar in the mission at the Purgatory settlement, Laura had used her skills with chemicals to save everyone from a mob of crazed men.

But there was something in the way she spoke, the way she glanced at Caleb, that told Jilly blowing things up wasn't as exciting to Laura as building this trestle was to Jilly.

Laura had a lot of nerve badgering Jilly to tell her about her nightmares when Laura wouldn't talk about what bothered her about something as wonderful as blowing a hole in a mountain. Maybe Jilly could do the blasting. Laura could teach her. And Michelle could teach Jilly how to boss people around. Jilly liked doing that but had to admit—if only to herself—Michelle was better at it.

Jilly needed to be twenty-five to inherit her share of Stiles Lumber. The shortcut to inheriting was to get married. Laura, the baby of the family, had found Caleb. That'd been easy. Well, easy except for explosions and Caleb being beaten nearly to death.

Michelle, the oldest, a stunning brunette, had married rancher Zane Hart in what could be called a panic. Michelle had been found by the son of Horace Benteen, the man Edgar had accepted money from in exchange for Michelle's hand in marriage. Michelle and Zane's wedding had been held with only a few hours' notice, but things were working out very well from what Michelle said in her letters.

Michelle and Laura now had controlling interest in Stiles Lumber, so they'd tossed Edgar out of the company and out of the house, ending his cruelty toward Mama and horrible management of the company.

Jilly didn't need to have shares to run the company, not if her sisters didn't object. Michelle lived far away on a ranch, and Laura seemed devoted to being a parson's wife. They might willingly hand the reins to her.

Jilly couldn't wait for that, either.

She needed four more years to get her inheritance legally in her hands, and she saw no reason not to wait out those years as a single woman running a lumber dynasty.

And in the meantime, she'd build her trestle.

There was no better way to practice than to actually do something. She wanted that practice and more. In order for the trestles to bear the weight of the train, it all had to be done right: selecting the building material and calculating the vibration of the train, wind, and, in the case of the river, the current, erosion, and flooding. The track was going to be on a steep incline, but it couldn't be too steep or no train engine could climb up nor could brakes control the load heading down. She knew all the grading, all the curves to lessen the rate of descent.

She had figured, planned, and calculated. The only thing left was to build the tracks.

As she led the way outside, she clutched the pages and pages of perfectly detailed blueprints in her hands. She'd also included mathematical calculations using force, weight, depth, altitude, and deterioration. She'd studied many other architects who'd done the same thing, and she'd visited construction sites with Papa, and even though she was young, she'd talked with the men building those structures, worked with them for days to understand what they were doing.

She was ready.

FOUR

RIDING ALONGSIDE JILLY to the bottom of the gorge, Nick considered how his life had completely changed in the last year. Nick had been a cowhand for Zane's Two Harts Ranch when he realized three of the women in the mission group on the edge of the property were the daughters of Liam Stiles. When Zane and Nick had found out about the sisters' plight, as well as the danger their mother was in, Nick had quit on the spot and run to the Stiles mansion to help. He'd previously worked as a lumberjack for Stiles Lumber, and he knew distantly of the beautiful, brilliant Stiles sisters, and how Mrs. Stiles was revered by the lumberjacks for her kind and generous treatment of the men who worked for her.

Nick had come to Margaret Stiles in a white-hot fury and been a bodyguard to her until Beaumont left the mansion.

Beaumont had been so incompetent, greedy, and cruel to his family and employees alike, he'd been well on his way to ruining all Liam Stiles had built. With him gone, and

Laura and Caleb here to help guard Mrs. Stiles, Nick was free to spend more time learning how to manage a lumber company under the tutelage of Old Tom and to help rebuild what Beaumont had nearly destroyed.

Nick didn't have much education. He figured he was smart enough, but he'd seen the drawings and mathematical strings of numbers on Jilly's papers and knew he had no idea what she was doing.

He'd seen plenty of bridges, or *trestles* in this case, though to him, they were the same thing. Put 'em up, brace 'em good, and you're done.

But he didn't even put such thoughts into words, knowing he'd reveal the depth of his lack of understanding of what Jilly was doing.

Still, he could put up this trestle, and it'd hold. He was sure of it.

Rather than try to prove that, he let Jilly stand before the massive pile of timber and set everyone to working.

And Nick threw in and helped. Happy not to be in charge of this undertaking.

LAURA ROSE FROM HER CHAIR in the office to get another sheet of paper. She had more to write to Michelle, but she had to do something else first. "I need to order dynamite."

Laura watched Mama nod absently. She was focused on a long column of figures. A very long column. Obviously, this train track was going to cost a lot of money, so Mama was very attentive to the money going out. But it would make them a fortune—double, maybe triple, their annual income by supplying far more logs to their sawmills, in the end. If all went well and they got the track built before it ruined them.

Right now, all wasn't well.

Laura wasn't happy with California Ironworks. They'd promised to have those rails in a week ago. Nothing had come.

"I'm about two days from riding to San Francisco," Mama muttered. "Maybe you shouldn't order the dynamite. Just go with me to town and pick it up." She started on a new column of figures.

Laura looked at Caleb, who arched a brow.

A trip to San Francisco? There'd been no mention of that before now.

Caleb cleared his throat. "Mama Stiles, is something wrong?"

She snapped her pen down on the desk so hard Laura jumped.

Frowning at Caleb, Mama said, "I'm afraid something is *very* wrong. Those rails should have been here by now. I didn't want to bother Jilly with their excuses when she has such a busy morning, but as I get one weak response after the other from them, I keep picturing those men Edgar arranged as husbands for you girls. All of them were on that board. And they put their hands on you, Laura. What else might they be up to?"

"Horace Benteen isn't powerful anymore." Laura felt a savage satisfaction that the man was locked up in prison for life. "And Myron Gibbons should have given up all hope of marrying me."

30

"Gibbons might be motivated by his anger over losing his chance to marry you, Laura." Caleb came to her side.

She leaned into him and shuddered to think she might have ended up married to Myron Gibbons. Cruel beast of a man. "You saved me from that, Mama. You and Caleb."

"We all worked together to save you girls from that fate. But one man remains, and he's shrewd. He'll know by now that Jilly isn't married," Mama said. "All three men paid thousands of dollars to get Edgar's promise you'd marry them. When you and Michelle cut Edgar out of Stiles Lumber, that money was in there, right along with the company money. We got it, so he can't pay it back. He's safe from Benteen. Gibbons is wealthy beyond belief, but it's mostly inherited. I don't know how hard he'd fight to get his money back. He might do spiteful things to Edgar, but it would be pointless to bother trying to get ahold of you, Laura."

Caleb slid his arm around Laura's waist. "You're worried about Carlisle and Jilly."

"I'm worried Carlisle has done something to interrupt the shipment of rails," Mama said. "I'm worried we haven't found all the men loyal to Edgar who work for us. And yes, I'm worried about Carlisle and Jilly."

Laura patted Caleb's hand on her waist and went to where Mama sat at her desk. "You're worried about so much. I'm sorry."

"No, I'm sorry, Laura. I'm sorry I brought Edgar into our lives. But I'm also done apologizing. He was a skilled liar. He became, as Caleb said, exactly what I wanted him to be. I believed him because I am an honest, trusting woman. He victimized all of us." Mama shoved her chair back and rose from the desk. "And I'm done hoping for the best when it is clear the worst is happening. I'm going to San Francisco."

She swept around the desk and marched toward the door as if she were leaving right now.

"Mama, stop!"

When she whirled around to face her, Mama's face was grim. "What is it, Laura?"

Laura almost smiled. Her mama had always run this household with a firm grip. Loving and encouraging, but the girls didn't get away with much misbehavior. But as a married woman, Laura was beyond her discipline.

To prove it, she walked right up to her angry mother and wagged a finger right under her nose. "You're not charging out of here with no one to protect you. Nick is too busy, and Caleb can't go because I'd have to go because he wants to keep me safe, too. That would leave Jilly and Nick alone here in the house unchaperoned. Go if you want. It needs to be done, Mama, but plan first."

Mama smiled sheepishly. "You're right. Of course, I can't go alone." She crossed her arms. "But I do need to go. I could write to Michelle and ask her to go, but it's a terribly busy time on the ranch. She said in her last letter that the cows are calving, and Zane is working long, hard hours. You and Caleb could go if I stayed out at the work site with Jilly and Nick. Or—"

An odd, crafty look came across Mama's face. "Or the three of us could go and leave Nick and Jilly unchaperoned and hope the two of them stop being foolish and fall in love."

Laura had to fight down a laugh. She knew Mama saw it.

Caleb came up beside them again. "No, we're not going to do that."

32

Parson Caleb was very aware of what was proper and what was not. But he was grinning. "What we need to do is take both of them with us."

"Jilly won't leave the trestle," Laura said.

"She might," Mama said, "if she can't get her rails."

"I think one meeting would do it," Laura said. "We'll just tell Mr. Barritt what's going on. Somehow Carlisle has gotten between our order and the people filling it. Apparently, he's got someone intercepting our telegrams so Mr. Barritt doesn't see them. Or he might be up to some shenanigans with the bank or the shipping."

"He's not our banker." Mama scowled. "But he's probably got connections there."

"Zane's money is in Wells Fargo. We could talk with them, transfer our accounts there."

"Lloyd Tevis, yes." Mama snapped her fingers. "We could trust Lloyd not to choose Carlisle over us. And yes, Jilly will have to go along."

Lloyd Tevis was the president of the Wells Fargo bank and another close friend of the Stiles family. What's more, he was a man of honor. A man who wouldn't be manipulated by Carlisle.

"Carlisle is heavily involved in trains, too." Mama rubbed her chin, thinking. "He could be misdirecting shipments that way."

"Maybe Old Tom and a couple of others from here could go with you instead of me and Laura," Caleb said, probably realizing that Laura and Mama had stopped planning how to make the trip and started on what they'd do there.

"Tom, yes." Mama frowned. "But will you both be safe here?"

"We will be," Caleb said, "if we start helping Jilly and Nick build the trestle. We'll stay at the work site with everyone else."

Nodding silently for a time, Mama said, "I'll go pack, you go talk to Tom."

"I'll send a servant out for him, Mama Stiles," Caleb said with determination. "Even believing Edgar is long gone, we're not leaving you in the house alone."

"Alone with the cook and maids, the porters, and the men in the stable near to hand."

"One of them can run out and find Old Tom and bring him in," Caleb said. "We're not leaving."

And that look crossed Mama's face, the look of anger and guilt. The look that said she felt like she'd brought this on them all. The look that said she was through apologizing because she'd done it enough. She'd been fooled, they all had, and they were still paying for it.

She headed upstairs. When she was well out of earshot, Laura said to Caleb, "Nick's going to be upset when he comes in and finds Mama gone without him guarding her."

"Crazy as a rabid badger is more like it."

"Will she be safe?" Laura looked in the direction Mama had gone.

"You know Old Tom better than I do. Will she be safe?"

"I think she will, but I want Tom to handpick two men to go with him. Men who were here before Edgar. And I'm going to send a telegram to Uncle Newt. Make sure he knows Mama is going to San Francisco."

With a quiet sigh, Caleb said, "You really should call him Governor Booth."

"Sorry, I keep trying to remember." Another personal friend of the Stiles family.

"Maybe send one to Marshal Irving, too." The man who'd arrested Horace Benteen. The man the governor called on when he wanted a law enforcement job done right.

Heading for the desk, Laura said, "I'll write them. You go get someone to bring Tom to the house. But you and I are going to send these telegrams ourselves. I know Morse code."

"Of course you do."

Laura grinned. She knew Caleb had come to accept that she knew practically everything.

"Don't you trust your own telegraph operator?" They had their own telegraph wire up here for the lumber business they conducted.

All amusement faded from Laura. "I don't trust anyone outside of the family."

"That's a grim way to live. But you trust Old Tom."

Still solemn, Laura nodded. "I do trust him, but right now, I only trust him because I have no choice."

Caleb was right. It was grim. It had to stop.

"I'll talk to the porter." Caleb rushed out.

Laura wrote fast. The telegrams needed to be away before Mama got here and objected to bothering the governor with her problems.

Laura thought of those long columns of figures. The supplies for the railroad were terribly expensive. The venture would pay off soon, and pay well, but they couldn't just pour money out forever. They had to get this train track built.

And it needed to be done before the cold weather shut them down. Then they could start up operations in the spring to begin to get a return on their outlay.

If they only got the track halfway built, if anything stopped Jilly from doing it and doing it fast, they could bring Stiles Lumber down around their ears.

Laura decided she'd stand by to get a reply, not trusting the telegraph operator with the return message.

Grim indeed.

FIVE

WITH EVERY TURN OF THE SHOVEL, every hour of labor, the railroad track was costing them a fortune. Jilly needed to get it built quickly so the hemorrhage of money would stop.

Jilly felt the weight of it because it was Papa's dream. She'd been raised, educated, and trained to handle this. Papa had been talking about it for years, and Jilly had sensed he was waiting for her and her sisters to grow up enough so that they could be part of building it. Now it fell to Jilly to build it without Papa's wise, guiding hand. It had to be done fast and right and before winter closed them down.

They had twelve deep foundation holes to dig. And in the stony soil at the bottom of the ravine, that was a big job. She thought of the other trestles she needed to build. Much wider spans. Much deeper gullies. This was a simple project by comparison, and they all needed the practice they'd get from dealing with this first gorge.

Jilly had ten men from the lumberjack crew digging those holes for two days, and they had six of them mostly done.

She had twelve massive logs for the foundation legs. She'd chosen each log personally. Not even ten massively strong men would be able to lift the trunks and set them for foundation timbers. A pulley with ropes tied to the teams of mules would make the weight manageable.

The pulley was rigged at the top of the ravine, around thirty feet overhead. The men only needed to guide the timbers into place. The logs were forty-six feet long and carefully cut so they would stand at the same height—accounting for the uneven bottom of the gorge—when they were buried ten feet deep. They'd use the wooden cross braces and the massive bolts to connect the timbers. Then they needed more complex cross braces at the top to hold up the railroad tracks. And heavy, squared-off timbers to fasten the rails to. To think this was the simplest of the trestles they'd build.

Drilling the holes in the timbers and the braces was an all-morning job for everyone who wasn't digging. This was a crew who lived and worked all day, every day, with lumber. Jilly didn't stand over them, pointing. She worked over the logs she'd brought down. She trimmed a few remaining branches, estimated where the braces would go, and marked each spot carefully. When she was done with that, she used a hand drill on the logs and braces, where the two would connect.

The camp cook sent down lunch and pitchers of cool water, not hard in the mountaintops, where the spring runoff was melted snow.

The men went back to digging, and when the first holes were finished, five men stayed down and five went up top.

"Nick, go up there and make sure the men are handling the pulley right." Jilly did some bossing now.

"I sent Dub. He knows what he's doing. He helped build the pulley." Nick set aside his drill and came close enough their conversation wouldn't be overheard. Speaking quietly but firmly, a blaze shining in his mismatched eyes, he said, "I'm not leaving you alone down here."

Jilly gestured to the five men left digging but kept her voice down, too. "This hardly counts as alone."

"I'm staying down here with you, Jilly." He leaned very close. "And what's more, you know I need to, and you know why. You pride yourself on efficiency and yet here you stand, wasting time." His two-colored eyes flashed with stubborn amusement. "Dub can do it."

Jilly felt the frustration of not truly being in charge, not with Nick. He seemed to mostly take orders well, but it occurred to her that he probably only took orders for things he was already planning to do.

That made her a strange kind of boss.

Short of throwing a temper tantrum, which would embarrass her and still wouldn't get Nick to do as she asked, there wasn't much she could think of to do to impose her will on him.

It didn't matter anyway. Dublin O'Malley, a redheaded Irishman who'd been a lumberjack here for years, was already heading up, and Nick had taken over digging the hole Dub was working on.

She went back to drilling holes and used her irritation at Nick's insubordination to make the drilling go faster.

"WHAT DO YOU MEAN Margaret's gone?"

Jilly stopped working when she heard Nick holler like his head was going to blow off.

Caleb and Laura had come down to the work site, and they were explaining about Mama's sudden determination to get to the bottom of the delayed steel order.

Nick was furious.

And Jilly was on a rampage. "We should have gone with her."

Caleb glanced at Laura. "We considered it. But you can get a lot of work done here even without the rails. And she's got three strong men with her. Loyal men. Old Tom, Carl, and Willie."

Jilly almost relaxed, but Nick didn't. "That's not enough. She should have discussed it with us."

"She discussed it with Caleb and me," Laura assured him. "We couldn't go and leave you two alone in the house. It's out of the question."

"I could have slept with the lumberjacks." Nick as good as growled.

"Then Jilly would have been alone in the house. We don't trust Edgar or Carlisle to stay away. One or both of them probably messed up the delivery for the exact purpose of drawing Jilly back to San Francisco, where she'd be more vulnerable, or separating us so she wouldn't be as safe up here."

Jilly looked over at the crew. They had the first six foundation timbers in place and the next six holes nearly dug. They'd begun bolting on the braces on the ground level. Laura was right. She could get a lot done without those rails.

"Carlisle shouldn't have this kind of power over a company." Jilly was angry at everything that made this job run less smoothly. And now it was possible Mama had endangered herself. "California Ironworks, regardless of what strings Carlisle pulled, should have better oversight than this."

"We're on the board," Laura said. "We're going to make sure everyone there knows how Carlisle meddled in C.I.'s business affairs. I intend to make him sorry he did it. Mama is going to move our money out of the bank it's in, on the assumption he's got influence over that bank. We'll do business with Wells Fargo instead."

Caleb gestured to posts that towered thirty feet in the air. "How can I help?"

Jilly shook her head to dislodge the temper from her thoughts. "There's plenty to do. We need braces at intervals all the way to the top. It's enough to keep all of us busy for the next two weeks. Follow me."

Nick shook his head, too, but it didn't seem to dislodge his temper. Instead, he said, "She's in danger. I have to go."

"Nick, we need you here." Laura and Caleb each grabbed him by the arm. Laura said, "I sent a telegram to Michelle. I told her what was going on. I'm hoping she goes to meet Mama."

"Zane can't get away this time of year," Nick said.

Laura and Jilly looked at each other. They knew Michelle had done a lot of work making Zane's home better, and after Zane found gold, he'd raised his men's wages, improved their living conditions—thanks to Michelle's inventions—and added men to ease the workload. And they knew Michelle and Zane were deeply in love. There wasn't much Zane wouldn't do for Michelle.

"He'll find a way to take her." Jilly was sure.

Laura gave her head a firm nod.

Nick hesitated but finally said, "All right. Let's get back to work."

MICHELLE HAD HOOKED UP a ceiling fan in the kitchen and another in each bedroom in the main house. The fans themselves were simple. What wasn't simple was putting a water tank up on stilts. With the tank up high, it gave the water enough pressure to spin the waterwheel and operate the fans. She'd also figured out how to make the water recirculate, so they didn't just run through gallons and gallons of water to make the fans spin. So now pipes that drove the waterwheel were all through the ceiling, downstairs and up.

She wanted to put a fan in each cabin. Her goal was to have them all in place by the heat of summer.

She'd also found a way to use waterpower to churn a machine that would wash the laundry. That had made the women's lives much easier. She'd applied for a patent for that and the ceiling fans, and both were granted.

Correctly hooked up, the waterwheels could create an electric spark to light the fireplaces and the kitchen stove, too.

She'd experimented with a powered beater for making cakes, a sewing machine, and a dozen other household appliances, but none satisfied her. Her waterwheel, small as it was, was clunky.

She needed that four-stroke cycle engine.

And to that end, she'd come near to blowing herself up a number of times.

It made a mess for her. It really upset Zane. It scared his sisters to death.

But they were small explosions. She'd explained that in painstaking detail, a number of times. True, she'd singed her eyelashes once and come in covered with black smoke a few times, but progress came at a price.

And to create that engine, to do it first . . . It was a patent she wanted in her name so badly. It would change the world in wonderful ways, and she wanted to be part of it.

As Michelle stood on the stepladder she'd built to reach the ceiling fixtures more easily, she smiled. She was making life better for everyone here. She truly believed it. Zane's sisters, Annie and Beth Ellen, were so thrilled with the washing machine that they encouraged Michelle to invent day and night.

Two Harts Ranch was on the way to being a small town. Four of the cowhands were married, all to women who'd been part of the mission group Caleb had started at the edge of Zane's ranch. And Two Harts Ranch had celebrated the married men and built cabins for them. Normally, cowhands were prone to being wanderers, but married men stayed put. Zane paid top wages since he'd found gold on his property, so he got top men. He now encouraged the men to find wives and bring them home. That made for a different kind of working man, and Michelle hoped it would give the ranch a steady, dependable workforce year-round. And Josh, Zane's brother, a seafaring man, had given up that life to move home. He helped with the ranch tremendously.

Heinrich and Gretel Steinmeyer had also been part of the mission group. They had a tiny newborn son, Gustaf, and their daughter, Willa, was now two and toddling everywhere. Heinrich had become a decent cowhand and dependable enough that Zane named him ramrod. Gretel worked as a housekeeper alongside Zane's sisters.

Michelle loved it here. She loved the fertile meadows full of the pretty red-and-white Hereford cattle. She loved the waterwheels irrigating those meadows and the windmills that filled ponds and water tanks and kept the cattle from suffering during dry spells.

She'd thought her life was pointed at running Stiles Lumber. She'd always wanted that and planned for it, only fretting to think of the struggle to be in charge when Jilly wanted to run things as badly as she did.

But living on the Two Harts was wonderful. And they didn't have to stay here all the time, even though Zane had rarely gone to even a nearby town before they'd married. They'd spent a month in San Francisco this winter, living at Mama's house on Nob Hill with her sisters.

Beth Ellen stuck her head through the doorway as Michelle climbed down the stepladder from her now-turning bedroom ceiling fan.

"You got a telegram from your sister." Beth Ellen waved the little piece of pleasure. Her sisters always had exciting things to say. And now it would be even better because Jilly's last letter said she was ready to start building. The anticipation echoed in Jilly's letter. Michelle grabbed the telegram and saw Laura's name.

Not Jilly. But Michelle enjoyed hearing from either of them.

She tore it open and sat at the couch that sided the fireplace. Beth Ellen ducked out, to give her privacy. In a house with all four adult Hart children and Michelle living together, privacy was much longed for, and they all knew it.

Laura's telegram shocked Michelle into anger.

Royce Carlisle had apparently teamed up with Edgar Beaumont, and the two were causing mischief. Jilly would be so upset.

An upset Jilly was something to stir fear in the strongest of hearts.

And Mama on her way to San Francisco? With only a few lumberjacks to protect her? Yes, those men were tough and loyal, but what authority did they have over a man's wife, if Edgar should choose to enforce a husband's power?

Reading Laura's rationale for it, Michelle had to admit no one from the family could be spared. Not unless Jilly went to cower in some corner of the dark basement, gun aimed.

But Mama wasn't safe.

She ran to the back door and yelled, "Zane?"

He was working all the hours God made. From before sunrise until long after sunset. The calves were dropping, the rivers and streams threatened to overflow their banks with every rain. All the spring work beyond those pressing daily needs never let up, though Zane had said the waterways were lowering and the calves were mostly here.

He was exhausted, starving, and occasionally short-tempered because he was exhausted and starving.

Still, he poked his head out of the barn. He had an oversized bottle in his hand with a giant nipple attached to the narrow neck. They'd taken in an orphaned calf just last night when a mama had twins and wouldn't accept one of them.

"What's the matter?"

"I have to go to San Francisco. Mama is there, and I'm afraid she's in danger. I need you to go with me."

Zane stared at her for a long moment, then turned away and shouted, "Josh, I've got to go to San Francisco."

He set the bottle on the ground as he jogged to the house. She'd never loved him more.

JILLY DIDN'T CLIMB the timber. Lifting, positioning, and hammering the bolts, it was all very heavy work, even with the horse-drawn pulleys helping from overhead.

She'd've needed a lot of assistance to do it, and she wasn't about to insist on doing something that would make this job harder for the men. She would only slow things down.

But Nick was going up. She'd worked with him enough to know he was an old hand with all things lumber, and it appeared that extended to bracing timbers.

The first brace could be put in place with men standing on the ground. The men held the brace steady. Nick lined his side up and slid in a bolt that needed to be hammered to go all the way through. Once the braces at ground level were tightened, the men swarmed up the timbers.

Men still on the ground, men climbing, men overhead. The clank of hammers, the shouts for braces to be lifted and aligned.

Jilly loved every minute of it.

She watched with cool satisfaction as the teams of men put the braces in place. This was her railroad coming to life. A heavy weight she enjoyed bearing on her shoulders.

Ross used his wrench to tighten a nut to the end of the bolt.

It was almost a dance. The hammering was like beating drums. The shouting could have been words to a song. It all gave Jilly a thrill to watch it, hear it. Nick and Ross moved up again ten more feet. They slung sturdy belts around the timber. That, combined with the climbing spurs, made ascent fast and easy. Or at least they made it look easy.

Jilly knew how to climb a tree just this way. Her papa had taught his daughters all aspects of the lumber business.

Another brace began to rise on Nick's side, and Jilly saw the other team go up, all of them working together like a smooth-running machine.

NICK HAD ONE MORE CLIMB, then he and Ross would be done with this pair of foundation timbers.

As he slung his climbing belt around his waist to free his hands for lifting and bolting, Nick smiled to think again of this unusual turn his life had taken. He was getting used to having a woman boss on a job.

It had startled him a little at first. He'd always lived in a man's world. Worked with them, was ordered around by them, got his pay from them.

Not here at Stiles Lumber.

He kinda liked it.

Mainly because Jilly was brilliant.

There was just no denying she knew what she wanted and how to get it. And she had this trestle better designed and planned than he could have—way better. It might've pinched his manly feelings to admit it if she wasn't just so competent.

He even respected that she was starting with a fairly narrow gorge. It was a good test of their skills. Jilly had picked well to build the first trestle here.

In fact, she hadn't put a foot wrong in the way she treated the men, the way she worked hard at their sides, and even the way she stepped back when a job needed brute strength.

With pride in his boss and pleasure at how well it was working and how fast he'd be done here, Nick pushed hard, with Ross across from him matching his pace.

Ross was a youngster, but he knew tools, timber, and how to take an order and learn from someone who'd done it before.

The kid was also about halfway in love with Jilly. But she handled Ross well, never encouraged him, yet didn't insult him or brush him off like a pest. It wasn't easy to find that middle ground, and Jilly managed it perfectly.

With the second brace finished, Nick climbed up to stand on it. He steadied himself to go on up. He glanced down and saw the braces he'd need to bolt were already rising. They'd been lined up and tied off by the men below, and were now being towed up using the strength of the horses with the guiding hands of the men above, using a pulley system Jilly had designed and installed.

He'd better climb fast, or the braces would beat him to the next spot.

He adjusted his climbing belt around the post and lifted his spurred right boot to jab it into the timber.

Before he could set his foot, a sharp crack from under his left boot shook the brace.

The sturdy wood he stood on wobbled. With a sudden jolt, it dropped beneath him.

An involuntary shout echoed from his throat.

Jilly screamed.

Someone below bellowed, "Nick, hang on!"

Ross screamed. That hit Nick harder, sounded worse than anything else.

Nick didn't have time to even look at the kid. He was too busy trying to grab hold of something, anything.

"Hold it, up there!" Jilly cried out. "Hold tight up there."

But the call came too late. The fall was too sudden. Nick smashed into the brace being raised and bashed his head. His weight ripped the ropes out of the hands above.

The brace plunged down, Nick straddling it.

Nick clawed at the brace they passed below, but his fingers wouldn't latch on.

The wicked whip of something flashed past his face. Ropes from overhead, he thought.

Before he could snatch at them, Nick crashed to the ground. His knees hit hard enough they bounced. His head hammered against the brace he still straddled. Shouts, wood crashing, it was a jumble, blurred from the blow to his head.

Rolling off the timber, he toppled against Ross and saw the kid's face crimson with blood.

Nick reached for him, or he tried, but his hands wouldn't work. Nothing worked. All he was aware of was pain and motion and noise echoing in his head.

Then he was aware of only utter darkness.

CHAPTER

SEVEN

JILLY SCREAMED AND RAN FOR THE FALLING MEN.
Scrambling over braces and timbers, she rushed with the others to the rescue.

No one got there in time.

She saw one of her lumberjacks, Garvey Bates, get hit by the falling brace. It pinned him to the ground.

Ross hit the ground with a sickening thud, and a second later, Nick smashed into the dirt. Men bellowed from overhead.

Jilly looked sideways, and to the first man who caught her eye, she said, "Get those other men down off the timbers." All work had to stop.

"Get that brace off Garvey," she continued. He was trapped under it, but he was moving, conscious.

Nick and Ross weren't.

Men rushed to help Garvey, and others knelt beside Ross.

Jilly reached Nick's side before anyone else. Blood coated his face from a gash in his forehead. His eyes were closed, and he wasn't moving. She saw blood under rips in the knees of his canvas pants, and his fingers bled from torn fingernails.

"Get me the first aid supplies." Jilly snapped out orders though she could barely think straight.

She ran her hands along Nick's arms, then his legs. She hoped she was a judge of broken bones because she didn't think he had any.

"Get the wagon over here. We'll move them as soon as we can and get them to Doc Sandy." She looked up into the anxious faces of the men overhead who were manning the pulleys. "Go tell Doc we're coming in with three injured men."

The faces vanished. It crossed her mind that she worked with good men who she trusted to do everything possible. Including these good men who'd fallen during work she'd ordered them to do. A simple job that had somehow turned dangerous.

Nick, Ross, and Garvey. All three hurt. Nick was bad enough, but Ross was the worst. She'd seen him hit the hardest. Had the fall killed him? Panic closed her throat, and she shouted no more orders because she couldn't force out a word.

Her crew swarmed all of them, helping in whatever way was needed.

Caleb was at Ross's side. "I've got a pulse."

The worst of Jilly's sick fear eased. But only a bit.

Laura rushed over with a bundle of bandages. Laura keeping her head. It helped Jilly gather herself, and she could talk again without weeping.

"Help me get a gauze pad on his forehead. I don't feel any

obviously broken bones. His knees are bleeding and swollen. I think he hit them really hard, but they aren't noticeably broken." Jilly caught Laura's gaze. The two of them shared such a moment of fear and deep love. "I'm so glad you're here."

Laura pressed a pad of cloth to Nick's head. "This looks like a nasty cut but not deep."

"How's Ross, Caleb?" Jilly's voice snapped. Back to herself. This was her work site. Her accident site. What had gone wrong?

"He's breathing." Caleb kept working without looking up. "It's hard to judge his injuries. He hit hard, landing on the edge of this timber pile."

"Is Garvey bad?" Jilly asked.

Two of her crew had lifted the brace off him with extreme care.

One of them hollered, "He's awake. Looks like he's got a broken arm, but nothing else I can see." The man didn't sound overly confident.

A broken arm would need to be set, and done right, or he'd be finished with lumberjacking for good. And that was the job he loved. Garvey was a giant of a man who could yell *timber* in a voice as big as his body. He'd been with Stiles Lumber for years.

Jilly should have kept the crew below well back. She should have tied the climbing men to safety harnesses from overhead. She should have—

Her mind raced through safety measures she'd need to arrange as she rolled up the legs of Nick's sturdy pants. Men climbing timbers with belts and spurs was so common she'd never considered doing anything to make it safer.

She got a rolled bandage from Laura and began wrapping Nick's knees. Blood soaked the narrow white bandages as she wrapped around and around, not too tight but tight enough, she hoped.

She heard Laura quietly praying over Nick as she wrapped a bandage around his head. Prayer. She needed to pray.

How had it taken this long to turn to God? She needed to be a better person. A better believer. She needed her entire life grounded in her faith. She knew it, and yet she'd been slow to pray. She should have started before they'd fallen, before they'd bolted in the first brace. Before she'd gotten dressed this morning.

But just because she was late coming to it didn't mean she couldn't start now and pray with all her heart.

"Someone bring that brace that failed. Make sure the bolts are there, too. I want them taken up to the house. I need to find out what happened." Jilly knew her men would want to help. Need to help. They'd be eager to do anything to make this better.

"This bolt is snapped clean off, Miss Stiles."

Jilly looked in the direction of the voice and saw one of her men studying the sheared bolt sticking out of a brace hole. It shouldn't have broken. He removed it and handed it to her.

"Bring all the bolts, and I don't want anyone trusting their weight to the braces already up." She was relieved to see all the climbing men had reached the ground safely. "No one else goes up. If one bolt broke, another might."

Nick groaned. Jilly quit issuing orders. Done with his knees and not sure what to do next to help him or anyone, she moved so her face was only inches from Nick's. Watching him closely, she saw the moment his eyes fluttered open.

He looked dazed. She wasn't sure he even knew who was taking care of him.

"Nick, we think you're going to be fine."

"R-Ross?"

That was Nick, thinking of someone else before himself.

"He's unconscious but alive. Caleb is working with him."

"Just a kid. Who e-else? Someone broke my fall . . . saved me."

"It was Garvey. He's got a broken arm, but he's alert."

Alert enough to be in agony.

"Doc Sandy knows how to set bones." Nick tossed his head as if he planned to roll to his side. Probably to go to work tending Ross and Garvey single-handedly.

Jilly pressed her hands to his shoulders. "Lay still. Settle down now, Nick. All the men are working, tending Ross and Garvey. Your knees are scraped, and you've got a cut on your forehead. You hit hard enough to be knocked unconscious. I don't know if it'll need stitches, the doc will decide that. You'll be laid up awhile, but you'll be all right."

Laura leaned in, too. "There's nothing for you to do except heal. Ross just needs to wake up again. We'll get a cast on Garvey's arm."

"The wagon's ready." Caleb's voice rang with authority.

The men had used one of their climbing belts to rig Garvey a sling. With care, they helped him onto the tailgate. They guided him all the way into the wagon bed so his back could rest against the high driver's seat.

"You're next," Jilly said to Nick.

"N-no, Ross next."

Jilly's jaw tensed. "They're not ready to move him yet."

She saw two other men working to stop Ross's bleeding, to do whatever they could.

Four burly lumberjacks eased Nick up into their arms, two on each side with him still stretched out flat. They walked with him over to the wagon.

Once Nick was settled in the wagon bed, they went to carry Ross.

Caleb moved with them, one hand under the back of Ross's neck. One hand pressed to a wound on his head. Caleb's lips moved silently, and it sent Jilly back to her own prayers as she stood beside the men who'd carried Nick.

"What happened? Why'd we fall?" Nick's eyes had sharpened.

"The brace collapsed," Jilly said. "A bolt sheared off under your weight."

"Those bolts are supposed to hold up under the weight of a train."

"Yes." Jilly studied the shiny bolt that had broken—but it wasn't shiny inside, only on the outside. "Yes, it surely was supposed to do that."

"Not the right bolts?"

"They *are* the right bolts." Jilly was furious. "Or at least they should have been. I'm afraid they've been tampered with."

Poor quality metal? Acid used to undermine their strength? Old bolts painted to look new? Maybe . . . maybe . . . maybe. Her mind swirled with suspicion.

She'd find out.

To make room for Ross, Nick was slid farther into the wagon, close to where Garvey sat cradling his painful arm.

"Lucky thing we fell." Nick closed his eyes, looking like he hurt enough to dread the ride to the house.

Garvey, his face gray and drawn with pain, growled, "Lucky? How's this lucky? I'll be laid up for weeks."

Nick didn't answer, but Jilly knew what he meant. She hated it and wanted to deny it, but she knew.

She watched grimly as Ross, his face ashen under the blood, gauze wrapped tightly around his head, was eased into the wagon beside Nick. He'd shown no signs of regaining consciousness. He had a pulse and no visibly broken bones, but internal injuries could be invisible and impossible to repair.

Jilly watched the young man who'd flirted with her, who'd treated her with such awed respect. A young man with a good heart.

Nick finally said, "If that bolt had held, we'd've gotten this trestle finished and called it good. The whole trestle would have collapsed when the first train passed over. A train with riders. They'd've plunged to the bottom of the gorge and died in a fiery explosion."

Just because that would have been a horror and a tragedy didn't mean Jilly was going to call this mess lucky. But she had a feeling that was exactly what had been intended. Just as her rails not arriving was intentional. Someone didn't want her to build this railroad track. And if she got it done, that same someone wanted this trestle to collapse.

One name popped front and center into her head. Edgar Beaumont, her stepfather. The man who still had ugly plans to force Jilly into marriage with a loathsome, but very powerful man.

Royce Carlisle.

Now she had two names.

And one was as bad as the other.

She climbed up on the wagon seat beside the driver and rode home with her badly injured crew. The only break in the grim silence was an occasional groan from Garvey when they hit a bump in the rugged trail. A sound he quickly silenced. A good man. Three good men all hurt because she'd been careless.

Careless in trusting a company with a reputation that was beyond reproach. And yet somehow, someone had substituted substandard bolts for the ones she'd ordered.

Carlisle most likely. He had the connections to do it. And that meant Carlisle still thought he had a chance to marry her. It would earn him, for the price of a simple set of wedding vows, a third of Stiles Lumber. But she had a dreadful feeling that Carlisle's interest in her wasn't driven by greed. It was personal. He wanted her, not the company—that would just be icing on the cake.

She had to marry. She had no choice. And the very thought made her sick to her stomach.

EIGHT

THE TRIP UP THE MOUNTAIN on the steep trail was a nightmare of jolts and switchbacks. Trees scraped the sides of the wagon. The mules drawing the wagon leaned hard into what wasn't too heavy of a load, but made harder by the incline.

When they finally reached the mansion, riding in the wagon, the first person Jilly saw was the company medic, Doc Sandy.

She'd sent men ahead to warn him of the injuries. Now the men all stood at Doc Sandy's side, ready to help.

Doc Sandy had stretchers at hand. After a quick check of the men, he moved to Ross first. He told the stretcher bearers to get him settled on one of the two high examining tables. Beyond them was the infirmary with four more beds made up and ready for patients who needed to stay overnight.

Next, he pointed to Nick, who shook his head. "Take Garvey. I got knocked into a good sleep, but I'm all right."

Doc studied him through narrowed eyes. Jilly had climbed

down and now stood beside the medic, assessing Nick for herself. He was ashen. The bleeding contrasted sharply with his terribly pale skin. He was none-too-alert-looking, lying flat on his back. If he was really feeling so good, why hadn't he tried to sit up?

"All right, Garvey, can you stand unassisted?"

Garvey scooted toward the back end of the wagon, carefully keeping his broken arm tight against his body. When he reached the open tailgate, he slid off the wagon and stood. He braced himself with his right hand as his knees wobbled, then straightened. He wasn't overly steady, and one of the men slung an arm behind Garvey's back. Together they staggered inside. Two other men walked along close, ready should he topple over.

Without sitting up, Nick slid on his back to the end of the wagon, much more slowly than Garvey. He gripped the wagon's side and, an inch at a time, sat up.

Jilly clenched her teeth to keep herself from scolding Nick for trying to be stronger than a head wound. The idiot.

"Give my head a minute to clear." Nick sat there, his eyes open but dazed. At last he said, "If I try to stand, I th-think I'm gonna fall down, Doc. I'm sure once I lie down here in the wagon awhile more, I'll be fine. You go on in and take care of Ross and Garvey. I'll be in soon."

Doc held three fingers up in front of his face. "How many? Count."

"H-how many what?"

Not a good sign. Jilly went to Nick's side, unable to stay away.

"Fingers," Doc said. "How many fingers am I holding up?"

Nick's eyes closed, then she could see the fight to open them.

Doc waved four men over with the stretcher.

With the stretcher coming and Doc lifting the lids of Nick's eyes to examine his pupils, Jilly did her best to stay out of the way and still stay close.

After another ten seconds without an answer to the question, Doc said, "Concussion."

"I can't feel anything broken." Nick spoke unsteadily. "Nothing hurting in my gut."

He was clearly doing his best to sound tough. Even though he'd just failed the most basic concussion test. "My head's just good and bashed in. Knees are killing me. Nothin' that'll keep me from sitting up to the table at suppertime."

Jilly wanted to say a few sharp words to Nick about going to bed and staying there a good long while. It was just as well the stretcher came close enough she had to step back. The men didn't need to hear her growling.

Laura came to her side. She and Caleb had ridden their horses back, and the rest of the crew was alighting from another wagon, coming to see how the men were.

Laura drew Jilly away. Caleb came up on Jilly's right while Laura walked on her left. They followed Nick and his bearers and Doc Sandy, a regular procession, into the doctor's office.

That's when Jilly found out Doc considered her to have the second-most medical knowledge on the mountain.

Which must mean the rest of them had none.

Doc set Garvey's arm, got the plaster mixed and the cast started, then left Jilly to bind up the broken arm while Laura helped.

Caleb followed the medic's orders, too, and through every-thing he kept up his prayers and encouragement.

Jilly might not be wounded, but she was sick at heart that a job she headed had led to these injuries.

Ross had barely stirred. He still wasn't awake, but he was alive. Jilly prayed fervently the kid had no mortal injuries.

The kid. That's how she thought of him. An earnest, hardworking, polite kid. He was probably the same age she was.

NICK'S EYES FLICKERED OPEN in full daylight. He heard the murmur of quiet voices around him. As he came awake, his head ticked like a wound-up clock. Every tick he managed to remember one thing at a time.

He was Nick Ryder.

He was a lumberjack.

Falling, he remembered falling.

A trestle had collapsed under him.

Looking around, he could see he was on one of the exam-ining tables in the doctor's office off the side of the lumber-camp dining hall.

Looking around helped him to realize he was in terrible pain.

It all rushed back with sickening precision.

His eyes shot wide as he thought of Ross.

Turning his head, which hurt like mad, he saw Ross with his head bandaged, scrapes and bruises discoloring his face, but he was awake and talking to the camp medic.

He remembered how still the boy had been. Caleb had found a pulse, but Nick had feared the worst.

Relief surged through Nick, and as the fear and tension eased, his thoughts clouded up. As if the tension was all that kept him conscious.

His eyes went on past Ross. Jilly sat in a chair, studying a bolt. A broken bolt.

Anger replaced relief, and his focus returned.

"Figure out where you went wrong, Jilly?" He'd been calling her Jilly for weeks now. He considered her ma, Margaret Stiles Beaumont, to be the next thing to a mother to him. That made the Stiles sisters his sisters, though that word bothered him to no end because his feelings, at least for Jilly, weren't those of a brother.

But Margaret. Yes, a mother. Protecting her, warning Edgar to never touch her again. Nick loved that woman like he'd loved his own ma.

Jilly rose and came to his side, leaned down, and turned her head so he could look straight up at her. It was a lot less painful than having to turn his head, and it struck Nick that Jilly was a thoughtful woman with a mind to his comfort.

"Do you see he's awake, Doc?" she called over her shoulder.

"I'll be right over."

Jilly turned back to Nick and held up three fingers. "How many?"

"Are you the doctor now?"

Jilly smiled, but her face showed strain, and her color was high. A worried, upset woman, for a fact.

"I suppose I'd qualify to be called a nurse. Are you saying you can't see well enough to count my fingers?"

"It's three. Stop examining me and tell me what happened out there."

"I'll tell you everything, but first you should know we've stopped all work on the railroad track until I find out why I was sent substandard bolts from California Ironworks. Right now, I don't trust a single thing I get from that company. As soon as you're able, we're heading for San Francisco. Mama's already gone, remember? Laura and Caleb brought that news out not long after the noon meal."

His head ached, but that did seem familiar. "Okay, I do remember. We need to chase that woman down."

"We'll leave as soon as you're able to travel. Once I get to San Francisco, I'll go straight to Eric Barritt, the president of California Ironworks. I will make sure I get top-quality steel, and while I'm at it, if I tell my story right, I might get my beloved stepfather, along with Royce Carlisle, thrown in jail for the harm they did you, Ross, and Garvey. They can renew their acquaintance with Jarvis and Horace Benteen in San Quentin."

"Is Garvey all right?"

"He has a broken arm. It wasn't too nasty of a break, and Doc feels like he got it set straight, so he'll eventually be fine. But he's going to be laid up for a while. Doc has him resting in the infirmary. We'll have our hands full keeping him from going to his own cabin to sleep."

"And Ross?" That's who had Nick really worried. Although for a man who worked with his arms and his strength as Garvey did, a broken arm could end his career.

Jilly's brow furrowed with worry, and her voice dropped to a whisper. "He was unconscious a long time. He's seeing two or more of everything, and he keeps falling asleep. Doc is really worried about him still."

For a second, her eyes brimmed with unshed tears, and Nick thought she might cry. He had to fight the urge to pull her close and hold her while she wept.

"It's my fault. I trusted California Ironworks. It's a mistake I won't make again. Everything, *every single thing*, we have shipped gets checked and double-checked." Jilly straightened, then paused and leaned back down, but she wasn't whispering anymore. "And if I can't get Edgar and Carlisle arrested, I might just strangle both of them."

"Only if you get to them before I do."

Jilly gave her chin a firm jerk of agreement, then stepped aside so Doc could take a turn examining him.

NINE

NICK DIDN'T MAKE IT TO SUPPER for three days, and even then he nearly had to crawl to do it, but finally, he sat with the Stiles family—not counting the runaway Margaret. He sat up straight, too. Of course, his back hurt so badly he couldn't bend, so sitting up straight was his only option.

The gash on his forehead was bandaged, but he had a bruise spreading down the whole left side of his face and his left eye was mostly swollen shut.

His knees wouldn't bend . . . or rather, he made them bend, but they made him pay for it.

Four nails were torn all the way off his fingers, and the rest were broken below the quick from his trying to claw a grip into the collapsing brace.

He was glad they didn't serve anything hard to cut, hard to chew, or that he had to see well to scoop onto a fork. It seemed the cook had known about his injuries, or he was really lucky. He ate mashed potatoes with a thick shredded-chicken stew poured over it. And he was relieved to get some food into his belly. He needed to regain his strength for the trip to San Francisco, which he was determined to force them to go on tomorrow and get to Margaret before something happened to her.

Nick had spent time training with Old Tom to learn more about Stiles Lumber, and he'd felt safe being away from the house as long as Zane and Caleb were close by. Once Zane left, Nick had found himself pressed into the job of assisting Jilly in building the railroad. With Edgar gone and Caleb with Margaret and Laura, Nick had agreed to help.

He should have never trusted a headstrong Stiles woman.

Margaret had gone to town to fight. She'd taken good men along. Nick knew it, but for some reason, he'd come to believe he was needed to protect Margaret, and by extension, Jilly. The two most vulnerable Stiles women needed to stick together. Vulnerable because one of them wasn't married, and one of them was.

He didn't intend to shirk his duty.

And that meant sitting up straight enough that Jilly would cooperate when he headed for San Francisco in the morning.

"Nick, you need to go lie down before you fall down." Jilly frowned at him. Even with a frown twisting her face, she was still the prettiest thing he'd ever seen.

Her green eyes flashed with concern. Her red hair was twisted in a careless bun. She had little patience for fancy dress and elaborate hairstyles, even though wealthy women such as her often focused on such things.

Instead, she wanted efficiency. She wanted fast. She wanted to dress in such a way that nothing slowed her down.

"California Ironworks did a nice job of interfering with your train tracks, didn't they?" Nick wondered what exactly she intended to do about it.

"Those bolts were old, rusted, maybe washed in acid, then painted to look new. I should have examined them more closely and made sure I got what I ordered." Jilly scooped more chicken gravy over a new pile of mashed potatoes, then tapped the ladle sharply on her plate.

"I thought I could trust them, and that makes me a fool."

"Why on earth would you have thought you couldn't trust Mr. Barritt and California Ironworks?" Laura asked.

"Because I know some of the men on the board aren't happy about missing their chance to marry into Stiles Lumber. I trusted C.I., but I should have looked closer. I should have been expecting trouble."

"Horace Benteen is in jail, and Myron Gibbons can't marry me."

Nick saw Caleb lace his fingers with Laura's. She gave him a look so full of love that Nick looked away to not intrude on such an intimate moment.

"Just because Gibbons knows he's missed his chance with you doesn't mean he won't conspire to cause trouble out of spite," Nick added. "And even if he's given up, that leaves Royce Carlisle. And I'm sure he's furious at losing his chance to gain a stake in your company."

"But he hasn't lost his chance, has he?" Laura asked.

"We have controlling interest in the company," Jilly said. "Now that we've ousted Edgar, we are running this company right. No man can marry me and hope to have any power over the company."

"No power over the company, maybe," Caleb said, "but he could have power over a third of the profits. You'd still make a valuable wife."

"And he might threaten you, big sister." Laura gave Jilly a worried look. "He might threaten to hurt you if we didn't agree to do things his way. I'm sorry, but you're still in danger, and the company, too, as long as you're unmarried."

Nick studied Laura's expression. He had expected impatience with the one remaining unmarried Stiles sister and concern for her safety, of course. But . . . Laura seemed worried about something else. Something deeper. And why had she said she was sorry? Laura and Michelle had married quickly and, no one could deny, with some recklessness, but they'd done it. Why not Jilly?

Nick didn't ask. He was a little worried about the answer himself.

He hoped the battered face he was wearing masked his expression.

Jilly focused on her meal so hard you'd think she hadn't eaten for a month. With swift concentrated bites, she finished her chicken, tapped her lips primly with her napkin, and put her hands on the table to scoot her chair back, obviously ready to end this uncomfortable conversation.

"Just a minute." Caleb, a mild-mannered preacher whose ministry focused on loving others, could find a voice that cracked like a whip.

Nick had one himself, though he had to admit that Caleb used his with good effect, probably because it was so unexpected.

Jilly froze even though Caleb had no authority over her.

"Let's pray before you leave, Jilly. Pray for your ma's safety. Pray for the success of our trip. And pray for healing. For Nick here and for Ross, who's still fragile, and Garvey, who needs his arm to heal well for him to be able to continue as a logger."

Jilly folded her hands and bowed her head. Nick suspected it was with some reluctance, as she'd been solely concerned with escaping her sister's and brother-in-law's comments urging her to marry without delay.

Nick bowed his head and listened to Caleb. Nick's prayers went up, as they'd done since the accident, for Ross and Garvey. For Margaret's safety. For his own body to heal and his strength to hold while he went running off to San Francisco. Riding horseback all the way down a mountain, through the little town of Hatcher's Creek and on to Placerville, the nearest town with a train station.

It's why Jilly was building a train track up here, and they needed it badly. It would speed up getting logs to the sawmill and make a huge difference in getting supplies up the mountain. In the end, it would raise everyone's profits.

But it had to be done safely, and for that, Nick prayed hard that they'd get to the bottom of what had happened out at that trestle.

And getting there began with a long ride tomorrow.

Caleb finished with the hope that they'd all find joy in their lives and find an end to all the burdens they bore. Then Jilly went on up to bed. The rest of them followed soon after.

TEN

J ILLY, LAURA, what are you doing here?" Michelle exclaimed. "Why aren't you building a train track?"

"Michelle!" Jilly threw her arms wide and ran to her big sister, Laura only a pace behind.

Zane grinned fondly at the sisters, then his eyes went on past them to Caleb. Then he shifted his gaze again and locked on Nick. He rounded the little knot of women standing outside the Nob Hill mansion, knowing Margaret would be coming out to join them, too. He walked straight for Nick.

"What happened?" He wasn't just talking about Nick's face. They'd abandoned something Jilly was wildly eager to do way too soon after they'd started.

Watching the women chatter and hug, Nick quietly said one word, "Sabotage."

"Tell me."

Nick gave a quick summary of the snapped bolt, substandard metal, and delayed shipment. Caleb threw in a detail or two.

"How far did you fall?" Zane asked.

"About twenty feet. I'm the lucky one. Another logger fell as far and hit harder. He's still not fully alert, though we're hoping he'll mend. And that heavy wooden brace landed on a third man who was trying to break our fall and ended up breaking his arm instead."

Zane considered it all. He'd already talked with Margaret about the delayed rails when he and Michelle had arrived late yesterday afternoon.

Michelle had been downright shocked to hear Margaret had escaped Nick's vigilance. Of course, to do it, Margaret had to sneak.

"What brought you to town?" Nick asked.

"We were lucky enough to have one of the men in Dorada Rio when Laura's telegram first came. He brought it straight back. Michelle read it and started hollering. We were on the train before the end of the day."

"Busy time of year to be away from the ranch."

"Yep." Zane didn't say more.

Nick shook his head. "We would have been right behind her if I hadn't been knocked silly. I was a while coming around, then my head wasn't clear."

Margaret emerged from the house and joined in the babbling. Probably smart babbling, but that's what it sounded like to Zane.

"Margaret's already been to California Ironworks once, and we were headed back just now." He glanced at Nick. The man looked used up and that was only the honest truth. Quietly, Zane said, "She was just going to fuss at the poor man some more. Not that he doesn't deserve it. But Margaret is determined to oversee every step of those rails being shipped. Now with that trestle accident, she'll want to stand and watch the bolts being made. We can look after the Stiles women. You go in and rest up from the trip."

"I've done nothing but sit all day."

Jilly must've told her what happened, because Margaret spun around and her eyes locked on Nick's battered face. She came straight for him, so fast Zane had to jump out of the way.

She got close, her arms outstretched, then she hesitated and didn't touch him. "You look like you hurt everywhere."

Nick shrugged, then winced. "I took a beating when that bolt snapped, no doubt about it. But I was hurt a lot less than Ross or Garvey."

"You go on in and rest."

"Nope, I've been sitting all day. And you shouldn't've taken off without me."

Zane watched Margaret's sincere concern. He wasn't a sensitive man, so it didn't bother him overly that Margaret liked Nick a lot more than she liked her sons-in-law. Caleb was for certain second, which made Zane her least favorite. But third wasn't so bad. Out of three, though.

He turned to see how Nick would handle this strong-willed, kindhearted woman.

"If there's trouble facing me, there is no one I'd want at my side more than you, Nick." Then she started fussing. "You said Garvey is hurt worse than you?"

A woman who knew the men who worked so hard for the family's company.

"A broken arm. We're trying to convince him to heal up

with his wife down the mountain. But he says he'll find some work to do, even if he has to help cook."

A lot of the men were married. They spent the harvesting months in the mountains and the winters in their own homes with their families. "If it heals straight, he'll be fine, but—"

"Garvey has always used his strength to make his living." Furrows lined Margaret's face. "I'll make sure he knows we will find a job for him while he heals as soon as he feels up to working. I'll keep him on the payroll, but he'll see sitting around as shameful, and drawing a wage while he sits around even more so. We'll hope he gets back to full strength. But if he doesn't, we'll keep him on wherever he ends up. He can work with you and Tom for now."

Old Tom had followed Margaret out of the house and come up to demand an explanation for Nick's bruises and what else was going on. "I can use him. There's plenty to do for the lumber company even with one broken wing. Ross too. I hope that kid heals. Likeable young man, good heart, hard worker." Then Tom said solemnly, "Can you and Caleb take over here, along with Zane? I want to get back to the mountaintop. Too many of the people in charge are away. They'll need someone to give orders."

"We can handle it," Zane said, overriding whatever the rest of them were going to say. "Even with Nick laid up. Trust us to take care of Margaret."

Jilly turned to Tom and hugged him. "And thank you for looking after her until we got here."

"There's a train coming through in an hour. If we hurry, we can catch it." Tom tugged on the brim of his hat. He and the two men who'd come along turned and walked away.

They didn't even go back into the house to pick up whatever clothes they'd brought along. Anything they'd left behind would catch up to them soon enough.

"I was going to spend another hour or so nagging Eric Barritt," Margaret said. "All my scolding was going to be about the late shipment of rails. Now I intend to demand he personally inspect every bolt we buy and see that each and every shipment isn't tampered with in any way until it's delivered to our doorstep. I want to get to the bottom of how these bolts were replaced with inferior ones. I suspect I know the truth, but I want someone to go to jail."

She rested one hand on Nick's shoulder. "But my nagging can wait until I hear all about the damaged bolts. Let's go inside and discuss what's to be done next."

Zane saw Margaret's concerned gaze rest on Nick. His black eye was the green one, and there was only a slit of the bright color showing. His blue eye was wide open and laced with pain and exhaustion—sitting all day notwithstanding.

The family headed inside. Zane suspected, even if no one admitted it, that the delay in all of them charging to the ironworks was about Nick.

He was a trusted family friend now, and they took care of their own.

ELEVEN

JILLY STILES ALWAYS came back to the mansion on Nob Hill.

She was alone, walking down the dark hallway, a candle in her hand the only light.

And then she wasn't alone. There was Edgar. Laughing. There were flames. No escape. The room she was trapped in burned around her. Edgar's painful grip on her wrist, his leering face looming over her, whispering terrifying threats, accusations, all her fault.

Then she heard a terrible crack overhead. Even caught in the dream, she knew this was different. She'd never dreamed this way before.

She was no longer trapped in her burning bedroom. She stood outside, in the mountains, under a half-built train trestle, watching it collapse.

Nick falling, being battered by the timbers. Falling and falling, he hit tumbling braces. The fall was endless, the gorge she stood in was a bottomless pit.

She cried out his name, knowing he'd die. Knowing it was because she'd failed. She'd caused this. She'd killed him, just as her actions with Edgar would kill Mama.

She tore against Edgar's grip, clawed at the hand holding her, the man laughing at Nick's fall, his vicious face lit up by flames.

She trembled in fear, then trembled as if the whole world was shaking. An earthquake. It set her free from Edgar, from the dream.

She jerked awake.

Nick was beside her, shaking her, pressing a cool cloth to her face.

"Are you awake?"

"Am I . . . am I . . . what?" Jilly was so confused that her fine memory failed her.

With a sigh of relief, he said, "You are. I'm glad."

She realized he'd turned the lantern up, and the room was well lit. She glanced at where he had a grip on her wrist . . . or no, that had been Edgar. Nick, with his bruised face, had a grip on one shoulder and a damp, cool cloth in his other hand, still bathing her face. She saw what might be claw marks on the back of his hand. He didn't mention them as he sat on her bed beside her.

In her bedroom.

Dismayed, she resorted to outrage. "What are you doing in here?"

"You called out to me." Nick was only calm, only gentle. "I happened to be walking down the hall."

"What are you doing in the hall outside my door?"

Nick was silent as he looked at her. He lifted the damp cloth from her face and tossed it into the bowl by her bed.

Then he studied her face for too long. "Why did you call out for me? I assumed, as I walked past your door, somehow you knew I was there, saw me or heard me. You sounded . . . well, upset. I thought you needed help. I came in. I asked what you wanted. It took me a few seconds to realize you were in bed, caught in a dream. I turned up the light, hoping that would wake you, but soon saw it wouldn't. I shook you and such to pull you out of what sounded like a really horrible nightmare. Then I thought maybe the wet cloth would help."

Instead of the outrage, she should be thanking him.

"Do you have them often?"

"Doesn't everyone have nightmares sometimes?"

His kind expression suddenly bleak, he said, "I reckon they do. What was it about?"

And that was a question she'd never answer.

Instead, she asked, "What time is it?"

Nick glanced at the red-and-gold ormolu clock on her bedside table. "Three in the morning."

"What are you doing up, wandering the halls?"

"You're fully awake and back in fighting shape. Good."

"That's no answer."

"I'm awake because you all sent me to bed yesterday when we arrived in town, that was about five o'clock. I thought I'd rest awhile, then come down for dinner. I just now woke up after a ten-hour nap. I couldn't get back to sleep and was hungry, so I was headed down to the kitchen to scrounge some food. I'll get on my way if you've escaped from your nightmare."

Jilly didn't want him in here. The only stronger urge was not to be left alone in this room with her dream haunting her. She knew she would sleep no more tonight.

Forcing a small grin that grew as the idea took hold, she said, "The chef skipped his fancy food tonight, probably because we didn't give him any notice of you and I and Caleb and Laura arriving. He made fried chicken instead. There's some left. And he made a custard."

She arched her brows twice, to tempt him. "I know where he keeps the key to the icebox."

Nick straightened sharply, but she saw the amusement in his eyes. "He locks up the food?"

"He's French. He's temperamental."

"Let's go. We'll throw him off if he was planning to serve leftovers."

"Monsieur Rouviere would die before he'd serve leftovers. I suspect he planned to eat it all himself. As much as he turns up his nose at *nourriture américaine ennuyeus.*"

"What?"

"It means 'boring American food.'" Jilly was glad to talk about something besides her nightmare.

"Is he really from France?"

"He speaks French. He cooks French. He *acts* French."

"Whatever it means to act French."

Jilly shrugged. "Papa had him checked out before he hired him. He's from Omaha."

"Well, he's a good cook, so he can speak and act any way he wants." Nick rose from her bed.

Jilly shivered a little when she thought about a man rising from her bed.

He turned away, found her lightweight silk robe that she wore in the summer draped over the foot of her bed, tossed it at her, then walked away.

"I'll wait in the hall."

Which was very decent. Relieved not to be alone with her thoughts, she hopped up, pulled the robe on, twisted her wild red hair into a knot at the back of her neck, and slid on a pair of green knit slippers that matched her robe. Suddenly afraid Nick would leave her, she rushed out into the hall. She almost barreled into him as he stood a few feet back from the door, waiting patiently.

He caught her by her shoulders in time to avoid a collision, then in gentlemanly fashion, which she thought was sweet, he offered her his arm. He was being deliberately formal to balance her being in nightclothes.

They descended the grand staircase together in silence, neither of them wanting to disturb the household.

Or maybe that's why he was quiet. She just didn't want anyone else to hear them and come looking for a midnight snack with them. With the dream still haunting her, being alone with Nick sounded right.

They reached the bottom of the stairs and walked through the entrance hall to the back of the house to the kitchen. Once in the kitchen, with the door closed, Jilly felt it was safe to speak, at least quietly.

While Nick turned one lantern up to dimly light the kitchen, Jilly found the key to the larder and took out two chicken legs. She gave him a conspiratorial grin and handed one over.

"No plates?" He took the chicken and got a quick bite.

"Think of it as a picnic." The chicken had really been good. Monsieur Rouviere had probably used his mama's recipe he learned in Omaha.

"Nick, part of my dream was about you falling. I haven't apologized enough for that. I failed to inspect those bolts. I shouldn't have had to, but now I see part of being responsible for a project includes not assuming things are as ordered. Instead, I need to—"

"Stop, Jilly." Easygoing, hardworking, overprotective Nick glared at her. "Just stop with your apology."

NICK WATCHED Jilly's eyes widen in shock, then her temper flared.

Good. It was exactly what he wanted.

She'd been subdued, even wounded since the accident. All her bright, fiery energy was snuffed out like a guttered candle flame. She'd been treating him like he was her doddering grandfather, and he'd been too battered to do much but let her.

Now she'd included him in her nightmares.

That was going to stop.

He was feeling better, and there was nothing about him that wanted her so beaten down. "I'm not going to sit here and listen to this. It's wrong, and worse, you know it's wrong."

She took a bite of chicken, listening.

He was impressed that she listened to old Grandpa Nick. "Why are you letting Carlisle or Edgar or whoever is behind this make you think you're so terrible?"

"I don't think I'm—"

Nick swept his chicken leg in a slash that'd do justice to a saber. "Where is your passion for this project? It was all you talked about. Now I don't see any excitement in you for the train track. Are you really going to quit because you were betrayed? Are you going to let nightmares invade your sleep, torment you, and put that defeated look in your eyes over someone who cheated you?"

Her chin came up. Her green eyes flashed. No defeat there. Good.

"You were given substandard material by a company that prides itself on being the best in the business. You said just that, many times, while talking about working with them, and while complaining that your order was late."

"They are the best." Her protest was weak. She took another bite of chicken and chewed thoughtfully.

Nick snorted. "California Ironworks owes you damages. Mr. Barritt can make excuses all day and all night, but somewhere in his supply chain, someone got lax, got greedy, got tricked, got something. So he's got people working for him taking bribes to send out damaged bolts. Those bolts aren't your fault. My fall isn't your fault. We had people badly hurt, could've been killed because of those bolts. And that's laid right smack at the feet of Eric Barritt."

He watched Jilly stand a little straighter with every word he spoke. Fiery, but now that anger wasn't aimed at him for telling her to shut up.

He hoped.

She tore a bite out of that chicken leg like she was tearing a stripe off an army private who'd been caught deserting.

"You're going to *demand* Barritt get to the bottom of what happened. You're going to *demand* he make good the lost time your injured men will be out of work. You're going to *demand*—"

"I can think of my own demands." Jilly used the chicken leg to jab at him. "I am going to tell Eric Barritt to fill my order correctly and immediately even if he has to go into the foundry, forge that steel himself, load it personally on train cars, and haul it to the top of a mountain with armed guards. He can't be sending out poor quality material like that. He'll be ruined. California Ironworks will be ruined. And I'll lead the ruination."

She found a small stack of linen napkins on a shelf, grabbed two, and went to the table where the servants ate. A table adequate for six people, which was all the staff Nick had seen in this monstrosity of a house . . . which was half the size of the one on the mountain.

She slapped a napkin on the table in front of her and another one right around the corner. Nick got the head of the table. They sat and munched in the flickering glow of the lantern light.

Nick got up for a second piece of chicken. A breast this time. "More?" He waggled the crispy brown meat at her.

"Sure, I'll take another leg."

He brought them over, and they ate in companionable silence. "So is Monsieur Rover, or whatever his name is . . ."

"Rouviere. *Rooo-vee-air.*"

Nick didn't try it. "Is he going to kick up a fuss about the missing chicken?"

"Not to me." Jilly grinned, and they finished eating like

83

a couple of naughty kids who'd stolen a cooling pie off a windowsill.

When Nick was full, and starting to wonder if he could actually sleep a couple more hours, he set the chicken bones on one half of the snowy white napkin and wiped his fingers off on the other half.

Then, knowing it was probably a mistake, he gently asked, "What was the rest of the dream about?"

All her fire extinguished like he'd thrown a bucket of cold water on her newly crackling flame.

Yep. Mistake.

Slumped shoulders, chin down, she chewed. Then, her chicken gone, she looked at him, right in the eye. "You said everyone has them. It occurs to me, Nick Ryder, that you've been plunged into my family's mess, and you know just about every intimate detail of my life."

Nick wondered what she meant by "just about." What didn't he know?

"How about quid pro quo?"

"Quid . . . uh . . . what's that? You've got another cook around here named that?"

"Quid pro quo. It's Latin. It means a favor for a favor. Give and take."

"And that's your dream? Someone doing you a favor and asking for one in return."

Her eyes narrowed. "You're avoiding my question. You want me to tell you what haunts my dreams, but you won't tell me what you have nightmares about. In fact, Nick, I realize now I don't know a thing about you."

"Sure you do. I protected your mama from Edgar. What else do you need to know?"

"I don't need to know a thing." Jilly paused and licked her fingers slowly.

Nick couldn't help but watch.

"But I'd like to know about you. I'd like to be a kind enough person that I want to get to know a man who protected my mama. Where did you grow up?"

"I was born in Michigan." It had been a long time since he had really talked about himself.

"I knew that. You told me you know lumbering from working in camps in Michigan and Minnesota. You know all about my family. Tell me about yours."

"Uh . . . my ma is dead."

Jilly reached out, her face etched with compassion. "I'm sorry."

He suspected she really was. "I left home to work when I . . . when I was, well, very young.

"You were thirteen. I remember when I first met you, you said, 'I'm older than you, and here you are building a church. I've been working, wandering, most of my life. I started in lumber, running errands when I was thirteen. Then as a lumberjack when I was sixteen.'"

"With your memory, I'm sure that's exactly what I said."

"What else?"

It almost wouldn't come out of his mouth. Not because he didn't want to talk about it, just because he was so out of the habit. "I'm the fourth born of ten children. The first son. My three older sisters married very young and left home before I did."

"Why did you leave so young?"

"Pa said it was time. He had a lot of mouths to feed." He wondered now if his sisters had married out of desperation to escape the always perilously hungry household, or if Father had told them to get out, too, and as women that had been their only escape.

Jilly's eyes narrowed. She was listening, thinking. Remembering whatever he said.

"I had six younger brothers and sisters at home when I left. I wonder if each of them was cast out just as early. My ma was always exhausted and frail, and the babies came one after another nearly every year. I went home once, years after I left, before I headed to Minnesota. Ma was dead, and I'd never heard. Pa had remarried. His new wife was round with a coming child."

"Are you in contact with any of them?" Jilly reached over and rested her fingertips on his hand.

Shaking his head, he said, "I'm not sure I can remember all their names. I've never tried to find any of them. I was too busy scrambling to survive on my own."

"How did you start in lumbering?"

"Pa spoke to his boss, who owned a lumber company in the forests of Michigan. At first I was terrified of the big, rugged men. I was a boy used to hunger and cold but also used to being surrounded by family."

Her fingertips shifted so her hand rested on his.

"Gradually, I came to trust the men and love the life. For the first time, I had plenty to eat and a warm fire at night. I learned the smaller jobs, running errands, carrying around whatever needed carrying. I handled horses, forked hay to them, and cleaned dirty stalls. Later, I helped with the cooking and just did whatever was asked of me until I was old enough and strong enough to work the two-man saw and heave the logs with pry bars and lots of hands onto the horse-drawn sledges. A buddy told me he'd heard they paid better wages in Minnesota forests, so I teamed up with him to head west. I stopped by to say goodbye to my family, a good number of my siblings were gone, and the new woman was there. I didn't stay long. I've never seen them again, and learned to never think of them."

"Never?"

"Mostly never."

"Were you born with heterochromia?"

Nick grinned. "That's a twenty-dollar gold piece of a word, Jilly."

She shrugged. "Were you?"

"No, I got socked in the eye in a schoolyard tussle when I was a kid, real young. I barely remember it. When my eye stopped being swollen shut, I looked like this." He pointed at the green one.

Then his grin faded. "Your turn."

Jilly rose from the table.

Nick was on his feet and caught her wrist, turning her to face him.

Looking him in the eyes, she said, "Just like the bolts, the rest of the nightmare isn't my fault, either. But I have to live with it, it seems."

Their eyes held for too long. Then they held longer.

With Edgar for a stepfather, waiting until she turned twenty-five might be too late to save her. "I think we should get married, Jilly. It would protect you from Edgar. Protect you from Carlisle. And I'd do my best to . . ." He cleared his throat. "To make sure you were never alone and scared in the night again."

She didn't slap him.

Instead, tears brimmed in her eyes, and it was worse than a slap.

"I'd never do that to you, Nick. I like you too much to do such a thing to you." She tugged loose from his grip and swept around him. He let her go, when his hands itched to grab her again. Drag her back. Drag her close.

But those tears. Jilly didn't cry. That was what Mama Stiles said. Laura was her crier. Michelle and Jilly weren't prone to tears.

So what about a marriage proposal, one she honestly needed pretty desperately, would bring tears to a woman's eyes?

Nick was afraid of the answer, so he didn't ask the question.

TWELVE

JILLY FOUND she had a rare knack for terrorizing Eric Barritt, president of one of the biggest companies in San Francisco.

"Look at this." She thrust her hand forward, holding the bolt that had snapped under Nick's weight. "It's substandard iron."

The bolt was painted a metallic gray, but inside it was something other than solid steel. It was corroded and rusty, as if taken from some long-collapsed building.

"I inspected the bolts you sent, Mr. Barritt. Hundreds of bolts were exactly as ordered with dozens of faulty bolts mixed in. At a glance, they seemed fine. I picked up a handful of them to start the project and saw nothing wrong, and I left the higher up work to others. One of these old bolts gave way, and three of my men were badly injured."

At her wave, Nick stepped forward. He looked very battered. A good sample of the damage.

Mama had come into Mr. Barritt's office with her and

Nick. The rest of the family had agreed to wait in Mr. Barritt's outer office rather than pack into this room. But Barritt knew they were here. He knew she spoke for the whole Stiles family.

"Mr. Ryder was the least badly injured of my men. Neither of the others will be back to work anytime soon. And that's *if* their injuries aren't permanent. I'm now going to have to hand-inspect every bolt you send me. And this is no simple mistake. It's sabotage. This company is liable—"

"You"—Mr. Barritt cut her off, fire flashing in his eyes—"are absolutely right, Miss Stiles."

That surprised her enough she quit ranting.

"Our company sending you those bolts is outrageous. We stand firmly behind our products. This didn't just sabotage *your* construction. It sabotages California Ironworks, our reputation, the pride we take in being the very best. I'm going to shake up the whole production line. Every square inch of this place from the man who takes the original orders to the man who ships out crates of iron. Our orders do *not* go out late, and certainly if we ran into a delay, we'd inform you clearly and quickly."

Jilly had to get her last point across. "We suspect Edgar Beaumont of being behind this."

Mr. Barritt gave a firm nod of agreement.

But Jilly had more to say. "And he's in cahoots with Royce Carlisle."

Mr. Barritt seemed taken aback. Possibly even a little nervous, if Jilly read him right.

Carlisle was a powerful man. Edgar wasn't, not anymore. Accusing Edgar Beaumont of a crime would suit many people in San Francisco now that the source of Edgar's wealth and influence had been cut off.

It was entirely different to accuse Royce Carlisle of industrial sabotage, and yet, in Jilly's opinion, Carlisle was a much more likely suspect. The power he wielded reached deep into many companies. Unlike Edgar, who'd lost his seat on every board.

Jilly looked at Nick. His poor battered face. The blow to the head. Would he have been hurt if she'd gotten married?

Jilly shuddered to think of it, because she was sure his danger would only get worse if they married.

Except when Nick had suggested it, in that quiet kitchen, during their foolish picnic, giggling over stolen food, she hadn't shuddered for the first time ever. In fact, she'd been tempted to say yes. And that was worse than if she could just ignore it. Wave it aside.

Temptation had called like a siren song. To be protected by a strong man. A good and decent man, as her father had been. It brought out a side of her she was surprised even existed. A very feminine side. To her mind, a weak side.

She needed to stand straight and strong on her own two feet. Instead, she badly wanted to lean on Nick.

"What makes you suspect Carlisle?" Mr. Barritt asked.

Jilly felt Nick shift just a bit to stand closer to her. As if he'd let her lean on his strong shoulders no matter what there was between them.

"He wanted to marry me." Jilly had debated with her family whether to be honest about this. It was a disgrace, but Mr. Barritt would need a solid reason to truly suspect Carlisle. He might be careful with a new order, but fearing

Carlisle was essential to his vigilance. They decided to tell a shortened version of the truth.

"Mr. Carlisle tried to arrange a marriage through my stepfather without my consent. He now knows I'm unwilling, and Edgar knows not to do such a thing again. I think this is Carlisle's way of getting revenge." She wondered if Carlisle would aim his temper at Edgar, too. "Possibly even ruining our train track construction to damage my ability to take care of myself and my company in hopes he can still engineer a wedding."

"Serious accusations, Miss Stiles. I can see how Carlisle especially would have the means to apply pressure, bribe or threaten someone into doing dirty work for him within my company. Yes, I've got some ideas, and I can promise you . . ."

His promises were sincerely given, and she believed him, to the extent she believed he was capable of delivering on those promises.

He promised her bolts and rails would be delivered quickly. She told him she suspected her rails were even now being rerouted somewhere and possibly being replaced with poor quality workmanship.

"You'll get a new order that I will personally oversee. We'll start again and cancel any order already shipped. You'll be lucky to get back to the mountaintop ahead of the new rails and bolts."

"I know you'll do your very best." Jilly reached across the broad desk to shake his hand. He took it and shook with vigorous professionalism.

Once she had her hand back, she added, "But I'm still

going to have to inspect everything. My building project just got a big setback, and I lay that at the feet of your company."

"I can send a work crew up with the shipment. In fact, you've shown me the path you plan for your rail line. I'll send a full crew there to start the switching station at Placerville and build out toward you. I'll build up, you can build down, and we'll meet in the middle. My work crew will make up for the time you've lost, and the cost of that will be on C.I. I'll pay their wages for the summer in exchange for the time you're going to have to spend inspecting my hardware."

A generous offer.

"I'd appreciate the extra workers, Mr. Barritt, thank you. Now I need to get back to my mountain and back to work."

"Your supplies will be coming so fast you might see them catching you, if you look over your shoulder."

Jilly turned to Mama, who stood quietly behind her. Mama had let Jilly handle everything, but the esteem Mr. Barritt held for Margaret Stiles had added weight to all Jilly's charges. A mama who respected her daughter enough to let her wield the power.

Then Jilly glanced at Nick, who'd stood quietly at her side. A man who hadn't tried to take over. A man who'd proposed to her last night in the kitchen of the Nob Hill mansion.

She thought of how, in her nightmare, she always came back to the mansion on Nob Hill. And now she had a chance to shift those nightmares, changing them so she wasn't alone with Edgar in that mansion. If she accepted Nick's proposal, she'd never have to be alone again.

Jilly gave her thoughts a mental shake to again escape

the temptation. She led the way out of the office to meet her family, and quickly told them of the results of the meeting. Before she could finish, Mr. Barritt came out of his office. He greeted them, then told them he was headed straight for his foundry to arrange their order. He headed out at a near run.

"Zane and I are going back to the ranch," Michelle said. "We came to San Francisco to make sure Mama was protected. Now that you're all here, we can get Zane back to his baby calves."

Zane patted her on the back. "The calves are nearly all here. We'll spend time branding, then there's some slower times while we let the babies grow a little, let the older steers fatten up. My brother, Josh, can handle that. In a few weeks, Michelle and I will come up to the mountain and help build the train track."

Mama flung her arms around Zane's neck. "I'm as lucky in my sons-in-law as I've always been in my daughters."

Zane's cheeks turned a ruddy pink, but he hugged Mama back with gentle strength.

They all got on the streetcar and rode along, the streetcar running on rails to make the way easier for the horses.

They finally reached the bustling train station where Michelle and Zane could take a train to Lodi, then ride home on horseback.

Jilly smiled at her very bossy big sister. "I really miss you, even if I do like taking charge of building the railroad."

"I'm sure things would run more smoothly if I were there."

Jilly laughed and hugged Michelle tightly. "Except for the extra time spent bickering."

Michelle laughed back. "We'll be up to visit soon. In a month or two, I hope."

Everyone was hugging and saying a few last desperately important words.

Zane spoke quietly to Nick, studying his battered face. Jilly caught only the words *Be careful* and *Take care of them*.

Then the train whistle blasted, and Zane hustled Michelle on board. Jilly noticed how comfortable he looked. He hadn't done much traveling until he'd met and married Michelle. Now he jumped on the train like a seasoned traveler.

They found seats so Michelle could wave out the window.

"We've broken up the team." Jilly spoke softly, almost to herself, then she turned to see Laura nodding and dabbing her eyes.

Caleb slung an arm around Laura's neck and pulled her close. "No, you've added to the team."

Laura sniffled and leaned fully into Caleb's strong arms.

"We have. I know. And it's a good team, just different." Jilly didn't say more as she watched Laura and Caleb, a good team all their own. A beautiful picture of two people in love. But it hurt to know the three Stiles sisters would never be just the three of them again. As much as she and Michelle sometimes rubbed each other wrong, that's how Jilly had seen the three of them. A team. One unit with three distinct heads. She'd never again be as tightly bound to her two best friends in the world. Now husbands were their closest family, and that was as it should be.

But she felt the weight of the loss as she stood with Nick, Mama, Laura, and Caleb, waving as the train pulled out of the station. Jilly didn't cry because she just wasn't a crier, but she felt the burn of unshed tears in her eyes and almost wished she'd said yes to Nick last night. Then she could lean against him for comfort the way Laura leaned on Caleb.

A whistle blasted steam out of the locomotive's smokestack, and the wheels squealed as they were forced to roll. Michelle waved out the window, and they all waved back. The train engine hissed and roared, making even cries of farewell impossible to hear.

The train picked up speed, and Michelle withdrew from the window as the train rolled out of sight.

The rest of them headed for home to change into traveling clothes. They had enough time to go back to the Nob Hill mansion, pack, and get back to the station before their own train left, heading, Jilly lamented, in a different direction.

"YOU'RE A FOOL if you think I'm just going to forget thousands of dollars, Edgar." Royce hadn't gotten to be one of the richest men in America by accepting failure.

And he wasn't going to get his money back. He knew it. Edgar didn't have it. Which left him to get what he'd paid for himself.

Jillian Stiles.

Ever since he'd seen her in the flesh at a theater performance several years ago, he'd wanted her. He'd very discreetly allowed Margaret Stiles to discover his interest and judged her reaction. When she'd adamantly told his messenger it was unthinkable, Royce bristled. An arrogant woman, Margaret Stiles, as her husband had been an arrogant man.

A lot of work had gone into getting Beaumont to agree to an arranged marriage, and the fool had demanded a very high bride price.

Then, without Royce knowing about it, Edgar had lined up two more husbands. He had three stepdaughters, after all.

Worse, he'd been sloppy enough that word had reached Margaret, and things had gone downhill swiftly.

But it wasn't enough to change Royce's plans. A father had rights. A daughter could be brought to heel. And Royce wanted a spirited woman. His wife of twenty years had been spirited at first. But she'd faded over the years, gotten weepy and quiet until he'd had to grit his teeth to be in her presence.

Finally, she'd passed from this life and left him alone. What he felt for Jillian Stiles could be allowed free rein.

Royce had plans and plenty of them. The bolts were just the beginning. He didn't want a wife who acted in manly ways. It was outrageous. Destroying her building project was just the first step he'd take in bringing her to heel.

"What else can I do, Royce?" Edgar said. "I've been locked out of the town house and the mansion, but I'm willing to help. I still have some confederates on the mountaintop, though they thinned out the men loyal to me. Whatever we do, we need to plan it carefully."

"Tell me what that place is like. I might just send my own men up there to grab her."

He'd never been to the Stiles mansion. He was among the highest social elites in San Francisco, just as the Stileses were, but Liam Stiles was a man of rigid ethics. And Royce had been of another mindset. There was great wealth to be found if a man was willing to look away from unsavory things that added to his pocketbook.

Stiles's ethics and Royce's averted looks didn't mix well, and the men had never dealt with each other while Liam was alive. However, the Stiles Lumber accounts were in the bank Royce had recently gained control of. Word had reached Royce almost immediately when Edgar's name had been removed from the Stileses' accounts. They went so far as to completely close those accounts and open new ones to make sure no mistake could be made about granting Edgar access.

Today he'd received word the money had been moved, every penny of every account associated with Stiles Lumber and the family personally, to Wells Fargo. It infuriated Carlisle to know his money, as well as Gibbons's and Benteen's, was lost.

The Stiles women were certainly known for their intelligence. They knew full well they'd moved money paid as bride prices. They'd as good as stolen it. But to get it back, he'd have to sue, and to do that, he'd have to admit he'd as good as bought a wife, then had his offer thrown back in his face.

His pride wouldn't permit that.

There was no getting it back. Which meant Edgar owed him. So Edgar would pay. When the time came, Edgar would pay dearly . . . and so would Margaret Stiles.

"I've got a few ideas, and yes, the men you have up there can help. I have to move a few pieces on my chessboard first, but when I need you to contact those men, be ready."

Edgar nodded, as eager to please as a puppy. A puppy would have had better survival instincts.

THIRTEEN

THE STILES FAMILY had been back from San Francisco for two days when a foursome of handsome brown Clydesdales pulling a massive wagon loped into the yard that surrounded the mansion. A sedate quarter horse was tied to the back of the wagon.

It had to have started up before dawn to get here before the noon meal. The trail wound back and forth across the side of the mountain because the path straight down was impossibly steep.

Another wagon pulled in behind that one, then a third and fourth. These wagons were pulled by sturdy mule teams, six drawing each wagon.

The long overdue rails. There would be spikes to drive through the wooden railroad ties, too. And the replacement supply of bolts.

Cases and cases of bolts. Grim at the thought of the massive chore ahead of her, Jilly accepted this discouraging new task as part of being responsible.

The stout man driving the Clydesdales threw the brake on his wagon and swung down. The men behind followed suit but stayed with their teams. Jilly noticed they were unhitching the mules.

The teamster approached her. He was hugely muscled and wore a vest instead of a shirt, his arms bulging as he moved. His face was a mess of unshaven beard, his hair long and black, pulled back and tied off with a leather thong. The man looked rough, but his hands had been gentle and steady on the reins of these spectacular horses.

"Name's Hawley, Miss. I'm looking for Jillian Stiles."

"That's me." Jilly had been standing on the porch, two hours after breakfast, chafing over the delays in her train track and providing no fit company for anyone.

"I've been told to leave the wagons as well as this team of Clydesdales with you, Miss Stiles. Mr. Barritt knows you use draft horses up here, and he's hoping four good Clydesdales will be of service to you. He's sending them by way of an apology for the delays and poorly made bolts. There's to be no charge for the bolts, nor rails, either."

Jilly's eyes shifted to the four massive horses. They were beautiful. A perfectly matched foursome. Shining dark brown coats, black mane and tails, and white feathery hair around their hooves that matched the white blazes on their faces. The curves of their muscled bodies gleamed. It struck her that the Clydesdales were a likely match for Mr. Hawley.

She and her sisters had seen a few Clydesdales in San Francisco and talked of getting such beautiful horses. They'd do a lot of hard work up here and be very well treated. But Clydesdales were rare and very costly. They would have only been purchasing them for the love of a beautiful animal, and their mules and Belgians did fine work.

The team of Clydesdales had beautiful leather traces, and the wagons were brand-new and sturdy. And the rails and bolts for no charge?

"We're to take the mules back with us, but the wagons are all yours."

It was a fine gift Mr. Barritt was giving them. The man truly did not want them to blacken the reputation of California Ironworks.

"You can use the team to haul the rails out to your railroad bed." Mr. Hawley sounded as if he feared she'd reject the gift. "The team is well trained, and they've been used to haul logs before, too. I'll leave the rails on the wagon and unload the bolts for inspection. Of course, you're welcome to inspect the rails, too, but maybe they can be checked without unloading them. They're mighty heavy things."

Mr. Hawley moved the quarter horse to the side, dropped the tailgate of the wagon, and set to work unloading the wooden crates with the help of the mule skinners. Jilly went to the Clydesdales. She picked the one nearest her and ran a hand over its shoulder, enjoying the scent of the horse and the smooth silk of its coat.

The horse twisted its head to nuzzle her shoulder, and she turned to pet him on his rounded nose while Mr. Hawley worked. A brass plate on its bridle read *Samson*. Amused, she wondered what the other horses were named. Strong names, she had no doubt.

Several lumberjacks saw the unloading start and hurried over to help.

"We have our own wagons and supplies for the rails we'll build out of Placerville, Miss Stiles," Mr. Hawley continued. "These are for your use up here."

The drivers made short work of prying open the crates of bolts.

"Mr. Barritt's crew is already at work leveling the roadbed. They'll be laying the tracks down there while you work on the trestles up here."

Jilly felt as though she'd lost control of the project. She could just go inside and sit down, and the railroad would be built.

She was frustrated, but not so much that she'd fight over gaining all this help.

Mr. Hawley pulled his hat off his head and clutched it in such an abject, humble way Jilly had to wonder what Mr. Barritt had said to the poor man. "I'm to help you inspect these bolts if you wish, Miss Stiles. And my drivers along with me. Mr. Barritt told me to help in any way I could."

"I'm sorry to say, I want my own trusted men inspecting them. I'd love the help, but this is my responsibility, and I'll see it through."

He replaced his hat, tugged the brim, and gave her a slight bow. "We'll get on back, then. We'll be working toward the bridge that we'll need to cross the river at the bottom of the mountain. I was given to understand you'd be building that bridge while we built the rail line."

"Yes, we'll finish the trestle here that collapsed, then I'll come down the mountain and do that bridge next. I hope to have the bridge completed before you reach it."

With a hard nod, he untied the saddle horse from the

wagon and swung up on it. The other men each mounted one of their mules with the rest of their teams strung out behind, and together they rode down the trail.

Jilly went to work.

All she could figure to do was scratch at the bolts to make sure the steel wasn't painted on. Heft them for weight and toss them, one by one, into a bucket, counting them as inspected.

Garvey Bates came to join her. With his arm in a cast, and his long years with Stiles Lumber, Jilly couldn't find one single reason to mistrust him.

Ross Baker was in the infirmary. Still addled but mostly awake now. Poor kid.

She'd quickly told Garvey what to look for. Weight. Scratch at the bolt to see if rust was underneath a coat of paint, toss it into the slowly filling bucket.

Then Nick came. Jilly couldn't figure out how to suspect him of anything, either. Maybe Laura, Caleb, and Mama would join in this job, but she wouldn't ask them. It was her job, her responsibility.

They worked along, finding no defective bolts. And Jilly was more than sure they wouldn't find any.

Nick tossed an inspected bolt into the bucket and said, "We really were lucky those bolts broke." Nick's eye was still black, but the worst of the swelling was gone.

He'd said that before about being lucky. She knew there was truth in it. But it was such an ugly truth she couldn't bear it.

Garvey, working one-handed, grunted but didn't comment.

"We were *not* lucky." Jilly bent over the wooden crates of bolts, inspecting each and every one before she moved them into new boxes. As soon as she had enough for the trestle, she'd send the men back to work. This time with safety harnesses.

"Of all the stupid things to say." Though she admitted inside that in one huge sense they'd been lucky. "You could have been killed."

"Better than having it collapse under the weight of a train. Maybe a train with passengers besides the train crew. Maybe you'd've been on that train. Maybe I would've been on it. Maybe your whole family and the whole building crew would have wanted to be on as it crossed that trestle for the first time. Instead of a black eye and a bashed-in head, a lot of us might've died. Laura, Caleb, you, your ma."

"That had to be the intent—to have the trestle collapse under the weight of a train," Jilly agreed.

Nick nodded. Garvey's jaw went tight in anger.

"They hoped we'd get it all built, and it would collapse." Jilly glared at the perfectly made bolt, then tossed it. "It would be chalked up to a terrible accident and viewed as an incompetent woman being in charge. We'd've given up on Papa's dream of a train track up here—assuming we were alive to do that. And if I lived, I would have been ruined. I'd have a terrible reputation, and I'd've lost all confidence in myself."

"The kind of thing a man might do, an immoral man, who wanted you ruined. Wanted you to have no future in construction, which is what you have planned for your whole life."

Garvey looked away from his task. "You want me to head

104

on, Miss Stiles? It sounds like you've got troubles to talk through. I won't be spreading it around, but if you want it private, I'll go."

"No. In fact, you can help." Nick scratched a bolt. "You can keep your eyes and ears open. I don't think whoever did this is finished. I expect more trouble."

Jilly was inhaling at the wrong moment and started to choke.

Nick paused from his inspection of the new order of bolts and patted her on the back.

"Don't you agree? Carlisle will come at you from a different direction next time."

Once she could breathe again, she admitted the truth. "Of course he will. These bolts are fine, but I still have to be thorough about them, don't I?"

"Yep." With a clink, Nick tossed a bolt into the approved crate and reached for another one. Hundreds of bolts to go. A full day would go into this stupid effort.

She saw no choice but to plow forward.

"WE'RE STOPPING." Laura threw down a bolt in disgust and rose from the barrel she was sitting on. "You're wasting time, Jilly. Let's get back to building."

High noon.

Nick wondered if there'd be a showdown between the sisters.

"Now, Laura, honey." Mrs. Stiles always wanted her daughters to get along. She was sitting in a more comfortable chair, one with wooden legs and a padded seat. It'd been brought out for her when she came to help inspect bolts.

Laura was right. But Nick understood why Jilly did this. Her confidence was badly shaken by what had happened. His cheek was still tender, and his eye still black. His ribs were sore, though he'd decided they weren't cracked. And his knees were still swollen. They hurt, but they were working well enough he didn't limp.

"That accident happened because I trusted someone else to do my job," Jilly said. "That's not going to happen again."

"A *smarter* way to do this," Laura said, facing Jilly with her hands on her hips, "would be to train the construction crew to test each bolt before they use it. We're halfway through these bolts"—Laura swept her hand over the cases of bolts, both inspected and waiting to be inspected—"and we haven't found a single bad bolt. It's obvious that Mr. Barritt kept close watch, and no one was able to do any damage."

The whole family was out here working, plus Garvey, Doc Sandy, Old Tom, and Carl. They'd even pulled in Sarah, the maid who'd been so loyal to Mrs. Stiles. Everyone, in fact, the family felt they could trust.

Jilly threw a bolt hard into a crate of inspected bolts. "Don't tell me I'm not smart."

Nick saw a little color in Jilly's cheeks. She'd shown signs of a fighting spirit. Like when he'd lured her down to the kitchen to loot the family larder. The woman had regained control of the situation, but she'd regained control by taking complete control. And now Laura was challenging her to, instead, trust her men.

Nick rose slowly, not wanting to get in the middle of the

standoff, but he was an honest man, and maybe Jilly would listen to him. "Laura's right, Jilly. And the men building will be scaling those trestle timbers. They're going to check their bolts carefully."

He looked at the work crew that had been gathering for the last few minutes but had not been invited to work. "You know what we're looking for, right? You'll be able to be careful? Check each bolt before you use it?"

Jilly sputtered as Nick took over. She knew her control was slipping away and didn't like it.

Nick turned to her. "I liked the idea of looking for substandard material, but we've done it enough. It's clear that California Ironworks was careful with this shipment. Let's start building again. We can set a crew up at the top, as you suggested." He worked that in to remind her and the others that she was running this. "We'll put a rope around the waist of each man who's climbing the trestle, then no one needs to do a thing on the ground but keep back if something falls. Inspect each bolt as it's used. Safety ropes. That's enough."

Jilly, looking frustrated but slightly mollified by Nick's much more careful speech than Laura's, stiffly nodded. "You're right. We'll use the bolts we've already inspected first, then each of you men will inspect the bolts as you use them. Much better than this."

Everyone sitting around the crates, using barrels or chairs dragged outside the men's quarters, straightened with a sigh, so identical from every mouth that it set them all to laughing.

Jilly waved them toward the dining hall. "Eat a good meal. We'll get to work in one hour. With Mr. Barritt's crew working, we're going to have to hustle. We'll finish this trestle, then we've got to work from the bottom. We'll do that big bridge next to stay ahead of them. It'll mean camping down there. We won't have time to ride home every night."

The men nodded.

Nick knew she was right. There wasn't time to head down to the bottom of the mountain every morning and come home every night. They'd waste half the day just traveling. He was glad for the extra help. All those skilled workmen Barritt had sent would make this go so much faster. Assuming those workmen could be trusted. Assuming substandard bolts, rails, and spikes weren't being used down below by a strange crew.

Before Jilly could skip her meal to stand sentry, Nick said, "I'll eat out here to guard the inspected bolts. No sense undoing hours of work."

Nodding, Jilly said, "I'll get us two plates and stay out with you. Maybe bring Ross out. He's getting steadier."

Nick thought of the young man. He seemed ages younger than Nick. But Nick was only twenty-five. He'd just lived the kind of life that made a boy turn into a man fast.

Ross was only eighteen. And painfully infatuated with Jilly, who he watched with longing in his eyes.

Once in a while, Nick was tempted to handle the kid a little roughly to get his mind back on his work. For now, he said, "I'd like to see Ross up and around."

"I'll bring him." Garvey slapped Nick on the shoulder, and knowing the man's strength, Nick braced himself to keep from staggering forward.

Nick was glad they'd soon be getting back to building.

FOURTEEN

T HE MEN ARE REFUSING to work?" Jilly almost staggered when Nick delivered the news.

"A strike." Nick shrugged. "Most of them are with Barritt's crew. I think that's where this is coming from."

This morning they'd ridden down the mountain in two wagons with all the men who'd been working on the trestle. Jilly had sent other men ahead two days ago to collect the trimmed logs they sent daily down the flume and corral them until they had enough to form the foundation of the bridge. A train was a massively heavy thing, and the bridge had to be as sturdy as stone. The braces had to come from a sawmill and should be shipped from Placerville soon.

She'd left plenty of lumberjacks up on the mountain working hard. The demand for wood never eased, and they had a lumber business to run. She'd gotten a crew together to build the trestles but couldn't assign any more lumberjacks to her train track project.

And now this.

For a long moment, Jilly considered just quitting. They got along without a train, and this was Papa's dream. She'd taken it as her own, but that ugly accident with the collapsing trestle . . .

"It's the same sabotage as before, isn't it?" Jilly didn't think it was a question that needed an answer.

"I think so." Nick stepped closer to her. "I know what lumberjacks earn. Yours are very well paid. They're well fed. You give them comfortable shelter. They get their Sundays off, so once this train is built, they will be able to ride down the mountain almost weekly rather than be separated from their families all through the logging season."

"Yes, we've thought of that and told the men the ride down and back would be free for them."

"No one treats their men better than Stiles Lumber, and I've worked in lumber at several places, so I know. We can go talk to these men, find out what they want, but I think we're going to have to send Barritt's crew home. They've been working for a solid week and made good progress. They've prepared the roadbed and laid train tracks for ten miles from where this track connects with the main line. They've been saving this until you came down."

Jilly nodded. "We can finish it without them. I'll make sure Barritt knows what happened. They're his men. He's paying them. They might find it hard to get work back in San Francisco if the president of California Ironworks speaks against them."

"They're probably making money on the side to rabble-rouse. Edgar or, more likely, Carlisle is paying them." Nick rested one strong hand on her upper arm. "If we get the troublemakers out, the men will go back to work, but the tracks will be built slower without Barritt's men."

"We planned to do it all ourselves anyway. I should have known better than to let Barritt get involved. If they're bought and paid for by Carlisle, the work they're doing can't be trusted anyway. We're going to have to check every inch of it."

Nick's grim expression said he agreed.

"I'll go talk to them. I'll listen to their complaints, and if any of them are valid, I'll make adjustments. If that isn't enough, I'll fire Barritt's men and take the job back over with my own crew. Any of my men who stick with the strike can head down the road with the others."

Nick said quietly, "A strike can get dangerous. Do you want me to speak for Stiles Lumber? I'd hate for them to get ugly with you. I'd need to start cracking heads, and that'll slow down our building even more than firing Barritt's men."

Jilly met his gaze. Those odd eyes always drew her. She wanted to be indignant, but she knew he was right. The trouble was, this was her test. This was her job. She had to do it.

"Thank you, Nick, but no. If I can't handle this, then, well, I have to rethink my whole life. Let's go see if I'm capable of running this job."

"You don't have to handle it yourself. You can still build bridges and homes, even tall buildings if you want to. However this ends, you can still do all of that. Listening to ugly language and threats, standing close to men who might be violent, isn't necessary."

She managed a smile, but it felt like a sad smile. "I think it is necessary, Nick."

He studied her closely, his eyes flicking back and forth between hers as if he wanted to read her thoughts. Then, with a reluctant nod and a pat of encouragement, he said, "I'll be there beside you while you try to settle the crowd."

Jilly looked at Laura, Caleb, and the other men who'd ridden down the mountain with her this morning.

Loyal men.

The strikers, if there were any with the Stiles Lumber employees, had been staying in the tents down here with the California Ironworks crew for a couple of days, working with them and gathering the needed logs that came shooting down the flume. Maybe they'd been swayed, or maybe she still had men who were in Edgar's employ.

She turned to the men who'd ridden down with her wagon. "Are you men with me? Have I not given you fair wages? I know you all work very hard, but Stiles Lumber has always appreciated that and rewarded hard work. Do you have complaints about the conditions, food, the amount I ask you to work?"

To a man they shouted, "No." Someone said, "Best lumberjack wages in California." Another said, "We'll stand with you, Miss Stiles."

A couple waved their hats, shouting encouragement and loyalty.

These men were solidly with Jilly. They'd fight for her if called to do it.

She hoped and prayed no fight was necessary.

She turned to Nick. "Lead me to the strikers."

JILLY CLIMBED UP on a crate and shouted, "Please listen to me. I've come to hear your complaints."

Nick watched her wave her arms at a grumbling crowd of about twenty men. He'd been told a dozen. Was the crowd growing?

A few more men shouted. "Better pay. More men to share the work."

"Better food. We're working too long of days."

Other voices drowned Jilly's calls for their attention.

Just as Nick began to think he'd need to stand up there with her and start yelling, an earsplitting shriek cut through the air as Jilly whistled through two fingers. The angry men fell silent.

As the men realized they were looking at an unusually beautiful woman, the noise didn't fire up again, but the quiet wasn't exactly friendly. There was an edge to the men's attention that Nick didn't like.

"I am willing to listen to you. See if I can meet your demands and convince you to get back to work."

The men pressed forward. Nick shifted so he stood between Jilly and the crowd. Caleb came and stood shoulder to shoulder with him. Laura stayed behind Jilly. Nick thanked God for that.

Then others came to Nick's side, until all the men who'd ridden down from the mountaintop with them blocked the angry crowd from Jilly.

"We stand with Stiles Lumber, too." Men from the other side pressed past the strikers and turned to face the restless group.

"Do you have someone to speak for you?" Jilly asked. "Please, I'll listen. Stiles Lumber is known to be a good employer. We know how important the men working for us are to the success of our company."

One man shoved between two standing in front of him. "We're going to unionize."

Nick knew a union could serve good purposes. But he also knew these men weren't here to unionize. They were here to slow down the work, to harass Jilly and the whole Stiles family.

Carlisle and Edgar . . . their plotting was clearly behind this. Nick doubted there was a thing Jilly could offer the men because they were being paid not to cooperate.

"While you organize the union, do you intend not to work on the train track?" Jilly asked, her voice lower. And the men, whatever else they were, wanted to hear this beautiful woman's voice.

"No, we're calling a strike until the union is organized and our demands are met."

"And what are your demands? Maybe I can meet them right here, right now."

The men's grumbling dropped again. They seemed almost shocked that Jilly was so willing to listen.

The man who seemed to be speaking for the group said, "Shorter work days, higher wages, weekends off, better food, more men to ease the load on all of us."

Nothing too unreasonable—and all very vague.

Jilly's voice, still low, but still listened to keenly, asked, "Do you intend to take your demands to Mr. Barritt? He's the one who sent you up here. He's the one paying your salaries. I could shorten the workday and make sure you're getting good food. And I'm here right now with more men to lighten the load. But I can't change your salary, not without talking with Mr. Barritt."

"Mr. Barritt pays our salary?" said the man standing behind the ringleader. "We thought it was Stiles Lumber."

"Because of an order mix-up laid at the feet of California Ironworks, our work has been delayed," Jilly explained. "He sent you up here to make amends for that. He's handling your payroll. The men from Stiles Lumber are on my payroll. So what do you make?"

All the rabble-rousers fell silent. Nick suspected these men were well paid by Barritt, and their only real goal was to cause the work to stop.

The spokesman's face got red, and Nick braced himself to stop the man however was necessary.

"I'll send a wire as soon as possible to Mr. Barritt and explain what's going on and ask if he'll raise your salary."

"No need of that," a gruff voice sounded from deep in the crowd, which Nick thought had indeed grown.

"There's every need. I'll tell him you're demanding more money. We'll see what he says."

Nick knew exactly what he'd say. Unions were very unpopular among the owners of big companies. They often paid Pinkerton agents, or just tough men who'd swing a fist for a few coins, to break up strikes.

The spokesman strode forward until he hit Nick's shoulder with his own and almost knocked Nick sideways. Enough men stood with Nick that he kept his feet.

"What's your name?" Nick looked hard into the eyes of the man. Nick had never seen him before. That meant he was one of Barritt's men. Nick knew every man employed by Stiles Lumber.

The man clenched a fist. Nick knew this could turn violent

with one wrong word. Worse, he was sure that's what this man intended. The fact that there were even crowds on both sides was even better for him. More trouble. A bigger fight.

With Jilly and Laura easily dragged into the middle of it.

Nick studied the man, trying to figure out the right words to defuse the situation.

Then without any more words, the man swung a fist, knocked Nick onto his backside, and charged over the top of him right into the crowd of Stiles Lumber supporters.

As Nick took a heavy boot in the chest, an explosion ripped through the air.

Men behind the mob leader staggered forward. Flying shrapnel flew over Nick's head. The blast had deafened him. He heard Laura call to Jilly as if it were through a thick bale of cotton.

The man who'd just punched Nick fell flat on top of him in the throes of death. Nick shoved the man aside and got to his feet.

Dust and debris made it hard to breathe. The cries of the wounded echoed until Nick almost wished what was left of his hearing would quit.

He spun to find Jilly and Laura and saw them on the ground with Caleb clutching both of them, holding them beneath him. Caleb caught Nick's eyes.

"Get them out of here!" Nick said.

Caleb leapt to his feet and pulled Laura and Jilly up, shouting, "Run!"

Laura caught Jilly by the arm, and they ran, Caleb right behind them. Three other men were on their heels, acting as human shields in case there was another explosion.

Nick whirled around to see what could be done. The sight was a nightmare of blood and smoke, wails of pain. Men staggering, rolling, clutching themselves. Crying out for help. Other men lay bleeding, unmoving, dead or dying facedown in the dirt. Their backs peppered with metal bits from some kind of bomb.

Crawling to the nearest man, Nick judged him to be dead. He went on. Other men jumped in to doctor the wounded. Men who'd been shouting for a strike and threatening violence now turned to help their fellow man.

He saw Doc Sandy, who'd come down in the wagon to help work, attending men as fast as he could. Taking charge, snapping out orders.

Nick rushed to his side. "Tell me what to do."

Doc gave him one wild look, a look that reminded Nick this man was not a doctor—only a trained medic.

Doc gained control of himself through sheer will. His shoulders squared. His chin lowered with bulldog determination. "This man can be saved."

He jabbed a finger at the man lying in front of him. Only a few nasty-looking wounds on his back.

"No spinal involvement. Nothing deep. Rip his shirt off, use it to stanch the blood, then follow me."

Doc shouted for Old Tom, Carl, other men he knew. They were all alive and appeared to be unhurt, though they looked overwhelmed by the carnage. Doc's giving orders rallied them, and they jogged over.

Nick dropped to his knees beside the unconscious man. His head was bleeding the worst, but he could see the wound was a cut in the skin. No metal had sunk in.

The smell of blood and death almost froze him, but shaking away the shock, Nick pulled out his pocketknife and slit the man's shirt to get it off him, then cut the arms away and used them to bind up the wounds.

He pressed hard on the head wound to slow the bleeding.

The man groaned in pain. Nick felt cruel to hurt him like this, but he held the wound tightly until the bleeding slowed.

The man swung an arm toward his head with a feeble swipe.

"Hold on. Don't fight me. You're bleeding. I'm trying to get it to stop. You're going to be fine, but the more blood you lose, the slower you'll heal." Nick wasn't sure if that was true, but it was all he could think of to urge the man not to fight him.

The man turned his head sideways so he could look at Nick. "Wha . . . happened?"

Nick tied a bandage cut from the shirt around the man's head. "There was an accident. You're going to be fine. Just rest. We'll come for you when it's time to move."

The man lapsed from his struggles, having either calmed down or passed out again. Nick decided he'd done all he could and went after Doc.

Old Tom was working on one man with injuries similar to what Nick had tended. Carl knelt by another man, providing care. Every able-bodied man took orders and helped.

Nick waded through the bodies. Through the men helping.

Ahead, Doc bent over an injured man, shook his head, and moved on. He left one man after another in his wake, tending the wounded, abandoning the dead, a crowd of men falling away to obey Doc's orders.

Nick caught up to him when he'd assigned everyone a job. Doc's eyes were cold as if he had gained control but couldn't allow himself to feel anything.

"This man is dead." He swallowed hard and went on. "We're getting farther into the back of the mob. It looks like the worst harm was done in the back." Then the cold was laced with rage. "This bomb had to be set by the men striking, but why set it off at the back of the crowd? They only hurt their own men."

Doc's eyes skidded here and there. "Mostly their own."

It made Nick sick to think of who all might've been hit. It was nightmarish to see the dead and wounded, worse than nightmarish when he recognized men he knew. Men he'd led down here. Men who'd willingly put themselves between that mob and the Stiles sisters.

Doc moved, paused to check on an unconscious man, then moved on. Nick knew that meant there was no way to help that one. Doc found someone who could use treatment. But as they went farther into the crowd, more and more men were dead. Nick glanced around and counted a dozen men, more, too many to count at a glance. And there were many more who were wounded, being tended. He saw that Jilly, Caleb, and Laura had come back and were working over the men.

Nick wanted to get them away. Where there was one bomb, there could be another. He also hated that the women had to bear witness to such ugliness.

But he was busy and so were they. And they were smart

women, they knew the risk they were taking and the night-mares they might be bringing on themselves. Jilly and Laura had accepted it in order to help.

No one showed signs of protesting. Did that mean they were just too shocked to do anything but stumble around? Once the mayhem calmed, would the trouble start again? Would there be more explosions?

For whatever reason, the trouble seemed to be over. For now.

Unless you counted the travesty of all the dead and wounded men as trouble, and Nick certainly did.

FIFTEEN

JILLY NEVER CRIED. Almost.

The few times in her adult life she'd cried added up to being the exception that proved the rule.

Today was an exception.

She stood solemnly as men carried the dead and badly wounded to the edge of the work site and stretched them out to be taken away.

They had followed partially built railroad tracks to the small engine, with its tender car and a single flatbed car, not too far from where the bomb had gone off. The flatbed car had brought in a load of rails as far to the end of the line as possible. Then when the flatbed was empty, it would back up along the finished stretch of train tracks, drop off the empty car, and pick up a loaded one. This flatbed was empty and ready to back up for a new load.

And it did back up—but as a funeral and ambulance car.

The only dead men Jilly found who were Stiles Lumber employees were men she had thought she could trust, but they'd been siding with the strikers. She'd thought they'd cleared out all the men Edgar had hired. These men must have been swayed by some bribe or threat to side with Edgar against the Stiles family. Or maybe they really believed Stiles Lumber needed to treat them better.

There were also ten men who worked for her that were injured enough to need to ride on the ambulance-funeral car. Good men she knew well. The weight of it, the guilt, made tears push at her eyes and threaten to fall.

Fighting it, she stood at attention, paying all of the dead last respects. She'd spoken quietly to the wounded. Held a few hands. Promised they would receive the best possible medical attention.

Garvey, with his broken arm, had come down with the workers this morning, intending to ride the train from Placerville to his home in El Robles Blanco to stay with his wife until his arm was healed. Instead of an easy ride home, he sat as a mourner and as a caretaker to the best of his ability. The men would find medical care in Placerville, or some at least. It was a good-sized town, but this would be a burden on their doctors and what hospital facilities they had.

Garvey would make sure their treatment was the best—he carried a note from Jilly that promised to pay the bills of the men she'd specifically named—and bury the three of her employees who'd died.

She'd also ordered every man who'd threatened to strike to climb on the train, too. Their time of employment with Stiles Lumber was over.

That included all of Mr. Barritt's crew. Many dead, many wounded, among that group, but there were able-bodied men who were being sent away, too.

Any wounded among the Stiles employees who weren't seriously injured, and who'd stood with Jilly, were sent up the mountain on the wagons to be looked after in the infirmary. The rest of her crew went up, too. The work was done for the day.

They had sent word to Mama to wire Mr. Barritt to explain what had happened. He'd need to decide how to handle his employees' burials and their hospitalizations.

Mama was also to tell him the rest of his men were fired and would be returning to San Francisco. He had all his skilled labor back.

Jilly didn't know how to include sarcasm in a telegram, but she wanted to. None of this would have happened if she hadn't accepted Mr. Barritt's help. Another connection between Barritt, Carlisle, and trouble.

Three of her men dead. True, all three of them had turned against Stiles Lumber, but that didn't make their deaths hurt her stomach less.

Especially since she didn't know who'd set the bomb. One thing she couldn't deny was that it was far enough away from her that she'd never been in danger. Whoever did this wanted her ruined but alive.

Carlisle.

She turned, ready to make her own way home, and almost ran Nick down. His bruised face twisted her already aching gut.

He reached out and caught her before she stumbled into him. To hold her away? Or just to hold her?

Glancing around, she saw they were alone.

"We've got a bit of time. The last wagon was full, so

they'll bring horses down for us. Much faster than a wagon ride. Still, it's a long, slow trail. We've got a few hours, I'd say. I told Laura I'd wait with you, or she'd've never gone."

They stood face-to-face. Gently, he said, "I thought you might want time alone to let the worst of this shocking day fade, but I couldn't leave you down here completely alone. Is there anything I can do to make it easier?"

Jilly's throat was too tight for words. Her heart too heavy to be eased.

Nick, giving her all the time she might need to stop him, slowly pulled her close, then closer. Then pulled her fully into his arms.

The support, someone to hold her up . . . it was too much, the comfort too desperately needed. She broke down and cried.

NICK HAD NEVER THOUGHT much about women . . . well, a little, well, honestly, more than a little.

But he kept to manly places. His home growing up had been a place best left far behind, and he'd left before he was old enough to think about women.

Now here he stood, holding the toughest, most brilliant, and bravest of a tough, brilliant, brave bunch of women.

And here *she* stood, letting him hold her in his arms while she cried her eyes out.

Yep, right here and now, he was thinking about women, or more correct to say, a specific woman, and his thoughts were mighty . . . interested.

This brave woman's tears didn't count as a weakness because he'd had tears in his own eyes more than once today, working over the carnage. Seeing wounds on men he knew and respected. Seeing wounds on strangers. It all twisted his gut, broke his heart, and brought a few tears. Even now, a tear leaked from his eye as he thought of all those men so badly hurt, killed even. And he'd bet his life it was all aimed straight at Jilly Stiles.

Edgar trying to hurt Stiles Lumber, just striking out in vicious violence.

Carlisle because he still had his ratlike eyes on Jilly and wanted to put an end to any respect she earned that would give her a future as a builder.

Nick was sure that Carlisle was at the root of this evil.

With some discreet checking while they spent the winter in San Francisco, Nick had learned enough about Carlisle to sicken him. He'd seen the man just once. Little, skinny, and with stooped shoulders, Carlisle looked harmless until you heard of all he owned—and how he'd gotten it. Nick had heard of the brutal tactics Carlisle had used. Knowing what he knew, Nick had looked through the gold-framed glasses and seen the evil in Carlisle's eyes and the rot in his soul. The man made no attempt to disguise it. He reveled in it.

Nick suspected that the money and powerful connections Carlisle would make through a marriage to Jilly weren't truly at the root of Carlisle's treachery. The other men who'd contracted with Edgar to gain the hands of Michelle and Laura had given up with poor grace when those sisters had married. They hadn't wanted the women; they'd wanted the connection to the Stiles dynasty. They wanted the clout that came from moving in exalted financial circles in San Francisco, and Stiles Lumber was in the top echelon of those circles.

But not Carlisle.

Nick knew in his gut that Royce Carlisle wanted Jilly herself. He wanted her with the same hunger he felt for power. He wanted this spirited young woman. He wanted to own her and no doubt looked forward to crushing that spirit with relentless cruelty. He'd enjoy owning her and taming her.

And the bomb today was yet another attempt to intimidate her. Nick doubted the attempts would end while Carlisle lived.

The fear of what the man might do ended Nick's tears. Replaced them with anger and near desperation.

He held Jilly tighter until he might have crushed her, but her arms clung around his waist just as desperately. She allowed his grip. She might have even appreciated it.

Her tears slowed. Nick fumbled for a handkerchief and touched her beautiful face gently, the bit that wasn't buried against his chest.

She let loose of him with one arm only. He missed the feel of it, but she had nearly spent her tears. The sobbing changed to shudders. She mopped her face without looking up at him.

Pulling away, she turned from him and blew her nose rather loudly for such a feminine young lady.

Then, a final shudder or two breaking free, she at last squared her shoulders and turned back to Nick. She stood looking through him in that way all three Stiles sisters had of being lost inside their thoughts.

The handkerchief gripped in her hand as if she wanted

to strangle it, she stopped looking through him and looked him right in the eye.

"Is that offer of marriage still good?"

Nick blinked. Surprised. He'd hoped he could talk her around eventually, but that day had seemed far off. He held her gaze. Mismatched green and blue eyes studied her green ones awash in tears. Strength and beauty. Intelligence that he couldn't begin to match.

He'd come from nothing. And now here he stood with a woman beyond his dreams. Not only was the offer still good, he was delighted she'd asked.

"Yes." But he had to be as honest with her as she was about everything in her life. "Carlisle won't accept a marriage license and back away. He doesn't want a share of this company. He wants you."

Jilly's chin lifted. "You're right. He won't quit, and I endanger you by asking. He'll keep coming, but it wouldn't matter if he gave up."

"Why not?"

She flung her hand at the land behind him.

He turned and saw only blood on the ground. Everything else was gone. When he turned back, he saw that all her tears had burned away, replaced by fiery green fury.

"Because I am going to destroy him for this."

All her spirit and fire were alive and well.

"*We* will, for a fact." He gave a firm nod.

"If I marry, my sisters and I will own all of Stiles Lumber with Edgar wiped right out of the picture. We'll be, possibly, the most powerful women in the state. And I'm going to use every bit of that power to destroy Royce Carlisle. He's not going to come into *my* camp"—she jabbed a finger at the ground—"and kill *my* men"—she swept her finger around the bloody remains of the day's horror—"and expect to walk away from it. I need this company in my hands, under my control. Mine and my sisters', so I can wield every ounce of the power that it gives me to punish Carlisle for what he did today."

"We'd be truly married, Jilly." Nick should just say yes and marry her quick. He didn't want to do a thing to distract her from what looked like sheer determination. But he felt God was calling him to this bedrock bit of honesty. He didn't intend to wed Jilly and go on as a bodyguard. He intended to be a husband and every bit of what that implied.

Jilly looked at him. She looked into his eyes often. He'd never been sure if it showed her interest in him, or if she was just really interested in his eyes. What had she called it? Hetokrome? Something like that.

Right now, though, she looked deep. He did his best not to shield his thoughts. He had no wish to trick her into marrying him thinking it was nothing but a business contract.

She sighed. "I'm drawing you too close to danger. I suppose it's wrong of me to propose."

He smiled faintly. "Danger like being too close to an explosion? Or climbing a trestle built with defective hardware? Danger like that?"

"Just like that, only maybe worse because this danger was aimed at ruining me. The next time it might be aimed at killing my husband, so I'd be available for Royce Carlisle."

Nick shrugged one shoulder and drew one of his callused fingers down her tearstained cheek. "I'm right in the middle of the danger already, and I'm not going anywhere with or without marriage vows."

He leaned close and kissed her. Slowly, softly. Too long but not nearly long enough.

Then, leaning close to her ear, he said, "But I would much prefer it with marriage vows."

She drew back her head and looked at him, her face a little pale, her green eyes glittering, but not with happiness like a man wanted when he proposed.

Not with love.

"What is it, Jilly? Can you tell me?"

Jilly's gaze faltered and fell. And Jilly was one for looking a man in the eye.

He drew her close. She was stiff, didn't relax against him like she had when she'd cried.

He just held on. Rubbed her back like a man might comfort a sister or his ma. Nothing romantic about it. Only support.

"It's nothing. J-just fear of ending up in a bad marriage."

Nick knew she wasn't being fully truthful. Because of course it was the *why* that mattered.

He knew Edgar must have somehow terrorized her. He remembered how Edgar had cornered Laura at an unexpected spot at California Ironworks.

He'd picked his moment, caught her, and dragged her into a locked room, held her mouth closed against a cry for help, and scared her to death.

Laura had already married Caleb by that time, and when they found her, her whole body trembled with fear. Laura had told of Edgar's threats. Caleb had been able to comfort her. His love and her trust in him had brought the whole story to light.

Jilly had probably gone through something similar, or something worse. And earlier, before she and her sisters had run for their lives.

Before Nick met her.

Before there was anyone to protect her.

Well, there was someone now.

"Someday you'll be ready to talk about it."

"C-can we get married first? Can I tell you later?" Her voice was so faint he didn't think he'd've heard her if he wasn't holding her so tightly.

"Whatever you have to say changes nothing. I want to marry you. Tell me now. Tell me later. We can wait until it's something you want to say."

"And I feel best locked in my room at night. Alone."

He mentally stumbled over that. Leaning back, he saw she was still looking down. He touched her chin until she lifted her head and met his eyes.

"Do you mean you're planning to lock me out of our room? You don't want things . . . that is . . . married things . . . to pass between us?"

Jilly shook her head.

"I don't mind waiting for such things to happen. We don't know each other well yet. But I don't want the door locked against me. Let me sleep beside you. Let me hold you against the nightmares."

The bit of color she had on her face drained until her skin was ashen. He held on in case she fainted.

He could see he'd asked a lot of her. But was it too much?

Part of marrying her was to protect her, and to do that, he needed to be close.

At last she gave a tiny nod. "Yes, I'd like to . . . to wait for the intimacies of marriage, but I like the idea of someone holding me in the night. I like the idea of *you* holding me in the night. Yes. Thank you."

He kissed her, not sure if he should or not.

She didn't jump away, but she couldn't be said to show any enthusiasm for kissing.

When he pulled back, she sounded more herself. As solid and sure as the mountain she owned. A woman who never forgot a thing. Maybe that was at the root of her fear. That she heard every word Edgar had spoken, every threat. But was it more? That's what haunted Nick. Had Edgar done more than threaten? And was Jilly so terrorized by that she'd never welcome a husband's touch?

He was going to be her husband without knowing that.

And together they'd cast out her fear, whatever its root.

"Let's walk to meet the horses." Jilly extended her hand to him. "When we get home, we'll round up Caleb and speak some vows before this wretched day is done. Something good in the midst of madness."

"That sounds like a very good idea." He took her hand, and they turned and walked toward promises. Toward danger. Toward their future.

CHAPTER

SIXTEEN

MARGARET STILES hadn't known about Laura's wedding. Her daughters ran off to hide from Edgar's loathsome choices for bridegrooms with plans to find husbands and hurry home. She'd found out Laura was married when she came riding up to the Stiles mansion with Caleb in tow.

Margaret had almost put an end to Michelle's wedding. Once she was safe from Edgar's brutality and her thoughts had cleared, she'd realized urging her daughters to marry in haste to save themselves from Edgar's grooms was a terrible idea. She'd gone charging down to Dorada Rio, heard about the wedding in progress, and slammed into the church moments after the ceremony, shouting, "Stop the wedding!"

Now, she finally got to learn early about one of her daughters' weddings, and she could barely keep herself from clapping and laughing with glee.

Oh, she wanted this so badly it probably wasn't even wise.

But Nick was the strongest, kindest, most loyal man she'd ever met. And she'd as good as claimed him as a son almost from the first. Honestly, if Jilly hadn't agreed to marry him, Margaret might've adopted him.

But that hadn't been necessary. Jilly was bringing him into the family through a more traditional way.

Jilly, who Margaret had feared would never willingly marry.

And Margaret blamed herself for that because of how dreadfully she'd failed by marrying Edgar. But she shoved her guilt and regrets aside because they served no purpose and were a useless drag on her mind.

Without anyone needing to throw a net over her middle daughter and drag her down the aisle, the wedding was taking place.

When they'd gotten home from seeing the men off on the train car, they'd announced that they wanted to marry immediately.

Caleb had shaken Nick's hand and slapped him on the back. Laura had squealed with joy and hugged Jilly until her big sister had to stop her so she could breathe.

And Margaret felt like her children, her precious girls, were finally, fully safe.

And Nick and Jilly would live here, not like Michelle, who Margaret missed like she'd lost one of her arms. She liked Zane Hart very much, and Michelle was happy. And no rational mother could expect all of her children to stay within her grasp. Margaret had wished for it anyway.

It was a terrible day with the explosion, deaths, and injuries. Grim news had come bit by bit as injured men were brought up the mountain through the day.

Finally, the full story was brought by a badly shaken Laura and a deeply prayerful Caleb.

And Jilly hadn't come.

Margaret had twisted with fear until Jilly returned.

And when she did, she'd brought along an engagement and a wish to marry at once.

Nick had proposed.

No shotgun required to get Jilly to accept.

This marriage delighted Margaret as she watched the bride approach the groom.

Margaret was taken back to her own wedding to Edgar. How happy she'd been. So thrilled to find love again when she'd believed she had only room in her heart for her girls.

For a moment, panic rose in her chest, but she fought it down. She knew Nick by now. She'd seen him handle tough times. He was a good man.

Caleb held his Bible. Nick and Jilly stood in front of him. Laura stood as Jilly's bridesmaid. The four of them, the wedding party, stood in front of the crackling fireplace on this cool spring evening, in Margaret's favorite sitting room. She was settled on the love seat watching, a congregation of one. Oh, how she wished Liam could be here for this. The ache in her heart nearly broke it. Or broke what was left of it.

"Dearly beloved . . ." Caleb's solemn voice reminded Margaret that he'd been praying for the wounded and for the easing of the trauma of those who witnessed the carnage.

It was good for Caleb to have a joyful event today, too. Good for all of them.

Nick reached for Jilly's hand. Their fingers entwined. Jilly looked at him, so Margaret could only see half her daughter's face. And what Margaret saw was doubt. No glow of love. No happiness. Only doubt edged with fear.

It was almost enough to again make her stand up and yell, "Stop the wedding!"

JILLY SORT OF WISHED MAMA would yell *stop*. She'd done it for Michelle. What was holding her back now?

In the absence of shouting, Jilly had to make this decision herself. When Nick reached out his left hand for her right, she took it. With his fingers woven through hers, she felt his strength. Felt his courage.

"We are gathered here today in the sight of God, to join this man and this woman . . ."

Jilly had a nearly perfect memory. Every word Caleb said would forever be etched in her mind. She was being asked to vow before God—no little thing—to love Nick forever.

His hand tightened on hers as Caleb watched them closely. She listened intently.

Laura had found wild roses and brought them in. She'd wrapped their prickly stems around and around in a beautiful lawn handkerchief so Jilly wouldn't be scratched.

Mama had insisted she change into a green silk dress that was formal enough for a true society wedding, though usually the bride wouldn't be wearing it.

A bath and her hair fussed over.

Just as well, her dress, hair, and hands were streaked with blood and smelled of smoke.

Nick had to clean up, too. And Jilly saw he was wearing one of Papa's nice suits. Nick and Papa were of a size, and it fit very well.

One of the family porters had sometimes served as Papa's valet, though mostly Papa said a grown man should be able to dress himself.

Jilly suspected Ronald, the older of the two men who worked inside the Stiles mansion, and had for years, had helped Nick bathe and dress.

She wondered how loud and long Nick had protested.

But considering how well turned out Nick was, it looked like Ronald had won the day.

Nick's suit was black with a silk vest, white shirt, and an elaborately tied neckcloth. He looked every inch the high-society groom.

"If anyone should show just cause why they may not be joined together, let him speak now or forever hold his peace."

Jilly braced herself for Edgar to slam the door open, Royce Carlisle in his wake, shouting that Jilly was promised to another. Maybe blowing something else up. She realized she was strangling Nick's hand and forced herself to relax.

Silence prevailed.

Caleb went on.

He seemed so nice, so sincere. Laura had done well for herself.

Michelle too.

Now it was Jilly's turn. She held on to Nick's hand, she

hoped not to the point of pain, but she squeezed, hoping he'd know she was thinking she was getting a fine man.

"Do you, Jillian Stiles, take this man . . ."

It was time for huge promises. For a woman who dreaded the very thought of getting married, she found herself becoming surprisingly eager. "I do."

"And do you, Nicholas Ryder . . ."

It was her turn to feel his hand tighten on hers. She looked right in his different-colored eyes and saw a man she could trust. She certainly wouldn't have agreed to let him share a room with her if she didn't trust him completely.

"I do."

Mama clapped her hands a couple of times. Jilly was definitely doing what her mother wanted. And she imagined there were worse reasons to marry a man.

Caleb talked awhile longer, then he made a pretty gesture over them, sort of a sweeping arc with one hand, and said, "I now pronounce you man and wife. What God has joined together let no man put asunder." Then Caleb left off his solemn words, gave them a wide smile, and said, "I most sincerely pray that God will bless this marriage."

Then with an arch of both brows, he said, "It's customary now to kiss the bride."

Nick turned to her. She smiled, and he kissed her. She was glad he kept it short and gentle.

Mama hit them like a small tornado, hugging them both.

"I told Sarah to ask the cook for the best supper she could manage on such short notice." She took both of Jilly's hands in hers, the flowers now clutched by four hands. Mama's eyes brimmed with tears. "Congratulations, Jilly."

Her eyes turned to Nick. "Welcome to the family."

The tears trickled down. Nick handed her a white handkerchief, then rubbed her on the back. "Thank you, Mama Stiles."

More tears. Mama was lucky Nick's handkerchief was good-sized and very absorbent.

Nick slid his hand across Jilly's back and said, "Let's go have supper and celebrate this wedding. In fact, all three weddings. This is a big day. You ladies are now sole owners of Stiles Lumber."

From behind him, Caleb asked, "We don't have to go running off to San Francisco again, do we?"

Mama led the way out of the room. "No, we most certainly do not. Everything we need to do can be handled through the mail working with my solicitor. I think it's time we stayed home for a while."

"We should send a wedding announcement to the San Francisco papers," Jilly said. "And maybe convince some reporter to do a story on how the Stiles Lumber company is fully inherited by Liam Stiles's daughters."

They stepped into the family dining room. It wasn't built on a vast scale as many formal dining rooms were in Victorian mansions these days. The plain truth was, when they came up to their mountaintop mansion, the Stiles family did no formal dinners, no entertaining on any scale. This was their home, and it was built for their family. With room, of course, for a few guests, which was a good thing since they'd added to the family lately.

Mama hesitated over where to sit. She was always at the head of the table. When Edgar had come, he'd sat at the foot, though no one had called it that. They'd let him think it was the head. The girls had ranged between the two.

Nick went to her and said quietly, "You sit where you've always sat. This marriage doesn't change that you're the head of this family."

She gave him an uncertain smile and turned to her usual place. Nick helped slide her chair in.

Jilly noticed and thanked him for his good manners.

Nick smiled ruefully and told her he'd learned to do that only since he'd come to live here. Mama had instructed him in many things.

Then he helped seat Jilly while Caleb tended to Laura. The girls by their mama, the men next to their wives.

The table, covered with a snowy white damask tablecloth, gleamed with the best dishes and finely engraved silver. There were crystal water goblets at each place and two sets of candelabra on the table. Each held tall, white candles with burning wicks that scented the air with beeswax.

Mama signaled to the younger of the two porters to bring in the first course of the dinner as the family settled into place.

"While we wait for the solicitor to come, we've got a railroad to build," Nick said.

Jilly thought of the bomb and wondered if continuing was wise. But she didn't have to say that out loud. They were all no doubt thinking it. She thought of how important it was to have the project done before winter fell. That was going to be a challenge even without the sabotage she'd faced.

Caleb led the family in prayer, and tonight more than ever, those prayers were fervent.

Then the first course was there. A lovely, rich broth of spring vegetables.

She decided for now, she'd eat and pray and leave the future to God. She knew she wasn't good at that. She tried to manage everything for herself. And that was foolish because leaving the future to God was all anyone could do anyway.

CHAPTER

SEVENTEEN

JILLY WALKED INTO HER BEDROOM, and it took all the control in the world not to slam the door in Nick's face. She might've even reached for the edge of the door to swing it, but it wouldn't budge. A quick glance down told her why.

Nick had a firm grip on the door, as if he knew there was such a risk and wanted to spare them both an embarrassing tug-of-war.

He shut the door, and she only realized he hadn't come farther into the room when she glanced back wondering what he might be up to.

Leaning against the door, his arms folded, he looked steadily at her.

Her cheeks felt a temperature that probably meant she was blushing beet red. Not much made Jilly blush. She just wasn't given to such nonsense as weeping and blushes.

Already she'd wept in Nick's arms earlier today, and now her blushes were surely wretched with her fair skin and red hair. "I'd appreciate it if you'd step outside while I change into m-my n-nightclothes." She almost punched herself in the head to shake the words loose.

His eyes gleamed with amusement. "I will do that, but I came on in because I got to wondering if you'd lock your door against me if you got in ahead and got it closed."

Jilly thought of the key in her pocket. She'd hunted it up earlier with just such a thought in mind. Not that she'd fully decided whether to use it, but she had it. Only severe self-control kept her from sliding her hand in her pocket. A move that would indicate guilt as fully as a confession.

"Are you all right with me in here, Jilly? Tell me the truth."

The room wasn't fully dark, but dusk had settled. Two lanterns had been lit, one on each side of the bed, standing on matching bedside tables. The large canopy bed had enough room for three sisters to sleep comfortably side by side, as they had since Edgar had begun to scare them.

Suddenly, though, that bed seemed overly small to Jilly.

She wished he'd keep talking so she didn't have to. "I . . ."

Talking was exhausting.

"I'd be happy to sleep elsewhere for now and explain things to everyone, very honestly, if that is your wish," Nick went on. "I think Mama is really happy about our marriage. She's been so kind to me, and it's a wonderful thing to be wanted in a family like this. My own family wasn't so welcoming, not even to me."

He'd called her mother *mama*. Jilly felt her very fast-beating heart slide away from the fear and toward something softer.

"Your mother is a strong, wise woman."

"Edgar notwithstanding," Jilly added with some bitterness. "You know I was the only one who suggested she wait a bit. Get to know him a bit better."

Nick straightened from the door. His arms dropped to his sides. "No, I didn't know that. I thought you girls all said you really liked him, and that you were happy for Mama."

"We did like him. We were happy. But I wondered what Edgar would be like if he ever got angry or frustrated. We'd never seen him other than charming, full of smiles, full of kindness. Not before they were married."

"And you were bright enough to know everyone had bad moods. And you wanted to see what Edgar's were like."

"Yes, and I even did a few little things like keep him waiting when he'd come to escort us to some event. I sassed him a bit, nothing bad, but I wanted to test him. See if he'd react to a woman who was impertinent, but he was never impatient or even slightly annoyed, I think I felt the falseness of that. I didn't fully recognize it or admit it to myself really, but I know I wondered."

"Have you seen me angry or frustrated or in any way upset?"

"You weren't all that happy when you regained consciousness after the trestle collapsed under you. And you were stressed and, yes, angry, today after the bomb."

"And how did I act when I realized you were the Stiles sisters, and that Mama was in danger?"

"You were very upset and started rapping out orders."

"You couldn't say then that, in times of trouble, I've displayed an ugly, violent side or a falsely charming side? Well, not violent except wanting to beat Edgar into the ground."

"Yes, except for that." Jilly came toward him, as he'd stayed carefully away from her in this bedroom with the closed door. "On the contrary, Nick, I think you've come through many hard things with a strength of spirit that I admire."

Nodding, Nick said, "Good, so no surprises. I'm not going to change personalities now that I've got you in my clutches." He waggled his fingers like ten worms and put a phony sneer on his face.

Jilly giggled, which she also never did, right up there with crying and blushing.

She was the one who'd changed personalities.

"Um . . . I can hide in here." Nick looked around the room as if looking for something to crawl under. "Or I can stay in here until the household is asleep, go somewhere else for the night, then slip back here in the morning. I've considered it. But I assume eventually we'll get caught. Other people may wander in the night, sneak down to the kitchen to steal chicken, and they might catch me in the wrong room. I think it's best to either stay in here together or be honest that I'm not going to stay. There would be no harm in saying we've married in some haste."

Jilly snorted. "I've known you a lot longer than Laura knew Caleb or Michelle knew Zane."

"Well, I suppose we met when I came with Zane up to the Purgatory settlement when you were serving with Caleb's mission group. But I left that same day, and you came home not that long ago. I don't think you can count from the time we met when I immediately ran off to take care of Mama up here while you stayed with Michelle."

"I can count it if I want to."

Nick smiled. "Stay or go, Jilly, you get to decide. This is a very personal business, sleeping in the same room."

"The kind of personal thing a husband and wife do."

"True enough."

"I'd . . . like you to stay, but I have nightmares," she warned.

"I remember. If you have one with me here, I'd be able to wake you up and stop it from tormenting you. I'd be glad to be close at hand to do that."

Jilly swallowed hard. It really was quite a huge step to sleep next to a man, married or not. Well, married, because *not* was a ridiculous thing to throw in there.

"Then stay. I want you to stay. I have a changing room in here." She pointed to the side of the room where another door stood slightly ajar. "Mama had your nightclothes sent in there already."

"Your mother found my longhandles and brought them in?"

"She probably had Ronald bring them. I doubt she would go through your things."

Nick heaved a sigh of relief.

"You stay in here while I change, then we can trade places."

"Does the changing room have a lock?"

Jilly managed a smile, and she thought maybe her cheeks weren't quite so fiery hot after their talk. "Yes, but I promise not to lock you in there overnight. Although you could sleep on the floor. It's a large enough room you could stretch out."

"We'll see how sharing the bed goes, and if you want, you can send me to the changing room to sleep." He grinned at her.

She'd sassed him a little, and he'd liked it. She knew her straight talk and weird humor could be a problem. It'd be nice if it didn't offend her husband all the time.

"Go on then, Mrs. Ryder. I'll wait my turn."

Both her sisters were married. Jilly had personally witnessed them go into a bedroom with their husbands and close the door for the night.

She hadn't thought much about what it meant until it was her turn.

Changing into a floor-length, dark blue flannel nightgown—it got cold on the mountain most nights—she edged open the door and peeked out.

Nick saw her and politely turned his back. "Go on and get in bed, then I'll change."

"There's clean wash water. I used part of the pitcher and tossed it away. You can use the rest."

She almost ran to the bed. Then she pulled back the covers and slid in, drawing the sheet and blankets up to her chin.

"Go ahead now," she shooed him.

Nick watched her, grinning, then headed for the dressing room.

Was she on the wrong side of the bed? This was the side she usually slept on.

She fretted over that until the door to her dressing room cracked open. She couldn't quite control the glance she took. Then she giggled and pulled the covers over her face.

"These," Nick as good as growled, "are *not* my longhandles."

"Blue silk?" Her laughter broke free again.

"I'd've just worn my woolen longhandles except I took them off and left them behind when I dressed for our wedding."

"You took off from Zane's ranch to ride here with only the clothes on your back, but Zane sent what you had. That included silk?"

"My stuff took a while to get here. Mama ordered a few things for me, without me realizing it until the package arrived. She kept things from your father and passed them on to me a few times, too." He strode toward the bed, slid in beside her, and pulled the blankets up to *his* chin.

"I'd've gone to my room for my regular clothes if I hadn't already washed up and needed to come through this room on the way out. She must've bought these for me along with the spare shirts and pants. But she held this ridiculous getup back."

"It's very nice. Not your usual style, I imagine." She pulled the blanket down and peeked at him.

She'd seen enough before to know the silk top looked like a rather loose dress shirt with a pocket embroidered in white threads with an elaborate *N*. The pajama pants matched. Of course, she couldn't see them anymore. It struck her that he was as nervous as she was. It helped her calm down.

"She planned this. She hid these and waited for her moment." Nick lifted up the blanket so he could look down at himself. "Sneaky woman, Margaret Stiles."

"You'll get used to it. It's not scratchy like wool. And no one's going to see it. You can wear it every night for the rest of your life, and no one will ever know."

He dropped the blanket back over himself, then rolled onto his side. He propped his head up to look at her. "You've seen it."

"That's true. So there's no sense hiding from me. And I find I like the idea of my husband wearing silk."

Nick rolled his eyes. "Your mother should know me well enough not to buy me silk pajamas."

"A few minutes ago, you were calling her mama." Jilly shifted to her side, less embarrassed by her nightwear now that he was so unhappy about his. She propped her head up on her fist, mirroring Nick. She realized the beautifully globed lanterns were still burning on both sides of the bed. Night had fallen, but it was fully lit in this room, causing a shimmer on the collar of his pajamas. She reached over to touch the silk. It was wonderful. Soft and shining, smooth and rich. And a suspicion popped into Jilly's head.

"It occurs to me that Mama might have bought those pajamas not because she thought you'd like them but because she knew *I'd* like them."

Nick looked startled. "You mean she was hoping for this marriage?"

"Mama looked delighted today. Not once did she shout 'stop the wedding.'"

Nick nodded his head slightly, then with a little more energy. He poked Jilly's shoulder. "We're going to have to watch her like a hawk all our lives, or she'll be managing us without us even knowing it."

Jilly caught his pointy hand. "Mama is usually excellent at managing things. So that won't be so bad."

148

Nick didn't answer. Instead, he curled his own hand around hers, leaned in slowly, and kissed her.

She didn't jump up and run. Thought about it. But she stayed, figuring it might be right to share a good-night kiss.

He tilted his head, and the kiss deepened, though she knew nothing about kisses of any depth. But this one was gradually deeper. It was the only way to describe it.

Still holding her hand, he shifted and slid his other hand under her, holding her close, then closer.

A shudder went through her. He had to notice. He dropped her hand and slid that arm around her, too, and rolled her onto her back so he loomed over her.

Much like Edgar had.

She wrenched her head sideways and slapped a hand flat on his chest. "We agreed, Nick."

"We did, for a fact, agree." He was still over her, still looming. Those peculiar eyes studied her for too long. "Thank you for the good-night kiss, Mrs. Ryder."

He smiled at her and moved onto his back. He turned the lamp down to a barely visible glow.

Jilly did the same with the lantern on her side of the bed.

Then he reached out and took her hand as they lay side by side. She realized she hadn't felt this safe since Edgar had shown his true colors.

She wished she'd had the courage to do more than kiss Nick. But an inner dread kept her from speaking up about Edgar's threats. And that dread wasn't Nick's fault. He didn't deserve it. Though he wouldn't know why, she wove her fingers tighter through his in silent apology.

And she held on through a dreamless night.

"THREE OF MY MEN ARE DEAD, Carlisle." Edgar slammed a fist on Royce's desk.

The fist startled Royce, and he jumped, which struck him as weak and made him angry with himself. He couldn't abide weakness. All his life he'd been smaller than other men. Poor eyesight, not as strong physically, mocked by the boys he went to school with. Scoffed at by the girls.

Even his parents had sneered at him. His father was a blacksmith, and Royce's two older brothers had stopped their schooling by eighth grade when they'd finally grown big enough to do a man's work. They'd become blacksmiths alongside Pa. His family didn't respect education. They wanted a son strong enough to be proud of.

In San Francisco, with its cutthroat prices and shrewd business practices, most any man willing to work hard could do well for himself.

And Royce's father and brothers had worked hard.

But Royce wasn't ever going to be strong enough to swing one of those massive sledgehammers. He'd tried a few times, and his father and brothers laughed at him.

So Royce had gone off to college and found a way to pay for it all himself. He learned there were plenty of ways to make money that didn't include a sledgehammer and a burning forge. And none better than building railroads.

He didn't lay track or swing at spikes. He worked his way up through administration until he ran the company. He'd used every ruthless trick in the book, including having a few men who got in his way disappear.

And now here he stood at the very top of a rich heap of men, being raged at by Edgar Beaumont. Being startled by him.

It struck Royce how rarely he saw other men's anger. He had a reputation that kept other men firmly lower than him on any measuring stick someone would care to use. No one yelled at him. No one slammed their fist. Beaumont knew that, but for some reason—probably because of the power of being married into the Stiles fortune—he'd forgotten. He'd grown bold and arrogant.

Royce would have had him killed just because he had proven to be a useless failure, if it wouldn't have made Margaret Stiles Beaumont so happy.

Even that might not have stopped him if dozens of people hadn't seen Beaumont come into the Carlisle Building, demand to see Royce, and start shouting before he'd closed the door.

"Those were loyal men who would have stayed there, working on ways to help me get back into the house." Beaumont's face twisted into an ugly mask and revealed the true man. "But you decided to set a bomb." Beaumont swept a hand wildly across the desk. Royce didn't jump this time. He was too busy thinking of how much harm he could do to this fool with a sweep of his own hand.

"And most of the men killed worked for us. If the family wasn't suspicious before, they certainly will be now. You've made everything harder."

"No!" Royce lunged forward, his hands braced on his desk. Beaumont stepped back and swallowed nervously. "*You* did when we'd made a deal for Jillian's hand in marriage and you went hunting around for two more husbands instead of keeping your mouth shut."

Royce rose from his desk and still had to look up a foot to

meet Edgar's eyes. Edgar, if you overlooked the supreme ar-
rogance on his face, was handsome. Tall, broad-shouldered,
the man had straight white teeth and an excellent head of
dark hair. He'd spent his whole life using his looks to float
through life, while Royce had clawed his way up.

Looking at the striking man, Royce toyed with the idea
of killing him right there in the office.

How to get rid of the body, though? Even the San Francisco police force he'd mostly bought and paid for might
have trouble looking the other way.

"You couldn't keep being kind to Margaret until we made
the marriage arrangements?" Royce had planned to take Jillian away with him the night he was to go to the Stiles mansion. If she didn't quickly agree to the wedding, he'd keep
her secluded. She was a firebrand, and he'd expected resis-
tance. He'd looked forward to it. He'd had the place ready,
and she'd stay until she had no reputation left, and she had
no choice but to marry him.

"My wife is nothing but a complainer," Beaumont scoffed.
"An old woman who was so hard to be near I could barely
say 'I do' at the altar. And once we were married, the game
was over. She and her company were mine. Why should I
have bothered pretending anymore? I had everything nice
and tidy until those girls ran off."

"Which they wouldn't have done if you'd kept the women
in the dark about what we had planned."

Edgar flipped a dismissive hand at Royce, and it was a
hard task not to make Edgar very sorry for the disrespect.

"The old hag produced that stupid will. How was I to
know Liam Stiles would leave everything to a mob of stupid,

fussy girls? I had no inside information about Liam's dealings. It seems to me you'd be in a better position than I was to know the details of his will."

Stupid.

Royce's eyes closed on how painfully accurate that word was, except it was Beaumont who was colossally stupid. Carlisle had known the man wasn't smart. For years Beaumont had operated around the fringes of San Francisco high society. He had a strong knack for playing the handsome, wealthy charmer. Royce had been plotting to get Jillian Stiles under his thumb from the first moment he'd seen her. Royce sorted through the men he knew who might be capable of charming Margaret and settled on Beaumont. And it had worked perfectly.

Insinuate Beaumont into Jillian's life and use a stepfather's prerogatives to orchestrate a marriage bargain. All Edgar had to do was remain his phony, charming self. Instead, he'd turned back into his real self, and the Stiles women had been so disgusted by him they'd been suspicious.

The girls had run.

Margaret had stayed.

Even knowing her husband for a brute. She'd stayed and come up with that measles gambit. Driving Beaumont away for weeks had given her girls time to hide well.

Margaret Stiles was very smart. Very bold. Stupid and fussy? More like a warrior woman. Valiant and a true heroine. Beaumont hadn't the skill to pit himself against such a woman.

Carlisle had a visceral respect for Margaret Stiles Beaumont that burned itself into hate. There was little he hated more than a woman who thwarted him.

Although, a man thwarting him, or insulting him as Beaumont was doing now, also made him furious.

Edgar was a greedy man and a fool.

And of no more use.

Add to that, here he stood complaining about "his" men dying. As if Edgar paid for anything. They were Carlisle's men, and he hadn't minded sacrificing a few of them.

Infiltrating Barritt's railroad crew with well-paid men of his own had been simple. Most things were when there was money involved. Carlisle intended to break Jillian's spirit. He would start by ruining her chances of having a ridiculous career building train tracks. A women-led construction site was folly, and no wife of Royce's would humiliate him by doing such a thing.

Royce wouldn't put up with that from *any* woman. He would so enjoy breaking her fiery spirit. Royce couldn't think about her without imagining himself taming her.

The pleasurable daydream helped him keep from drawing a pistol out of the belly drawer in his desk.

Then Beaumont broke into the daydream. "I'm through letting you insult me, you stunted little banty rooster of a man."

Royce's famously cold ruthlessness crumbled into raging hot fury. He had two guns close to hand. He could shoot Beaumont right here and now. Then shoot a hole in the wall behind the desk with the second gun and drop it next to Beaumont's hand. Call it self-defense. No one would dare to gainsay him.

Yes.

Royce reached for the drawer.

A soft tap on his office door stayed his hand.

"Mr. Carlisle." His secretary stuck his head in the door. "You asked me to remind you of the meeting in the boardroom. Everyone is waiting for you, sir."

His faithful secretary had just saved Edgar Beaumont's life. Just as well. Royce had a very expensive rug, and it would be ruined if he shot Beaumont right on top of it. Another chance would no doubt present itself.

"If you'll excuse me." Royce rounded the desk, heading for the door.

Edgar caught his upper arm. "This isn't over. I need more money and more men."

At the feel of Edgar's hand on him, Royce's hot fury turned back to cold. Ice cold. No one had laid hands on Royce since his father. No one had done it and not dearly regretted it, his father included.

Killing Edgar was going to be a pleasure.

He listened as Edgar continued his demands, sounding strangely satisfied, as if insulting Royce hadn't cost him a thing.

And it most assuredly had. Doing his very best—and his best was excellent—to conceal his thoughts, Royce patted Edgar on the hand and said pleasantly, "You're right, this isn't over yet. I know where you're staying. Expect to hear from me soon. When we meet, I'll have everything you so richly deserve."

Edgar gave Royce a firm nod, not knowing he'd just agreed to die.

EIGHTEEN

WHEN BARRITT had sent his crew, Jilly made swift changes in her strategy.

She'd been working from the lumberyard. Building the railbed, then using handcarts, pulled by the sturdy mules and massive Belgian draft horses, to haul the rails and railroad ties as they laid the track in front of the horses.

These horses normally did much of the heavy work hauling logs. The Stiles family had a few of them, but mostly they used mule teams, as the big draft horses were expensive and rare. They had a few Belgians, and thanks to Mr. Barritt, they had added four Clydesdales to their stables. Jilly's horsemen were thrilled with the beautiful critters.

She'd planned to build the whole railroad track that way, working from the top of the mountain down, and every night all the men could go back to their cabins to sleep.

Now, with Barritt's men gone but with the beginning of the work coming out from the nearest train track and heading up, Jilly decided to go down there and build the bridges and trestles ahead of the track-laying crew.

Too far from home to make the trip every day.

So Jilly, Nick, and her building crew from Stiles Lumber camped at the bottom of the mountain. She divided her men into two crews. One to lay the track, and one to work with her. They'd be building the most complex structure of this whole project.

Her bridge across the river.

The river she and her sisters had landed in after their wild ride of escape down the flume. The first step was rerouting the river, and that was a big job because it was a big river.

Jilly didn't like changing her plans, but she considered herself a reasonable woman. It was inconvenient but more efficient, since Barritt's men had left behind their locomotive and train cars to haul logs. The train came out from the station and was always at the end of the line. The California Ironworks crew was gone, but they'd made a good start, and with what her own men had learned from them, they were making excellent time on the track.

Jilly had to get busy building that bridge.

She and Nick and a dozen other men set up a tent encampment. They worked just slightly upstream from the flume so the logging could continue, and logs came rushing down constantly. She'd carefully chosen the spot to divert the river. They were days working on that before they could begin building.

As they labored, Jilly's mathematical calculations were challenged by the difficulty on the actual building site. She'd known it would take longer and cost more than she'd planned, but she hadn't thought things would go quite this slowly.

Her blueprints and maps were constantly with her, though she remembered every detail of both. But to make the men see what she wanted, she needed her surveying equipment, her sketches, and lots of time.

Still, one step at a time. And there were no serious delays, no maliciousness leading to injuries, no evil men and their sabotage.

But she never stopped expecting any or all of that at any time. And she didn't think she was being one bit overly suspicious.

"AND WHAT IS THIS THING?" Nick couldn't remember half of what Jilly told him. But right now, he was pointing at one of her strange tools in hopes of distracting her while the men blasted a channel alongside the river to divert the water.

Nick could hardly breathe he was so impressed. Jilly knew how to do all of this. All he could do was try to keep up. And since Jilly's mind worked at about five times the speed of everyone else's, keeping up was one of his biggest problems.

"It's an alidade. It's part of my surveying equipment."

"But how does it help you survey? I wouldn't mind learning this and we've got some time."

Jilly watched with rapt attention the men hooking up the dynamite. Nick needed to keep her well back.

She was a smart woman, brilliant, for a fact, but she was also beset with curiosity and a desire to do everything herself.

Laura had planned to be down here handling the blasting,

but she'd come up with some kind of bellyache this morning and cried off. So Jilly had overseen everything, then only reluctantly stepped well back.

The explosion went as planned and cut a straight channel through an arc in the river, and they stood and watched the water flow exactly as Jilly had intended.

THE RIVERBED WAS FINALLY DRY, and the bridge construction could begin.

Jilly had the men heaving on the ropes to lift the timber into place, doing the slow, brutally heavy work, assisted by the horses and mules, as fast as they could.

She had a bad habit of shouting instructions or trying to rush forward to do things herself.

Nick's job was to keep her back . . . again. "Show me the model."

She whipped her head around to glare at him. At least she wasn't glaring at the work crew. She uncovered the model she'd made of the bridge she was building. "You've seen it sitting in Papa's office ten times."

"Yes, but it's different to look at it while the work is being done. You've actually built it so the center portion pivots?"

Jilly demonstrated, and the men worked in peace.

"What are you surveying next?"

She narrowed her eyes but answered. "After we blast our way through the mountain, we'll carve back the side of the mountain so we can follow the curve of solid rock and use that as a base to lay the tracks. The curve of a train is very specific. The turns can be only so sharp before the train engine can't manage to pull."

Jilly continued. Nick wasn't quite sure why since she rarely let him distract her, but for now, she proceeded to tell Nick how to survey land using the multitude of tools that were completely unknown to him.

She was a good teacher. He was a little surprised just how good. He'd have expected her to be so smart that she'd have no patience for a man who needed something explained twice, or three times.

Instead, she seemed to enjoy showing him how to survey. It occurred to Nick that he was learning a useful skill. She'd let him help with the dynamite, too. Blowing things up was useful. Add in building a railroad. Nick was learning things right and left.

CHAPTER

NINETEEN

JILLY STILES ALWAYS CAME BACK to the mansion on Nob Hill.

She was alone, walking down the dark hallway, a candle in her hand the only light.

And then she wasn't alone.

Edgar was there, looming over her. She knew to never be alone. She knew. And yet here she was. Jilly gasped and backed away. Her room. If she could get to her room, to her sisters.

She dropped her candle, and flames leapt up behind her. Leaping flames as impossible to go through as a stone fence.

Edgar laughed, and the flames seemed to leap higher, eat toward her. The heat burned her. Stopped her.

He grabbed her wrist, and laughing louder, he dragged her into another room. His room. No, she couldn't be in there alone with him.

"No! Let me go!"

He closed the door against the fire, but somehow the fire was in the room with them.

"No, Edgar, no!"

Suddenly Edgar's hands closed over her shoulders, and she was being shaken to death. She knew this was the end.

The shaking stopped.

Cold water splashed in her face.

The fire went out. Edgar gave her one last evil look and vanished as a demon might.

"Jilly, wake up. You're dreaming."

The shaking resumed. Her eyes flickered open. She looked right into Nick's blue and green eyes. The room was bright with lantern light.

"It's me, Jilly. You're safe. It was just a dream. Shhh, don't be afraid."

With a whimper she was ashamed of, she launched herself at him, her arms wrapping tightly around his waist. His closed hard around her.

Her heart pounded until she feared it couldn't bear such a strain.

Her eyes burned with unshed tears.

Gradually her breathing slowed and, with it, her heart and her rabbiting thoughts and fears.

"Tell me about the dream, Jilly."

"No, I don't dare." As she spoke those words, even those few words, her heart sped up again. The fear rushed back in. She never dared speak of it.

Nick closed his hands on her face so one palm rested on each cheek, and his fingers speared into her hair. He tilted her head just slightly, and he kissed her.

A kiss such as she'd never had before.

A kiss such as she'd never known existed.

It dragged her away from the dream and, even more, from his questions about the dream. She threw herself into the kiss. Her arms tightened, and she knew an exciting desire that she'd never even considered was contained in her body.

And she wanted to at last be fully and truly married. She kissed him back with the abandon she felt at escaping the nightmare.

After too long, and not nearly long enough, Nick turned his head aside. She felt the scrape of his whiskers on her lips. She liked the small abrasion and kissed his cheek to feel it again.

"No, Jilly. We're not going to be . . . together in any . . . married way while you're so upset by your nightmare. It's not right for you, and it's not fair to me."

The stern tone pulled Jilly out of the churned-up emotions that were flooding through her.

"I-I'm sorry." Jilly eased away. She pulled her arms from where they'd been wrapped around his neck. The terror of the dream, the longing awakened by his kiss. It was all so confusing. She felt next thing to addled—and she prided herself on her clear thinking.

She curled away from him and lay down, facing the wall. But he caught her arms and lifted her right back up until they were face-to-face.

Just as they'd been when she woke up.

Back to where she'd been when he'd pulled her out of her nightmare.

"Tell me, Jilly."

She shook her head.

"You have to."

"No."

"Jilly, whatever that dream is about, it's coming from something terrible. Keeping it locked inside you has turned it into even more of a horror. You're safe from him now."

"I'm not. Mama's not." And she realized saying even that was a type of admission.

"Yes, you're both safe." He pulled her closer, but this time into a hug. He pressed her head gently until it rested on his shoulder. His arms felt like a haven, a barrier against the world. But no barrier could protect Mama.

"Please, share this with me. Please."

"I-I can't."

"Because he—did he—did he harm you, Jilly? Did he hit you like he did your mama? Was it something worse? Did he touch you in a way he shouldn't have?"

"It's . . . Nick, I don't think I can say the words."

He just held her. She was calmer now. But she thought of what she needed to say and felt a trembling begin deep inside her. They were ugly, frightening words. And she wasn't safe. She'd never be safe. Edgar had told her so.

Something snapped together inside her. Snapped as if a bone had been broken and was suddenly whole again.

It was at least partly the fault of her photographic memory. The words he'd used, the threats, the expression on his face. They were vivid when she was awake, twisted and demonic when she was asleep.

She lifted her head.

"In the dream, I always go back to the mansion on Nob Hill."

Nick closed his eyes as if he didn't want her to see the

pain in them. But it was written all over his face, not just in his eyes.

"I'll tell you about the nightmares first. What happened is different from the nightmare. But what happened is why I have them."

Jilly swallowed hard, her throat felt bone-dry. "Can I have a drink of water?"

Nick let go of her, turned to the bedside, and grabbed a glass he always kept close. There was one on her side, too. She took his and drank deeply.

"Now you have no more reason to wait. Just say it, sweetheart. Speak the words out loud. We'll study them together and examine them for the lies Edgar is so good at, and we'll see them for what they are."

He pulled her close again, and now that she couldn't see his expression, it was possible to speak.

The fire. Being under Edgar's power. His bedroom. What could be more forbidden?

Nick held her tightly. Held her through it all. He kept her head resting on his shoulder. As she spoke, the trembling inside reached her voice, her hands, her lips, every inch of her shook until she thought she'd shake apart.

But Nick held her close, held her up, held her together.

"And how is what he did different?" Nick asked.

Jilly's trembling eased with the end of the nightmare, and now his questions were too much. Exhaustion dragged at her. "I should finish it now, Nick. Tell you the rest. But I'm falling asleep as I sit here. Can we put it off for another day? Please?"

The pleading in her voice made her ashamed. She wasn't

a woman who begged for things. She demanded them. She got them for herself. But tonight, she didn't have the strength.

Nick eased her away from him and studied her face. She had no idea what he saw, but he nodded.

"Rest now, sweetheart. Rest. We'll talk more tomorrow."

He helped her lie down as if he feared she was too exhausted to fall over on her back.

Then he stretched to reach the lamp by his bedside, lay down beside her, pulled her close so her head rested on his strong shoulder, and said, "Sleep."

She barely heard the word as she sank into slumber.

SIX WEEKS AND NO DISASTER.

No more strikes or explosions. And no more nightmares.

Jilly had avoided talking about her nightmare again by moving back to the base of the mountain and sleeping in a tent. Nick slept with her, but they were surrounded by crowded tents, and the snores all around her told her the men would hear her as well as she heard them.

She couldn't talk about such a terribly personal thing here.

They went up to the mansion on Saturday night and spent Sunday at home, but the days stretched long, and the travel was tedious and tiring. She managed to dodge Nick's questions with little trouble, though he had a way of looking at her that told her he wasn't fooled.

But he was working long hours, too, so he cooperated without much fuss.

And now they were done. Jilly stood looking at her completed pivot bridge with fierce triumph.

The end of the train track had been building toward the bridge fast. Today the track would connect with her bridge, and she'd get that locomotive across the river. A few yards of track were already laid on the other side so the locomotive could pull in there. Then the rail-laying crew could get back to work, and she could go on to the next gorge she needed to build a trestle across.

It would be another race against the oncoming train. The challenge of it made her smile because she'd beaten them but only just.

She'd worked hard alongside the men. She'd studied architectural drawings, read blueprints until her eyes crossed . . . for years. She'd seen pivot bridges, drawbridges, suspension bridges, for heaven's sake floating bridges. And she'd settled on this. And she'd done it. She'd had a vision of what she wanted, all while she tested and retested the quality of her steel.

Now here stood her bridge. Iron and wood, the center foundation. The men were even now rerouting the river so it flowed back under the bridge. She watched the water flow under her iron arches. She loved every bit of building this thing.

The pivot bridge used the current of the river to turn. Push the right lever, and the bridge turned until it reached one hundred eighty degrees and locked. With the bridge out of the way, any backed-up boats could pass. Then the bridge turned another one hundred eighty degrees and was clamped to the railroad tracks.

Finally, the biggest undertaking of this project was done.

Nick came up beside her and watched as she turned the bridge. "That is such a wonder, Jilly. I've never seen such a thing. And it's not just useful, it's a thing of beauty."

She looked away from the ironwork on her bridge to study her husband. "If it's done right, all architecture can be beautiful. And something like this that moves and is a practical, useful piece of the future, it's a fine accomplishment." She hooked her right hand through the crook of his elbow. "Johann Wolfgang von Goethe called architecture frozen music."

With a sniff, Nick said, "I bet Mr. Wolfie never built a thing this beautiful."

Jilly's heart, already soft toward her husband, who lay beside her every night, holding her hand, not pressuring her for more than that, melted all the way.

She was in love with Nick Ryder. So strange to think that. To know that. Love was such an odd thing, so hard to explain in a world limited to only a few hundred thousand words.

She didn't know what to say or how to say it, and that rarely happened to Jilly. She didn't even know if she should say it. So she just hugged his arm with hers, and they watched her pivot bridge swing to let boats through—there were none, this was just practicing—then swing again to connect the two sides.

"Goethe wasn't a builder, but he was a fine, successful man. A writer and a scientist. He said things that are still repeated to this day. 'A man sees in the world what he carries in his heart.'"

Nick shrugged. "That's pretty good. But I think lots of

people have said some version of that, including the Bible. A lot of similarity to the Golden Rule. Did he help write the Bible? I don't remember the book of Wolfgang anywhere. How old is Wolfgang?"

"Long dead, but not long enough to have written one of the Scriptures." Jilly giggled and squeezed his arm tighter.

"Are we ready, Mrs. Ryder?" Buddy Carville, an engineer who'd come along with the train engine when it had chugged down the newly built tracks, poked his head out of the loco-motive's side window with a wide smile on his face.

"We. Are. Ready." She felt like there should be fireworks or champagne corks popping. But the forests were flam-mable, and she didn't drink, so she made a grand gesture with the arm that wasn't clinging to Nick. The engine puffed and roared. Buddy blasted the whistle twice to draw everyone's attention, then slowly chugged across the river. He pulled a tender car and three cars bearing railroad ties and rails.

The tracks on the other side were reached without in-cident, and once the whole length of the train had cleared the bridge, the engine jerked to a halt with a hiss of steam escaping and the low squeal of the brakes.

"You can breathe now." Nick gently bumped his shoulder against hers.

She gasped for air. "I didn't know I was holding my breath." She looked at her bridge. "It's sturdy as the moun-tains, isn't it?"

"It's perfect. Jilly, I am in awe of what you've done here."

"Things have been going well for the last six weeks. I

don't believe in luck, but it feels like I'd be bringing bad luck down on our heads by thinking all our problems are over."

"It's not luck, good or bad. You have only men you know working on the train tracks, men who've been with you before Edgar came into the picture. Except for Buddy, but he's likely safe because I don't think he'd've driven across that bridge if he'd done something to sabotage it."

"It truly is a thing of beauty, isn't it?" Jilly watched, tempted to jump up and down and squeal . . . which was *not* the polished, professional image she hoped to convey.

"Two more months, you'll be done. This was the biggest thing you had to build, and it went perfectly."

"That's the timeline I hope for, but there's some rugged land to cross."

"From now on it's trestles, much simpler."

"Steep slopes to go up, two places we need to dynamite a hole in the mountain to get through, and a third place we need to dynamite a big bite out of the side of a mountain. Laura starts blasting tomorrow."

Nick smiled. "Can't quite see our little Laura with dynamite."

"She knows chemistry. She's done the reading, done the hands-on practice. She knows how to be careful and how to cover her ears."

"Then she's all set. Look, the wagons are here. A few months from now, we'll be coming down the mountain in a matter of minutes instead of a ride that takes hours. Let's head up."

The work crew climbed in the wagons. Buddy parked his train engine for the night and rode to the mountaintop with them. Tomorrow was Sunday, and as they'd done every Sunday, they would head home and take their well-earned day of rest.

Jilly thought of that explosion. Who had set it? She had no doubt that Carlisle had arranged it, but was the person who'd caused the harm one of Barritt's crew and hopefully long gone? Was he one of the men who'd died?

Jilly spent way too much time looking over her shoulder. Testing the quality of her building materials. Worrying.

She wondered if that would stop when the railroad track was done or if this was her new life, and she'd be nervous about everything from now on.

Nick put both his strong hands on her waist and lifted her into the back of one of the wagons, then he leapt up beside her with no effort at all.

She gave him an appreciative look. All his bruises had faded. All his aches were gone.

This was normal life. Nick was her normal. If she could go back to life before Edgar, then she'd have to go back before Nick.

Poor Mama might have chosen differently, but for right now, Jilly was happy and in love and flushed with triumph by the pivot bridge. And eager to begin the next phase of building. She was pushing hard, she knew it. The summer was wearing away, and the winter coming on like a . . . well, like an oncoming train. But she'd make it. She knew it!

However they'd gotten here, whatever rugged road they'd traveled, she liked where she was.

TWENTY

NICK HAD NEVER SEEN JILLY this annoyed nor this happy. The woman was almost in a dither.

Michelle was here.

She was happy to see her big sister. And she was annoyed with Michelle, who had a thousand questions and more than a thousand bits of advice.

Michelle and Zane were at the top of the mountain when Nick and Jilly arrived. If Michelle had known the bridge was being finished today, they'd've ridden on down the tracks to Placerville and come out to the bridge, then they could have seen it and ridden home in the wagon.

The two sisters were yammering at each other, and the mixed emotions were a complicated thing. Michelle wanted to go down the mountain to see the pivot bridge. And while it was far too late to change it, she was going on about drawbridges and the much simpler machinery involved. Especially since Michelle thought she could invent—

Jilly fumed, and Nick hoped she didn't decide to strangle

Michelle. Jilly would feel bad later, and dinner would be late for sure. And Nick was starving.

The two stood there. Dark-haired Michelle wearing a black riding skirt and a blouse the right color of blue to match her eyes. Redheaded Jilly with her flashing green eyes. They were a picture. A contrast and yet so much alike.

"I thought you were considering a suspension bridge," Michelle said. "They have a longer history. They've been building suspension bridges since before the Romans—"

"I told you the land along the railroad bed, where it needed to cross the river, had no proper outcroppings to suspend the cables from the—"

"But you could have built an incline on both sides of the—"

It'd been going on like this for about half an hour.

The hugging and squealing were long over. As well as the excitement that Michelle and Zane were going to be able to stay for a month since Zane's busy season was over, and his brother, Josh, was there to look after things.

Nick decided he'd get plenty of work out of Zane. Maybe logging and railroad building would appeal to the man. Maybe he'd decide to give up ranching and become a lumber baron.

Margaret had joined in the hugging, then stayed to referee. Apparently, Jilly and Michelle's arguing was a common enough thing.

Laura hung back, standing by Caleb, which was strange. Nick would have expected Laura to be right in there, holding her own.

She frowned at her sisters, the very picture of sulky discontent. She was smaller than them, more delicately built.

Blond and sweet and as informed as anybody Nick had heard speak on chemicals and reactions and something called the periodic table.

Nick had gone with her, everyone had, when she'd been in San Francisco to go to the Giant Powder Company and buy crates of dynamite. He'd listened as she talked with Mr. Bandmann, the owner of the company. Nick had heard all about how safe dynamite was compared to nitroglycerin, but he'd also heard about the explosion that had leveled the Giant Powder Company factory a few years ago.

Laura seemed fearless as she explored the factory and loaded the dynamite to transport it to the mountaintop, but Nick was glad to get out of the place, and later, Caleb admitted he was, too.

Nick had heard extensive descriptions of Alfred Nobel's work and the chemical makeup of dynamite. Jilly and Laura could talk about it for hours.

It tended to put Nick to sleep, which was probably unwise considering how big a blast the stuff made.

Nick couldn't even figure out what any of them were talking about most of the time. Jilly's math brain. Michelle's invention brain. Laura's chemical brain. They were a trio of mad scientists, for a fact.

It all made Nick want to go chop down a tree.

"Tell them," Caleb whispered to Laura. "Go on. You don't have to set off those blasts if you don't want to."

Though the two spoke quietly, Nick could hear every word.

"Oh, it probably won't kill me to blow up a couple of

mountains." Laura crossed her arms, and a furrow appeared on her smooth brow.

It was clear from the way they whispered together, that Laura and Caleb had already talked about this many times. Nick was standing on Caleb's right, while Laura was on his left, and beyond them, Zane looked on at his noisy family, smiling.

Probably happy he had a ranch to go home to. The man was never going to agree to leave off ranching.

Nick moved beside Laura, so she was caged between Caleb and him. He leaned close. "You could teach me how to use the dynamite. You could even say I asked if I could do it. In fact, I'm asking right now if I could do it, please."

Laura's gaze turned to Nick, and her surprised look was replaced with something soft and vulnerable. "You'd do that?"

Nick smiled and rested a hand on Laura's shoulder. "I want to do it. I know there's a lot more to it than just touching a match to the fuse. I don't know how much to use nor where to place the sticks of dynamite. You'd have to show me that or teach me how to figure it out myself. I also don't know how to chart the course. Or how to clear the debris—although that oughta be common sense. But how about making sure any loosened rocks from overhead come down so there's no cave-in? Do you have to build inside the tunnel? I mean more than the tracks, like steel beams to hold up the ceiling?"

"You'd have to know all of that and more. But a lot of it I could work on with you. And picking the spots to place the explosives, that's more Jilly's job than mine." Laura kept her voice lowered. "It's just too loud. I dread setting off those explosions when I'm so close, even though I wouldn't get too close. I know how much space to give myself. It's just that . . ." She gave Caleb a quick glance.

He smiled. "Probably oughta tell your sisters before Nick."

"Now?"

"It might quiet down the squabbling."

Which was, Nick decided, a job that badly needed to be done, and soon.

Michelle was shaking a finger under Jilly's nose.

Jilly had fists propped firmly on her hips.

Mama was standing mostly between them, holding them apart and doing plenty of scolding of her own.

All three of them were animated, brilliant, and beautiful. Well, all four of them, because Laura was all those things, too. Though not quite so animated right now.

But his Jilly outshone them all. He was so proud of her he was surprised his chest didn't swell up and pop the buttons off his shirt.

Zane leaned forward and spoke across Nick. "Let's hear your news, little sister."

Not raising her voice, though she certainly wasn't whispering anymore, Laura said, "I'm expecting a baby."

She wouldn't have caused a stronger reaction if she'd used dynamite.

The silence was complete as all three squabbling Stiles women spun around to look at her.

While they were quiet, Nick added, "I think using dynamite might be a little risky for a woman in . . . a delicate condition. Although I'm sure you're perfectly healthy and strong, as you need to be. But, well, would it be all right if you trained me on working with dynamite? I'm sure you could teach me how to do it, Laura. I'd really like to learn."

Then the little clutch of women squealed like hogs at slaughter time and rushed to hug Laura.

Caleb had his arm around her waist, so she didn't topple over when the onslaught hit.

Zane gave Nick an approving pat on the back. He'd gotten his offer in before the noise started, and he'd phrased it well. He didn't think even these very smart women would guess Laura didn't want to do the dynamite.

Caleb waited until he was sure Laura wasn't going to fall over, then he stepped closer to Zane and Nick and shook Nick's hand.

"Well done, brother."

The three of them fell back a bit so they could hear themselves over the raucous women.

Mama slid her arm around Laura's waist and said, "Come on inside, everyone. Laura, you should get off your feet."

"I've got a lot of questions for you, Mama."

"Of course you have questions, honey. I'll answer every one of them, and girls"—Margaret looked from Jilly to Michelle—"you might want to listen, too. Let's step away from the men."

The women headed for the house, still surrounding Laura, gentle with her as if she were made of the finest crystal . . . or maybe nitroglycerin.

Caleb's eyes went wide and a little frantic. "I-I hope she doesn't tell her anything that would, that is . . . anything that's going to-to upset her. I'd better go listen. I wouldn't mind knowing a little more than I do."

He took one step, and Nick wrapped an arm around his neck.

Zane stepped smack in front of him and slapped two hands flat on Caleb's chest. "Stay away. That's my advice. Let the women talk, and we can . . ." He looked around. "Where are horses that need grooming? Where are the cows?"

"All our animals are in the stable and the corral behind it. And we have stable hands to do that, including milk the few cows. Anyway, we're losing the light, too late to do much but go inside." Nick added in a conspiratorial whisper, "We could go in Liam's office. Maybe we can find brandy and cigars."

"I don't drink." Zane scowled at Nick.

"Neither do I, and neither do you, Nick." Caleb arched a brow at him. "And none of us smoke."

Nick figured they could still go in there and sit. Then he realized who he was dealing with. He said to Zane, "Hey, you want to see our new Clydesdales?"

Zane looked almost covetous. "Really, those big draft horses? You have one?"

"We have four." Nick gestured toward the stable. "Jilly—very subtly, in my opinion—threatened to sue California Ironworks and destroy their reputation because of those rusted-out bolts and the president has been extremely helpful ever since."

"She's got him the next thing to groveling." Caleb shook his head. "That is one scary woman."

"When she needs to be," Nick said with a smile.

"Nice job, Jilly." Zane headed for the horses.

The four Clydesdales were inside for now, but mostly the animals stayed outside when the weather was nice. The stable master brought in the horses and mules by turn to sleep inside so he had time to pamper them a bit as well as look each of them over for strained muscles and other injuries.

Tonight, by luck, it was the Clydesdales' turn.

The barn had six good-sized stalls. Zane's horse and Michelle's were in one together. A Belgian that had just given birth had another. Each Clydesdale had its own. When the men entered the barn, the friendly draft horses poked their heads over the stall doors.

"They are *huge*." Zane reached for the closest one and patted its silky neck. "You could drag a building around with these critters."

"Too bad you aren't dragging any buildings around," Nick said.

"True enough," Zane said ruefully.

"But we've got logs to drag off the mountain." Nick patted the Clydesdale next to the one Zane was fussing over. The big critters all looked a little jealous. Caleb went to the third one. The fourth snorted and shook its head.

Nick turned to give its neck a rub. "We've got steep inclines, and we need horses powerful enough to do the work without harming themselves. The mules pull sledges in pairs, and we have to limit the number of logs. One Belgian can work alone on a sledge, but we make sure those sledges aren't carrying a full load. These big fellas can handle a loaded sledge by themselves and show little sign of overwork, though we're careful."

"I have absolutely no use for an animal this big," Zane said. Then a smile lit up his face. "But I'm going to see how much time I can spend working with them for the next month."

Once they'd talked horses for as long as possible, Nick said, "Let's go on inside to Liam's office. We can think of something manly to do, like sit in beautifully made oak chairs and talk about blowing up mountains. How's the gold mining going, Zane?"

"There is no gold mining because we got it all. We've had a few incidents, but honestly, we haven't kept a close watch. We can tell there've been trespassers up there. We've left them alone to hunt. No one's found a single flake. I'd've heard about it if they had."

Caleb, who'd gotten most of the color back in his face that had drained to white when Margaret took Laura away, said, "The office sounds good. Let's go hide from the women."

"A BABY!" Mama threw her arms around Laura.

Jilly and Michelle smiled at each other while they waited their turn.

Quietly, Jilly said to Michelle, "The baby is having a baby."

Michelle grinned.

"Think of how we've been raised to run the company."

Michelle nodded. "I'm not doing my share. But I intend to spend the next month—"

"That's not what I mean." Jilly knew Michelle planned to do six months' worth of business in a month. It was annoying to think about it. "I was struck by the Bible verse about us being God's workmanship and how He ordained good works for us to do."

"You're thinking Laura's baby is already being prepared by God to run the company?"

It was all Jilly could do not to roll her eyes. "No, I'm thinking being a wonderful mama to her own babies and serving at Caleb's side as a parson's wife might be what God prepared in advance for her to do."

Michelle clamped her mouth shut. Nice for a change. They studied Laura hugging Mama.

"She's so happy," Jilly went on. "And she handed that dynamite job over to Nick without a qualm. I might add, Michelle, you were just as quick to hand off your share of the work for Stiles Lumber when you married Zane."

"I had a qualm." She sounded very casual about it.

"But not a big enough one to pick a man you could drag home."

"There was the matter of a man attacking me and another man wanting to claim me when he found out where I was. That prompted the speed. The qualm wasn't enough to stop me because I was already falling in love with Zane. Yes, you're right. I chose that life over this one."

"And that's as it should be, Michelle."

"Laura got to come home."

"But not to stay, I don't think. Caleb is here, supporting us for now, doing mission work among the lumberjacks. And he's content that he's doing the Lord's work. But if the Lord calls him away, then Laura will go. Of course she will."

Jilly turned to glare at Michelle. "What you don't seem

able to understand and accept is that I'm running this place. I am completely in charge. I'm keeping the books, paying the loggers, drawing the plans for the train tracks. You can *help* me, Michelle, and I'll welcome it. But you will *not* take over. I don't want to hear your opinion of my pivot bridge, my train bed construction, my surveying, or where I plan to blow up the mountain. You handed that job off to me as Laura is now doing, and I'll be thrilled to do it. Add to that, I seem to have married a man who is thrilled to help me. I want your help, ideas, and even advice, but you are *not* in charge, and that's final."

Michelle looked through Jilly, thinking. Jilly had given her a lot to think about.

NICK SAW PLENTY OF SIGNS of Edgar as they went into Liam's office. An open box of cigars, a crystal decanter of something brown, brandy or whiskey. Who knew?

A red silk jacket that Edgar had worn around the house during leisure hours. And for the most part, Edgar's hours were all leisure. It hung from a coatrack in the corner, and it was a jacket only a vain, pompous fool would wear. Not unlike silk pajamas, but no one needed to know about them besides Jilly.

And anyhow, Nick hadn't chosen them for himself.

Edgar left the coat hanging right out in the open like he was proud of it.

"Congratulations." Zane slapped Caleb on the shoulder. "A new generation of Stileses."

"It's gonna be named Tillman," Caleb said, then, with a smile, added, "But these Stiles women, I'd be real proud if my child was as smart, good-looking, and good-hearted as the lot of them."

Zane nodded.

Nick wondered when he'd be allowed to add to the Stiles population. He didn't mention to these newly acquired brothers that nothing went on between him and Jilly that could cause such a thing to occur.

Zane sat so his left side was closest to the fireplace. Nick picked a matching chair opposite him, with a low table between them.

Caleb looked a little dreamy-eyed as he dragged the rolling desk chair out from behind the huge desk and centered it between Zane and Nick. Everything was oak, a testament to the lumber that provided the foundation of the Stiles fortune.

Edgar had claimed the desk, but despite the stupid red jacket, cigars, and liquor, he hadn't changed the room much. It was all the work of Liam and Margaret Stiles. Jilly had told Nick a lot about it.

There was no fire going. It was a warm night, so none of them wanted to waste the wood. It occurred to Nick that if he did start a fire, he could toss that red jacket on it for fuel. He decided to do it soon, but he thought Jilly and Margaret oughta be here for that.

"Are you settling in here, Caleb?" Zane asked, reviving Caleb from the dazed pleasure on his face.

"I only know I'll go where I'm called. I will always listen for the voice of God. After all, God helped me be in the right place at the right time to find the love of my life. He led her safely down a dangerous flume and a fast-moving river. He led me around the Florida peninsula and up the Mississippi River and all the way across the country to be climbing on a train right when she was climbing on it. I actually got to stop and tell her to go first."

He smiled at the recollection. "God put me in the perfect spot when Laura and her sisters needed me. And the perfect place so we'd find each other, the woman I believe He's been preparing for me since before we were born. It's hard to imagine, but I know in my heart and soul that it's true."

For a moment, Nick fell silent, thinking about the long chance the Stiles sisters had taken. "Have you seen the flume, Zane?"

"Yep, I asked Michelle if she'd mind if I rode down it in a barrel just to see what she'd been through. She threatened to knock me over the head and drag my unconscious body all the way down the mountain and back to the ranch just to keep me safe."

It might've been right to laugh, but all Nick could think of was the deadly danger they'd been in. All because of Edgar Beaumont and his cruel plans for them.

The three husbands shared a solemn moment. Their beautiful, brilliant wives had taken such a risk.

Nick realized he'd rested his hand on his stomach, reacting to the twisting gut, the ache of dread. Beaumont was still out there. Carlisle still wanted Jilly. "None of us knew what had gone on before. None of us was in any position to protect them when they needed us most."

"I think"—Caleb glanced from Nick to Zane—"I want to name one or both of you as guardian to any children

Laura and I have. In case I die and Laura is fooled by some trickster into marrying. I'm not sure of the legalities, but I think Laura would agree to naming one of you."

"And she can't claim you insulted her because that very thing happened to their ma." Zane looked like he wanted to build on the idea to justify it when he talked with Michelle about the same thing.

Nick thought it was an idea with merit. "If you wrote it right, it might even be a deterrent to someone who wanted to charm his way into her life."

"I wonder how Edgar managed to hide his true nature long enough to fool all of them." Zane slouched lower in his chair, tapping one of his hands on the overstuffed arm.

"Jilly told me they'd never seen him be anything but charming, kind, and generous." Nick propped his elbows on his knees. "She even tried to do a few little things to test him, see how he'd act. But he never slipped. It's a lesson I reckon the women all learned because they seemed determined to frustrate each of us at every turn. None of them would be easy to lure into a second marriage. I'm surprised Margaret fell for Beaumont's masquerade."

Nick looked at Zane, then they both looked at Caleb. The three of them were solemn and worried about what the future held.

Nick began to wonder if it'd been long enough, and maybe they dared to go find the women. It had to be time to eat by now.

"You know Edgar's not done causing trouble," Caleb said.

That made Nick's gut churn until he was glad there was no food in his belly. "And neither is Royce Carlisle." Nick thought of him as the biggest threat. But he guessed Beaumont was in on all of this. Both of them were dangerous.

"Jilly writes to Michelle," Zane said, "and I've heard some from you two. But I want to know every bit of what's been going on around here."

They settled in for a talk that gave the women all the time they needed to speak of babies. All the time they needed and a whole lot more.

ROYCE STARED IN FURY at the message.

Jillian Stiles was married. Royce didn't know who this Ryder was, but it sounded like he was one of the lumberjacks. A filthy, sweating laborer. And now he had the rights of a husband to Jillian.

Sickened to think of Jillian belonging to someone besides him, Royce crushed the message and felt the pounding in his temples that had begun to haunt him every time he was thwarted in his quest to get his hands on Jillian.

He'd decided to first ruin her reputation as a construction engineer. It gave him vicious pleasure to damage her name, prevent her from working like a man. The woman needed to learn some hard lessons, and Royce had decided to begin teaching those lessons early, before he ever touched her. He'd taken pleasure in doing it slowly. And, admittedly, he'd been thwarted when he'd tried a direct assault with the marriage arrangement through Beaumont.

But he'd made a mistake by waiting, and he never made mistakes.

186

His fury building, he snapped at the failure of his hired associates.

He was done letting subordinates assist in this.

The cool, controlled thinking he prided himself on was gone. Rossiter had handled the bomb well, though he had survived the modifications meant to kill the bomber right along with the other victims.

Rossiter didn't seem to realize he was an intended victim. Royce didn't like to leave witnesses roaming around. But for the next step in this plan, Rossiter would be useful.

But Royce was ready to be done with one key witness. And he would handle that personally. The rightness of it bloomed along with the throbbing in his head. Carlisle needed to handle this himself.

He'd never wanted a woman like he wanted Jillian Stiles, and to truly possess her, he had to do for himself what needed doing.

Royce didn't mind the help, but he needed to make sure things were done right.

Beaumont barged into the warehouse where Royce had arranged a meeting.

"What's the meaning of dragging me down here, Carlisle? We could have met somewhere civilized." Beaumont was breathing hard. His eyes flashed with rage in the dim lantern light. The color on his cheeks was heightened with anger.

A foolish man to treat Carlisle so belligerently. But then Carlisle knew that Beaumont was a fool.

The decision to use him was a failure. And failure wasn't something Royce accepted, not from himself, and not from men he hired.

Royce always used others to handle the ugly details of his plans. But with Jillian, it was personal, so it was right that he handled the details personally. The throbbing in his head spread to his throat, his heart.

To be his, Jillian needed to be taken by him. The fury eased as the new plan came to him, alive and exciting. And Beaumont was undeniably no longer needed.

"I've had a change of heart about my plans."

Beaumont stopped charging forward. His chest heaving, he said, "Well, good. Why did you need to drag me down here to tell me?"

"I've got something to show you, over here." Royce led the way to a stack of crates to one side of the warehouse door. Beaumont followed along like a whining dog.

When he had Beaumont exactly in place, Royce pulled the gun from his coat pocket and fired.

Beaumont's face was laughable. To his surprise, in fact, Royce found himself actually laughing.

He hadn't expected to take such pleasure in killing a man.

Beaumont's face was etched with pain, yes, but mostly shock. Beaumont really had been stupid, or he'd have known this was the end result of treating Carlisle with such disrespect.

Beaumont stood there as if he was too stupid to know he was dead. Then his muscles failed him. He pitched over backward and fell into the wooden crate, his feet hanging over the edge.

A tidy clip of one loose end. A shame, really, that he'd let Margaret Stiles off the hook for her foolish marriage. Royce, just as he'd heard of Jillian's marriage, had heard of Margaret Stiles filing for divorce.

She might not ever get one because it was difficult, but she'd locked Beaumont away from her homes and, more importantly, away from her money.

Royce turned to the shadows off to his right. "Handle this, Rossiter."

A man who obeyed orders and didn't do any scheming of his own. How refreshing.

"Yes, sir. As we discussed." Rossiter approached the crate, shoved Beaumont's feet inside, then dropped a slab of wood on top of him. He picked up the hammer and nails resting nearby and set to work sealing the makeshift coffin.

Royce strode out of the warehouse. Glad he'd done it himself. The throbbing in his head seemed to take over his thoughts. He'd never killed anyone before. He'd destroyed them, but financially or through slandering their reputations. He'd never just plain killed. He'd been missing out.

He laughed a strange, high giggle that was like bubbles erupting from his soul.

It was a moment of pure power. Of godlike power. He couldn't give life, but he could take it away. And he longed to do it again.

He had a couple more plans in place to shake Jillian loose from that mountain and from her plans to do a man's job. He liked the damage his plans would cause, and the pain and suffering it would cause others, so he'd go forward with them before he settled this.

He walked swiftly up the street, away from the utter silence of the docks at night, toward a street where he could hail a ride. His footsteps echoed on the sidewalk, and they kept time to the pulse in his head and the laughter that escaped his soul.

It wasn't a safe part of town, and he wished someone would attack him. Give him a reason to kill again. He'd finally broken free of conventions. He'd never fully realized the power of this kind of evil.

He remembered he had Jillian's husband to kill. He hoped he got a chance to do that.

But he was a sensible man. He wouldn't let pleasure stop him from handing the job off to Rossiter if he found his hands full managing Jillian.

TWENTY-ONE

JILLY WALKED INTO THEIR ROOM, went straight to the bed, and fell over on her back with a loud sigh, arms flung wide. She bounced once, then lay there, looking like a landed trout.

Nick wandered toward her and looked down. "Happy to see your big sister?" He couldn't stop the smile.

She glared at him for a few seconds, then she propped herself up on her elbows. "Michelle has always been the one in charge of everything. Then she leaves for a few months, and when she comes back, she thinks she can just pick up where she left off making decisions and running everything. My big sister can't seem to understand that I'm in charge now." Her green eyes flashed with satisfaction. "But I don't mind repeating myself."

Since Nick didn't care to listen as Jilly listed all Michelle's faults, which, because Jilly loved her sister, would be followed with Jilly listing all Michelle's gifts, then growling over whether that made her a big help or a big old nuisance, he headed toward their dressing room and his silk pajamas.

He would never admit it out loud, but he'd gotten to like them, mainly because he could tell Jilly liked them. She often stroked the fine silk and while she was at it, she touched him. Oh yes, he'd come to like the pajamas very much. "I'll change first tonight."

He took time to wash thoroughly and shave, but even so, he was in and out fast. It had been a long day. A great day, but they were both exhausted. Before they both fell asleep, he had a few things he wanted to say to his wife.

He lay on the bed, waiting for her. She was in and out fast, too, though she usually lingered.

Jilly went around the foot of the bed and slid in beside him. The bed was on the wall opposite the door so they could see anyone who came in.

Lanterns stood on beautiful oak bedside tables. The chimneys were globes made of white glass, painted with delicate blue and pink flowers. They cast a light that made Jilly's beautiful eyes sparkle with intelligence. Nick had never been around furniture and fussy details like those lanterns before. His home had been bare bones. During a Michigan winter, they'd been happy enough with wood to burn and a meal. He had a bed, but three little brothers slept in it with him. Warm in the winter, but in the summers, he usually slept on the floor in front of the unlit fireplace.

Turning to her as she settled the blankets, he smiled. "When we stood by that new pivot bridge, and I watched it work exactly as you'd planned it, the pride I felt in you was almost overwhelming. The respect I felt, the joy at being bound to you . . . Something changed deep inside me. Or maybe better to say, I admitted to myself that my feelings for you go deep.

"I've known since I met you in the Purgatory settlement that you were an uncommonly beautiful woman, Jillian Stiles Ryder. And I knew before that how special all the Stiles sisters were. But none is so special to me as you, Jilly."

He leaned farther over her, and she reached up to draw a gentle finger down the side of his face.

"When you figured out who we were, it seemed impossible, a miracle," Jilly said. "Then you rode out within minutes of hearing Mama was in danger, to stand as a protector over her. You were my hero that day, and you still are."

She reached up, an inch at a time, and kissed him.

Drawing back just far enough that their gazes met and held, she said, "I realized today, Nick, that I-I . . ." She swallowed hard and gave her head a little shake, then smiled. "I love you, Nick. Of all the men I know, and all the hardworking, fine lumberjacks, my courageous brothers-in-law, every man I've met, none of them touched my heart. But you do. You are the man God chose for me to marry."

Nick stopped her words with a kiss deeper than any he'd given her before.

It was his turn to pull back. "I fell in love with you that day in Purgatory, or at least it was the beginning of love. There you stood with your sisters. Three women so beautiful it was stunning, breathtaking almost. But you alone drew me. Only you made me ache and want."

"And I spent far too much time pondering your unusual eyes. They stayed in my thoughts, and shone out of a handsome, heroic face. Heterochromia is interesting, but that alone didn't explain how often I thought of you."

"And when two people love each other, two very married people, who are alone together in their room at night, in each other's arms, what do you think those two people should do?"

Jilly's smile went from blinding to something else. Something warm and sweet. She rested her hands on both sides of his face and drew him close.

"I think they should be fully married."

She might have said more, but Nick lost track of the words and was left with only feeling. Only passion. Only love.

NICK WOKE with a beautiful woman in his arms.

The silk of her red curls spread across his chest, shining in the morning light. Her soft, warm breath caressed him while her head rested on his shoulder.

His first thought was to pray for this precious woman. His prayer began with thanks. Thanks to the point of feeling like he held a miracle in his arms.

Having someone of his own was wonderful. He'd grown used to being alone. Until this minute, he'd never realized how much he missed having a family. For a long moment, as he lay contented and happy, in love and in a comfortable home, he spent time in prayer for all of those long-left-behind brothers and sisters. He hoped they'd all found a safe haven in this world. He hoped they all had survived, and he wondered if there would ever be a way to find out.

He could offer any of them who were interested a fine job in Stiles Lumber.

Then his prayers turned to protection. For Jilly, for all the Stiles women, and for himself and all the new Stiles husbands. For the crew. For anyone who got in the way of Edgar Beaumont or Royce Carlisle. His prayers were fervent, and he sought God's peace, His strength. He reached up with his soul to touch God, to ask for reassurance and guidance.

"You're thinking what a bad bargain you've made."

Nick's eyes dropped from the canopy over the bed to the beautiful woman beside him. "You are doing the poorest possible job of reading my mind."

Her serious expression transformed to a smile. Her head raised until she leaned over him. "Is that right?"

He kissed her. "I'm thinking I am the most greatly blessed man on this earth. I'm thanking God with every breath that I have you for a wife. And I'm praying God's protection over all of us."

Her smile faded. "And that's what I meant. You were thinking you have lined yourself up like a duck in a shooting gallery. You're thinking there is danger aimed right at you from too many directions."

"At you, too, Jilly."

"Carlisle doesn't want me dead. He just wants me."

"His determination to have you for a wife is the worst sort of danger I can imagine."

"Worse than death," Jilly whispered.

"There is no possible way, married or not, I wouldn't stand between you and that despicable old monster. So since I'm not going away to spare myself a chance of danger, marrying you is pure blessing. The wonder of being your husband is beyond my finest dreams."

"I love you, Nick. I'm glad I have this chance to know love. I didn't think it would happen for me. I had such a fear of being married."

"You never told me why."

She brushed her fingertips to his lips. "It was like the nightmare only worse because it was real. I promised I'd tell you only . . . only . . ."

He felt her shudder, then she launched herself into his arms. Kissing him almost desperately. He knew she was trying to distract him.

He took her shoulders, and with some difficulty, because he was fighting himself as much as her, he held her away from him. "Jilly, stop, please, we need to talk. How often have you had the dream since we've been married?"

That question pulled her out of her dark dread. "You've been here to wake me up now twice."

"Maybe talking about it helped. What's at the root of the dream? What did Edgar do to make the nightmares begin?"

"Nick, I—"

"Stop. I see you arranging excuses not to tell me inside that brilliant brain of yours."

She smiled, but it wobbled. "I said I needed time, and you've given me more than I dared hope."

"If you don't want to tell me, let me just say that my imagination has gone wild with the ugly, violent things he might've done to you. I have trouble believing anything you say can be worse than what I'm imagining."

Nick held back a sigh of grief. He wouldn't impose his will

on her. Badger her until she talked. Only Jilly could release what she kept locked inside.

She lifted her hand from beneath his. "Edgar hadn't really done anything wrong yet during the winter in San Francisco. But his eyes when he looked at me . . . they made my skin crawl. I thought maybe I just couldn't accept him in Papa's place. I blamed myself for not being able to like and respect him. Even so, I'd made it a point to never be alone with him, and I never let my sisters be alone with him. Then one night he caught me alone."

Nick rested a hand on her wrist and stroked it gently.

She forced the story out, a slightly less fantastical version of what she'd told him about the dream, without the burning bedroom, but with the deep knowledge that this was real. This had truly happened to her.

As she finished, she said, "I believed at the time it was my fault. As if I'd driven him to long for me. Pulled him away from his love and devotion to Mama."

Nick kissed the top of her head, and his hand smoothed her hair. "He never, um . . ."

"His hands never moved beyond my wrists. But the threat in his eyes scared me half to death. Because of my memory, it's wildly vivid. And it plays over and over. Especially the end. He said if I told Mama, he'd kill her."

Nick tightened his arms with every word.

"And you never told anyone?"

"No, and the nightmares began. I've always believed I could do anything. But for the first time, I doubted I could protect Mama or myself and my sisters."

Nick held her close.

"We'll keep Mama safe, won't we?"

"We will keep all of you safe. You have my most solemn vow. But as much as I respect how you manage things, Jilly, I think you need to lean more on God. Take the work you do on your own strong, capable shoulders, but let God take the weight off your soul." He lay on his back and pulled her so her head rested on his shoulder and his arms were wrapped around her.

"I don't know if the nightmares will come again, but I do feel some of the weight lifting off my soul. I know I take on everything, and I know I'm too slow to pray as I go dashing along, fixing the world to suit myself."

"That sounds like something Michelle would do, not my sweet, easygoing Jilly."

She reached for a few of the hairs on his chest and gave them a good tug.

"Ouch!" He laughed and pressed her hand flat.

She laughed, too, then kissed away any pain she'd caused.

"Let's sleep like this tonight, Jilly. Maybe being held tight will keep the nightmares away."

She kissed him deeply and wrapped her arms tightly around his neck.

TWENTY-TWO

THE CONSTRUCTION OF THE TRAIN TRACK went faster now. The pivot bridge had been the biggest building project. The land was rough, and the smoothing of the train bed was in an area that was rugged and steep, but the crew worked well together. Michelle, though Jilly hated to admit it, was a huge help.

Michelle's head boiled over with ideas. She had an innovative way of looking at things, and she knew all the latest inventions. Beyond that, Michelle had them all organized right down to the ground. The building materials were always at hand. What Jilly needed was there before she needed it. Michelle had taken everything they'd figured out from surveying and done a masterful job of setting crews to work coming from both directions.

She had taken on nearly every aspect of this project except the actual building. She left that all to Jilly, and the separation of responsibilities seemed to work well. Jilly knew now that if Michelle had stayed and they'd tackled this together, they'd've have found their way. It helped her let go of a lot of the antagonism she felt toward her big sister.

And Nick seemed to really enjoy blowing up mountains. He came back from each day of work, where he had his own demolition crew, with flashing excitement in his eyes.

Ross had finally come back to work and seemed fine. He was less flirtatious with Jilly, but then Jilly was a married woman now, and besides, she mostly left him under Michelle's control.

He'd shown an interest in explosives, and Laura had trained him in their use right along with Nick. So the mountains were being cut through fast enough that Jilly could get to the tunnel and find it ready.

Jilly planned to assign him some less intensive labor than sawing down trees, at least at first. He still looked a little shaky to her.

A few days ago, they had finally brought the railroad tracks up high enough they could cut through a narrow stretch to connect with the old trail down the mountain. Home was finally close enough everyone could sleep in their own beds each night.

Sitting down with her family after they'd all washed up and eaten a fine dinner, Jilly said, "We'll be done with the train tracks before the winter makes it impossible to work. And I hope we'll be able to stretch out the logging for longer if we can run the train until late into the year. It'll be cold work, but I think we can manage it. The men being able to ride home weekly to visit their families will make them more agreeable, I hope, to a longer work year.

And we'll be able to get supplies sent up daily if we need them."

"I got a telegram from Eric Barritt today," Mama said. "All the bills for our supplies for the train came in marked paid in full. Every rail and bolt, every spike, all of it is compliments of California Ironworks"—Mama quirked a rather smug smile—"if we will agree not to sue him and not to spread the word about the defective supplies he sent us."

"Mama." Jilly's eyes went wide. "Think of how much that reduces the price of this project."

"A company as big as California Ironworks can't let its supply lines be adulterated by one evil man. Eric knows that. He's found proof of Carlisle's meddling. Bribes he paid to substitute inferior products for what we ordered. Men on Carlisle's payroll who were on our work crew who started the strike."

"Can he prove Carlisle was behind the explosion?" Nick asked. "Because that amounts to murder. And Carlisle needs to be behind bars. We've had a run of quiet work for quite a while now, but I know he's got plans to strike again."

Sobered by the truth of that, they all lounged in Mama's sitting room, wondering what Carlisle would think of next. They were using every safety measure Jilly could think of. They were carefully inspecting their materials. They made sure that any discontent among the men was listened to and corrected if it was within their power.

For all that, Jilly knew Carlisle would think of other ways to cause trouble. And trouble Carlisle's way could be deadly.

Jilly liked to talk through the day but not for long. She

worked long hours at a physically demanding job. She always retired early these days. And she took her handsome husband with her.

ROYCE WAITED PATIENTLY. He thought of himself as a cougar. Quiet, patient, powerful, deadly.

Tonight, no one would die if he was obeyed.

The door to the little hovel swung open on a cheery greeting.

"I have her." Royce cocked the pistol he held. The metallic sound drew the man's attention quickly.

First, he saw the gun, then he saw the dress. The dress his wife had been wearing when he'd left the house for an errand.

The dress now soaked in blood.

"Where's my wife? What—"

"Shut up or she dies." Royce knew the power of his voice. He knew the ability he had to chill others, silence them. Terrify them. He used the voice often to excellent effect.

"You'll do as I say, or she dies. And you have other loved ones. Each of them, one by one, will die."

"No, please, don't do it. I'll do anything you ask. But I have no money. I have—"

"Close your mouth and don't speak again unless I ask a question."

Like a coward, the man clamped his mouth shut.

"Your wife is alive and will stay alive unless you fail to follow my orders. And be assured, if you tell anyone, I'll know. I have people watching you all the time up at that lumber camp. The Stiles family may think they've gotten rid of all the men who are on my payroll, but they're wrong, and I'll know you've betrayed me before you get back here. And your wife will be dead. Then the others." Royce couldn't believe the pleasure he had watching the man shake, hands clenching together as if he were begging.

Gesturing with the gun, Royce pointed to a small box he'd carefully prepared. He gave the man instructions. "Head back to the camp immediately, and do as you're told. Fail and she dies. Others you love will die."

The man's head swung to the small box like he was drunk. "You're asking me to kill."

"No one will die. Not like when that bomb killed those strikers. This time, they'll suffer. Only your wife is in danger, for now." Royce wondered if the fool would believe him.

Those terrified eyes flicked from Royce's face to the gun to the box.

"Do you need more of her blood to convince you? She's got a pretty wedding band. I can bring you her finger with the ring still on it."

The man shook like an aspen in the wind.

"Go now. You can get there in time tonight to put the plan in place. Be back here to report on your success tomorrow night and see your wife again."

The man looked back at Royce, and tears flooded his eyes. The terror, the desire to defy such ugly orders, the knowledge that Royce meant every word.

With jerky movements, the man grabbed the box and said, "Don't hurt her. Please let her live. I'll do as you ask."

He rushed out of the house. Royce went to the window

and watched him swing up on the horse he'd left tied to a hitching post and kick it into a fast trot.

For a minute, Royce wondered if he'd fall. The man didn't look like much of a rider. And certainly riding with such fear in his heart made everything worse.

But the man kept his seat and disappeared from sight. Royce laughed. It was as much fun to terrorize people as to kill.

Almost.

Rossiter came out of the kitchen. "I'd hoped he'd need more persuading." He slid his brass knuckles off his right hand and dropped them into the pocket of his coat.

Brute strength. Useful but Carlisle found it distasteful, though the gun was brute force and the bloodstained dress qualified, too.

"We wait until dark to deal with our captive." Who knew what the man might've done if he'd known his wife was still here in the house? They couldn't march a bleeding woman out of here in full daylight. Fear had kept the man from thinking of that.

"I'll see her tucked away, sir. You can make yourself comfortable here and sleep in a real bed rather than rough it near where we'll keep our captive."

Royce glanced around the hovel and had to control a shudder to think of sleeping here. The throbbing began in his temples. He should have just sent Rossiter to do this. In the past, that's just what he would have done. But this was different.

"I used him so I could be closely involved in Jillian's downfall." The throbbing increased. It was only for a day. He could endure it when the reward was so rich.

When he tired of hurting her through her foolish construction project, he'd take her. And that day was coming soon.

He wanted to be at hand when the man came back. And he didn't want to be seen in town if he had to stay around for days. "He'll be back to report on how it went. After dark, go toss her into our neatly arranged hiding place, then come back. We both need to stay close."

TWENTY-THREE

NICK SAT ALONE in the back of the wagon that daily took him and his dynamite team to the current blasting site. He'd found six wild men who liked big booms, Ross among them. They were always rarin' to go. They loaded up the first wagon and headed out ahead of everyone else.

Except in the predawn hours today, there weren't any wild men. Even the lumberjacks weren't out and about. They usually headed out before full sunrise, and that beat the loggers, but still, there was always some sign the men were stirring.

In the predawn light, Nick saw Ross, his right-hand man when it came to explosions, slowly walking toward him.

"They're sick to their stomachs, Nick," Ross explained, looking a little green himself. "Runnin' to the privy too often, too. Some of 'em bad. Some of 'em just feeling puny. But you wouldn't want a single one of them working a blast job today. We've been struck by the grippe."

"How many are sick?" The *grippe*, Nick knew, was a

word that could mean most anything from mild bellyaches to fevers and even influenza or pneumonia leading to death. It could be more frightening things. Cholera. Diphtheria. Yellow fever. Contagious things. Deadly things. He hoped it was a simple bellyache.

"Better to ask how many are well. Whatever is spreading through the men has hit pert near everyone."

Including Ross, though he was on his feet at least, just barely.

"Go back to bed with the others."

Shaking his head violently, Ross stumbled and had to grab hold of the wagon to stay upright. "I'm not going back in there, Nick. It's an ugly business. It's a nice day. Maybe I can go lay down in the woods."

"I'd better talk to Doc Sandy."

"Best not to go near him. He's sick too. Old Tom. The cook. The cook don't matter none, as far as losing his help. Not a single man is interested in food. And whatever ails 'em doesn't seem to need doctoring. Just time. Leastways that's how it seems so far."

Nick walked to the tailgate and jumped down to the ground. "Go wherever you've a need to go, Ross. I'm giving everyone the day off. And you'll receive full pay, too."

Pete, the stable master, was sitting up on the wagon seat, ready to drive. He climbed down. He was overly careful, and Nick could see he wasn't in top shape.

"Go on with you, Pete. No sense you worrying about a drive with no men to ride along. And no sense me going alone. It's not a one-man job."

"I'll put up the horses."

Nick probably should have offered to do it. But Pete seemed to be staying upright, and honestly, Nick was a little afraid to get too close to him.

Pete and Ross might not have been hit hard by whatever had caused these collywobbles—they'd obviously come out thinking they were able to work—but they weren't well. And anyway, Nick didn't want any part of standing near them. The family had escaped the sickness so far. Nick had seen no sign of sickness among the house servants, but had he really been paying attention? After spending yesterday with the crew, if something was catching, then there was a good chance he and Jilly had caught it.

Nick headed for the house, wondering if Michelle and Zane ought to get out of here for a few days. Then, thinking of Laura, he wondered if a bellyache might harm a woman expecting a baby.

He'd reached the base of the stairs leading up to the front porch when Jilly swung the door open, Michelle on her heels, the two of them chattering and smiling.

Getting along fine, for the moment.

Then Jilly saw Nick. Her eyes went to the wagon being led back toward the stable. "What happened this time?"

He saw her fear, her worst suspicions. "No, nothing happened. Not like you mean, anyway, no sign of sabotage. Ross told me the grippe is going around with the men."

"The grippe?" Michelle looked toward the men's cabins. "That could mean anything."

"It sounds like they can't keep food in their bellies. Ross didn't seem to think it was serious. I told them to rest for the day. Sounds like most all of them are down with it."

"Why didn't we get it?" Jilly asked. "We spend every day with the men."

"Did they all eat out of the same pot of food?" Michelle asked.

"They all eat together in the hall," Jilly said.

Nick watched the two of them thinking fast, way faster than he could.

Seconds ticked by as they stared through each other. He was used to it by now, watching the Stiles women think.

Laura did the same thing.

Michelle's expression was very similar to her sisters', but Nick hadn't been around her as much.

"Spoiled food?" Michelle asked.

"Spoiled or poisoned?" Jilly whispered.

Their eyes widened, their matching frowns turning to scowls.

"Carlisle," Michelle said, clenching her fists.

"Edgar." Jilly spoke on top of Michelle's words. "Or both. And neither one of them has been anywhere around here. Which means—"

"We've still got traitors among us," Michelle finished.

Jilly turned to stare at the rows of cabins.

Nick hadn't considered it was anything other than some contagious sickness. Those swept through a place now and then.

"Do you trust the cook?" he asked.

Jilly and Michelle crossed their arms and glared in the direction of the dining hall.

Finally, Jilly said, "I don't trust anyone. Not anymore."

Nick hoped she didn't include him.

"WE'RE NOT GOING TO WORK on the track today." Jilly led the three of them back inside. Laura and Caleb were still at the breakfast table with Mama.

Zane had intended to ride down the hill with them and had gone to get his hat. He came back in a few paces behind them and went to Michelle. "What happened?"

Michelle and Jilly took turns telling them.

"We don't know for sure they were poisoned." Nick sounded reasonable.

Well, Jilly had no intention of being reasonable. "Better chance of that than every one of them—and none of us—all coming down with some stomachache at the same time."

She crossed her arms and looked from Mama to Laura to Caleb. "We are going to get to the bottom of this. Who did it? How did he do it? We've got to . . . to . . . to . . ." She threw her arms wide. "What are we going to do?"

"We hoped with all the men Edgar and Barritt had hired gone, we were safe." Caleb shook his head. "Is there any chance there are more men behind this than just Carlisle and Edgar?"

Michelle began pacing. "Horace Benteen, my suitor, is locked up in San Quentin."

"Suitor." Zane snorted. "Glad he's in prison."

"And I've had the impression Myron Gibbons has given up on me," Laura said.

Caleb slid an arm around her shoulders.

"Gibbons isn't like Carlisle," Mama said. "He's a greedy man, but once you were beyond his reach, I'm sure he turned his attention elsewhere."

"Every young heiress in San Francisco needs to be warned."

210

Jilly crossed her arms. "Is it possible Eric Barritt is somehow in cahoots with Carlisle?"

Silence ruled the room except for the sound of Michelle's footsteps. The men had no idea, and the women were busy thinking. Jilly mulled over all she knew about Mr. Barritt. He seemed honorable to her. But he was well acquainted with men who were not. Of course, having Carlisle, Gibbons, and Benteen on the board of California Ironworks didn't make Barritt a coconspirator. After all, Papa had been on the board. Then Mama after him.

"I don't think Barritt is in on this," Mama spoke thoughtfully. "But he is compromised. *He*, I believe, is an honest man. A man who, outwardly at least, seems to have things under control. But that doesn't speak for every man he employs. I fear the ironworks has been infiltrated. Everything we say to him might be passed on to ears we don't want hearing about what we're doing. I'm not willing to confide in him anymore."

"Then who can we ask about what Carlisle and Edgar are up to?" Laura rubbed her thumbnail on her bottom lip.

A longer silence.

"What about Lloyd Tevis?" Michelle paused her pacing. "He's got his Wells Fargo agents. They're good investigators. Could we ask about hiring some of his men to investigate Carlisle? See if we can catch him out in such a way he could be arrested?"

"I think they mainly chase down robbers who steal from Wells Fargo." Jilly stared into the middle distance, thinking.

"I've heard they're expanding." Laura had been mostly quiet. Probably afraid someone would force her to blow something up. Especially now that they were shorthanded.

"What about turning this over to Marshal Irving?" Mama asked. "He's a fine man."

"Let's try both." Michelle crossed her arms and began pacing again. "And I think we need to talk to them face-to-face. Let's run to Sacramento, then over to San Francisco. The men may be laid up for days. It's a good time to be away. If we're wrong about the poison, and it's something contagious, it's a *great* time to be away."

Mama turned toward the cabins as if she could see through the walls all the way to where the men lay sick. "I've got to go see what they need. I can't leave when so many men are ailing. It wouldn't be right. And if they *were* poisoned, we've got to make sure it never happens again."

"Michelle, can you go? If Zane goes with you, that's enough security, isn't it?" Jilly felt her forehead furrow. She wasn't sure if there was enough security in the world these days.

"Laura can come, too." Michelle looked up from the pacing that seemed to help her mind work better. "And Caleb, of course. We should get Laura away from here anyway, in case there's tampering with the food in our house. A bad bellyache probably wouldn't do any permanent damage to a healthy adult—"

"Let's hope." Mama didn't sound confident.

"But it might harm an unborn child," Michelle said. "We can't risk that. I'll talk with Marshal Irving about hiring security. It's time we did that. I'll tell Uncle Newt what's going on, too."

"Uncle Newt." Zane shook his head and plunked his hat on like he was ready to go.

"And I'll see what Mr. Tevis says about the Wells Fargo agents. I've heard they do a different kind of work than Pinkertons. The Pinkertons can be hired ruffians sometimes. The Wells Fargo agents are better at investigating. I'd prefer we hire them."

Jilly didn't know much about Pinkertons or Wells Fargo agents. She decided to let Michelle handle that.

"And while they're gone, Nick, you and I should spend time going over the laid tracks and the bridge. Check for sabotage. I've checked already, but I want it done again. These long weeks of peace are making me itchy. If someone is close enough to poison the men's food, then they are close enough to damage my train tracks."

"Are there any men left who were hired by Beaumont?" Nick looked at the Stiles sisters and their mama.

Slowly, as if picturing each and every person on the place, Mama shook her head. "There's not one. We've got two men working mainly inside as porters, Ronald and Delmont. There were several more when Edgar was here, but they're all gone now. And he didn't bring in any new maids or cooks. So I've known all indoor staff forever."

She looked at her daughters. "We employ a lot of men. The camp cook that Edgar brought in was dreadful. Not just a bad cook but also an arrogant man who treated everyone terribly and ran with tales to Edgar, getting several men fired. He was the first to go. Old Tom cleaned out the whole rat's nest of men Edgar hired. Besides the household help and the lumberjacks, there are the men who work with Pete in the stables, and the railroad workers Jilly hired. Am I forgetting anyone?"

Laura had been home longest, and Jilly had worked with the men most.

"We hired Ross just last winter, remember? Right before Mama got married," Jilly said. "We always hire a few new men to start in the spring. But *we* hired them, not Edgar."

"Could Edgar have known he'd be coming up, even before the wedding, and started hiring quietly back in San Francisco? Or sent men for you to hire?" Nick asked.

"Most of them were hired before I began seeing Edgar. Is it possible one of the new men might've been in cahoots with him because he planned ahead to set his sights on me?" Mama looked worried now.

It was Jilly, though, who said out loud what they were all thinking. "We have to accept that whoever did this is one of our own men. Someone Edgar didn't hire originally but was brought over to his side."

"But who?" Mama clutched her hands together at her chest as if in prayer. "We pay well. The men here know and like each other. Who would do such a thing?"

"Money's usually at the root of these things," Caleb said with a grim frown.

"I don't know who did it." Jilly was still thinking, sorting through the men. "But I know that, until we figure it out, we don't dare trust a single one of them."

Nick came to Jilly's side as solemn as the grave. "Let's go ask the camp cook a few questions."

"We'll saddle up and head down the mountain." Zane looked at Michelle, then Caleb and Laura, who all nodded and followed him.

"And I think I'll go speak to the house cook," Mama said.

"No, Mama." Jilly's urgent voice stopped everyone.

They turned to look at her.

"We're back where we started before Edgar left. Mama, I'm sure he'd like to hurt you if he could. And hiring someone to do it would suit him just fine. We don't know who to trust. You need to stick with me and Nick."

Mama's expression fell. All the weight of her choice of a husband was there in the downcast, deepened lines on her face.

"Maybe we shouldn't go." Michelle hesitated, and she rarely did that. She was a straight-ahead kind of woman. "Or at least not all of us."

Laura nodded. "I'm staying. Caleb, we're needed here." Then she added to Michelle, "Are you sure the two of you alone will be safe?"

"Zane and I will go to Sacramento first and see if Marshal Irving can suggest men he'd trust as guards. The two of us going might even be safest. At least my lousy suitor is locked up tight."

"Caleb and Laura can come with me to talk to our cook while you and Nick go talk to the camp cook." Mama's shoulders slumped.

Quietly, Caleb said, "I'd like us, as a family, to join together in a moment of prayer. We need God's guiding hand to keep us safe while we try to stop dangerous men who mean us harm. Everyone in this room needs to fight this battle within God's will. Many times in the Bible, kings went out to war, some with God on their side, some without even seeking the will of God. We need to be among the seekers, to find out what God's will is in this mess."

"But how can there be any doubt what God's will is when Edgar and Carlisle are doing such evil things?" Jilly frowned at Caleb, not liking even a hint that there could be two sides to this battle they had to wage.

Caleb looked at her, a direct, solemn expression, then his eyes shifted to Michelle, then Mama, as he took Laura's hand. "I love all of the Stiles women." He squeezed her hand. "None like my Laura, but I love you like sisters, like a mother. So when I say what I feel led to say, please take it with that in your minds."

Jilly's throat went dry, and she just nodded silently. Mama did, too. Michelle arched a brow at Caleb in a way that told Jilly her big sister never thought she was wrong about anything. Jilly had to admit the same notion lived in her own head.

"When someone is very smart and very strong, and when they are good people who want the best for everyone . . . at least everyone good, it's very easy to think you are up to any task that falls in your path."

"Of course we are up for anything." Michelle crossed her arms. Zane moved closer to her as if to protect her.

"Michelle, all of you, the battle you have to fight—and I know because I have to fight it, too—is not against Edgar or Carlisle."

"Of course it is," Michelle snapped.

"No, the battle is allowing yourselves to lean on God."

Jilly remembered Nick saying something similar to her. Take the weight on her shoulders but let God bear the weight on her soul.

Michelle opened her mouth as if to say something rude.

But no words came out. Instead, her mouth slowly closed, and she listened.

Jilly was proud of her.

"We all need to let Him take charge. Someone who is weak, even broken, like I was when I was in prison, can easily see he or she needs a heavenly Father."

Jilly knew that in his youth, Caleb had been a man similar to Edgar. A man who slid around the law with easy smiles and greasy charm. He hadn't been slick enough, though, and he'd ended up in prison and found God behind those bars.

"Or someone like me," Nick said. "On my own when I was too young and had no notion that I was strong enough to handle what came my way."

Jilly went to him and leaned on his strong shoulder.

"But when you're very strong," Caleb went on, "and, honestly, capable of most anything, having faith can be an afterthought, if it's a thought at all."

"I'm a woman of faith." Jilly scowled at her brother-in-law, feeling like this little talk of his was directed personally at her. After all, Laura was mild-mannered. Mama was, well, Mama. And Michelle had given up running things. That left her. She clamped her jaw shut, sorry she'd spoken when Caleb turned kind eyes on her.

"I know you're all believers, Jilly. I've listened to you and prayed with you and preached to all of you. I've worked at your side, and I know your faith. I'm just saying, especially right now, you're setting out in different directions to tackle a big problem with a powerful enemy. You all think you can handle it, and maybe in the ways of winning a fight, you can. But I want you to have God at your side in this time of

217

trouble. I want you to see that when it comes to this life, we are helpless without Him, and I don't think a single one of you really believes you are helpless."

Jilly heard the word *helpless* and almost spoke up again. She saw Michelle rub the side of her index finger against her mouth. Not unlike a person trying to stop words from escaping. Mama pulled a handkerchief out of a concealed pocket in her dress and twisted it.

"I'll pray now," Caleb said, "but each and every one of you needs to be open to God with every step we take in this ugly little war we're fighting."

Every person in the room bowed their heads. Even a couple that, Jilly assumed, were stiff-necked prayer partners.

Caleb's quiet words of prayer eased Jilly's rebellious heart, her dynamic mind, her stubborn will. No, their problems didn't go away with a prayer. But Jilly felt her heart open to God in a way it never had before. It struck her that as competent as she was at nearly everything, she really needed God to guide her down the right path. And not just through this rugged time of trouble but always.

As the prayer ended, she felt closer to God than she ever had as she and her family prepared to go their separate ways.

Jilly went to Caleb and rested one of her very able hands on his shoulder. "Wise words, brother. I'll bear the weight of my work on my own shoulders, but put the weight of my soul on God's."

"That's well said." He smiled.

"Nick said it to me the other night."

Caleb gave Nick a quick nod.

Michelle, Zane at her side, came up and said, "You're a brave man to talk to me that way."

Caleb grinned. "I *am* brave."

"And a decent man. I'll remember what you've said. Thank you."

Zane clapped him on the shoulder.

"We all have things we urgently need to do, but they have to wait for now," Mama said.

Michelle turned with her brows lowered. "What could be more important than trying to stop someone vicious enough to poison men, set off explosives in a crowd, and arrange to undermine a train track so it will collapse and possibly kill passengers?"

But then, just from listening through Michelle's question, Jilly knew. "We have to take care of the sick men."

Mama nodded. "During that prayer, I realized we were forgetting our first job is to our own, here at Stiles Lumber. We're already low on crew, and under the circumstances, I'm not willing to bring in men I don't know or trust. I'd guess none of them have eaten yet today. No one's up to cooking outside of those of us in the house. And we don't dare trust anyone else with the job anyway."

God had been talking to Mama. And more importantly, Mama had listened.

"Today and for however long it takes, we have to work together to get our men through this." Michelle looked at Zane.

Nodding, he said, "Let's go see what needs doing."

"We'll start on the farthest row of cabins and work toward the dining hall," Michelle said. "We'll visit everyone. See what we can do to help." She and Zane headed out.

Mama came and took Caleb's arm. "I've got three sons. All fine men. Let's go visit the sick, Parson."

"We'll do the middle row of cabins, Jilly." Mama on Caleb's arm, with his other hand holding Laura's, they set out for the cabins. Mama looked steady, but this trouble had worn her down.

Jilly knew how intelligent Mama was, how hardworking, how wise she was in her business dealings. This had struck her right at the foundation of all her confidence.

Nick came to her side. When Mama was out of earshot, Jilly said, "It's not fair that Mama takes the blame for all this. None of us saw through Edgar. He's a very talented liar."

"But did you *pray* about Edgar, Jilly? Did your family search for God's will?"

That threw a pall of silence between them.

"No, you're right about that." Jilly could feel the weight of that neglect. Now she could. She hadn't seen it at the time. "We didn't ask God to guide us. Instead, we just assumed Edgar was a wonderful gift from God. We were all content to be happy."

"I think that was at the heart of Caleb's prayer. Nothing will change the past. No amount of guilt or regret. The past is done, and we're left here to live with things as they are, not as we wish they had been. But we can learn from what's happened. From this moment on, we do our best—we do much better than in the past—to seek God's will."

"I'm realizing just how completely I depend on only myself. Even after all we went through with Edgar, I haven't fully laid my burdens at God's feet. Let's pray as we go help the men."

Nick slid his arm across Jilly's waist and guided her out. "And let's see if with God's help, we can identify a man who's willing to poison every single one of his good friends."

TWENTY-FOUR

SAYING THOSE WORDS jostled Nick's thinking as they walked toward the area where the men lived.

"Before we visit the cabins," Jilly said, "I want to see the dining hall and check on Doc."

They headed first for the kitchen. It stood empty. The fires out. No sign of preparation for the next meal.

Nick crossed his arms to study the barren kitchen. "When we're done talking to the men, I'm going to come back here and make a huge pot of soup. Beef broth maybe. Something that any man whose stomach can bear it will find ready when he's able to eat."

"Can you do that?" Jilly smiled at him with true respect.

"Yep, I can do that. Maybe you can help me, and we can both stand guard over the soup until everyone's eaten. We'll have to choose what we cook carefully. It's possible someone brought in spoiled food, or poisoned food. We need to be very mindful of the ingredients we use to cook that soup."

With her jaw locked tight, Jilly said, "I'll help, even if it's just standing guard. Next, let's see if anyone is in the infirmary and see how Doc Sandy is doing." She left the empty kitchen and headed for the doctor's office.

There were four hospital beds in the infirmary, and two high examining tables in the doctor's office. All were occupied. One by their medic.

Doc's eyes were open, and he waved a shaky hand to greet Jilly and Nick. He was on one of the examining tables.

They went to his side. Jilly asked, "How are you?"

"You should get out of here. This must be contagious considering every man here is sick. It looks like the house avoided it, so don't come close."

Jilly rested one hand on his shoulder. She leaned close enough to whisper. "We think you were poisoned."

Doc jerked, and his eyes gaped wide. "Poisoned? So we might yet die?" He fumbled to grab the edge of the bed and pull himself to a sitting position. "I have to get up. I have to help."

Nick pushed past Jilly and pinned the medic's shoulders to the bed. "Stay down."

"If my patients have been poisoned, I need to see to them. Maybe we can find an antidote."

"We don't know a thing for sure." Nick came close to Doc Sandy to keep their conversation private. The man on the examining table next to them was asleep and snoring. The rest in the infirmary were far enough away they couldn't hear quiet voices. "But we think someone slipped something into last night's supper."

"I emptied my stomach a couple of times, once last night and once this morning. Since then, I've been pretty settled.

But I'm so shaky. I'm just a worthless lump, lying here, not helping anyone else."

"We're going to tend the sick, Doc. We're hopeful everyone just needs to rest and get well." Nick watched the man who'd cared for him after the trestle collapsed and saw the acceptance in his eyes. He just was not up to anything right now.

"Thank you, Nick, Miss Stiles, uh, I mean, Mrs. Ryder."

Nick grinned and patted Doc on the arm. "You're going to have to learn her new name eventually because I'm here to stay."

A faint smile eased the worst of the pallor on Doc's face. He let his eyes sink shut.

Door to door they went. Knocking, responding to feeble calls to come in. A few men came to the door. Nick hustled them back to bed.

In a normal logging season, Stiles Lumber would have had two men in most of these cabins. It was the height of the cutting season. Winters were idle, but the other three seasons they pushed hard. This year, due to men being fired by Edgar, men loyal to Edgar being fired, and men quitting because of Edgar, they had a thin lumber crew, and the cabins that were built to house two men were private.

Nick listened to Jilly speak to each man, call him by name, ask after his family if he had one. She mentioned children by name and commented on the town they lived in. She always added some memory of what the man did for the Stiles family.

Nick knew she had a nearly perfect memory. He'd heard the term *photographic memory* used by her family. A few of the men spoke of it, too.

He hadn't quite realized what it meant. But he could see how touched each man was that his beautiful boss, Jillian Stiles Ryder, remembered him.

They seemed to almost heal under her gentle attentions. Whether they were wearing themselves out digging for strength to appear at their best for her, or she really was helping them rally, all Nick knew was that he'd underestimated her.

She was brilliant, no denying it.

Hardest-working person he'd ever seen.

Organized beyond reason.

And she was generous and passionate in his arms.

All good reasons to love his wife.

But this was a new side of her. A side that nearly shimmered with the kindness and thoughtfulness she showed the men.

While Jilly paid them such lovely attention, Nick kept busy tidying cabins, cleaning up some ghastly messes, and finding drinks of water for the men. He helped a few to the privy while he was there.

They were nearing the end of the front row of cabins. They found Old Tom in poor condition. He was older than most of the men and seemed especially fragile.

Jilly stayed with him a long time. Nick spent that time turning his hand to whatever needed doing. This cabin had really gotten the worst of Old Tom's sickness.

Nick's anger grew as he worked in the only way he knew how to care for this man who'd been so good to him.

They told everyone as they went that there would be soup if they could face a meal. Neither Nick nor Jilly mentioned poison beyond telling Doc Sandy. Not even food poisoning. The men believed they'd all caught some very contagious case of the grippe. Unsure what was the right way to handle it, Nick and Jilly decided to let that stand.

They knocked at the last cabin. The door creaked open, and Garvey Bates leaned in the doorway. The big man's complexion was ashen.

"Garvey." Jilly took a quick step forward. "You look near to collapsing. You didn't need to come to the door."

"I . . ." His voice faltered. Color, what little he had, drained from his face. He looked for a moment as if he'd fall. Nick pressed past Jilly and wrapped an arm around Garvey, then nearly staggered under the man's weight.

Nick righted himself and urged Garvey back into the cabin.

With corded muscles, Nick hauled Garvey the few steps to his unmade bed and let the man collapse flat on his back.

Jilly filled a tin cup with water and brought it to Garvey. "Help me sit him up, Nick."

Garvey shook his head, but Nick was strong, and Jilly was relentless. Finally, Garvey took a small drink, then, as if only now realizing how thirsty he was, he drank deeply, draining the cup.

"Th-thank you, Mrs. Ryder, Nick. Um . . . I s'pose it should be Mr. Ryder now. You're married to the boss, that makes you the boss, too."

"It's Nick, Garvey." Nick clapped Garvey gently on the shoulder, then left his hand on Garvey's back, which helped the man stay sitting upright. "You're more than just a man who works for us. You're a friend, too."

"I-I reckon." Garvey's eyes closed.

Where his lashes curved against his cheeks, there was a rim of moisture, maybe . . . Nick couldn't quite believe it, but maybe tears?

Nick glanced at Jilly, frowning. She saw the look and went back to studying the longtime lumberjack.

"Garvey, every man we've gone to see today has said 'stay back, you might catch this.' But not you." Nick watched the man. Yes, he was sick, but there was more. There was agony of another kind on his face. The agony of guilt. "Because you know this isn't contagious, don't you?"

Rather than answer, Garvey asked, "H-have any of the men died?" He spoke barely above a whisper.

"No, and none are going to." Jilly took one of Garvey's massive hands and held it in both of hers.

Nick thought of Old Tom and hoped that was the truth.

Garvey's eyes snapped open. "None?"

"They're all going to be fine. We missed a day of work, maybe a few days, but everyone will survive." Then very quietly, she added, "Old Tom is really sick, though. An old man like that, if he ate a full meal dosed with poison . . . What only made a strong young man sick might kill a thin old man."

Garvey's hand gripped hers as he looked hard into her eyes as if trying to read a terrible truth there.

"Tell me what's going on, Garvey. What do you know about the men being poisoned?"

"I did it. I deserve to hang."

"Where'd you get the poison, Garvey?" Her voice was steady, but Nick saw scarcely banked fury in her eyes.

Garvey shook his head, then covered his face with the hand that Jilly didn't have a firm grip on.

"What did they threaten you with if you didn't use it?" That's what had been jostling around in Nick's head. No man would poison all his friends unless he had a powerful reason, like a threat. "Did they hurt your wife or someone else? Or threaten to?"

"He'll kill her. He swore he would, and I believe him. The look on his face. I felt like I stood before the devil himself. He had her favorite dress in his hands, the one she'd been wearing when I left that morning, and it was soaked in blood. He said it was hers. He said he'd kill her slowly if I didn't do what he asked."

Jilly straightened away from Garvey, whirling so her back was to him. Nick saw the rage on her face. In his misery, Garvey didn't see it . . . yet.

"We'll find your wife." Nick tightened his grip on Garvey's shoulder. "You have my word, we will move heaven and earth to find your wife and get her to safety, but you have to tell us what's going on."

"I got home with my broken arm, and everything was fine. It was good seeing her. The young'uns are grown and gone now. Out of the house, though they're around. Finally, my arm healed, and I was ready to come on back up here to work. I went out to pick up a few things for my wife, and when I got home, she was gone. And that little man was there with her dress. Satan in a fancy suit. He wore glasses with rims that looked like real gold. He was mostly bald and had eyes so cold they made me think of ice on the mountaintop."

Carlisle. Nick gave Jilly one quick glance. She'd turned back when she recognized the description.

"He told me simple . . . take the bottle he'd brought and hide it in the evening meal, or my Mabel would die." Garvey was speaking to his toes as if shame weighed his head down. "Wouldn't kill them, he said. But he *would* kill my wife. Wasn't I willing to disrupt the work for a while, in exchange for her life? He said something about not deadly like the last time, the explosion."

"He said that? He mentioned the explosion?"

"Yep, seemed proud of it."

"He admitted to involvement in murder." Jilly wasn't asking questions now. She was thinking out loud. "And he kidnapped your wife and threatened to kill her."

All this made Garvey a witness to a confession of murder. Nick knew, and he was sure Jilly had realized, that Carlisle couldn't allow Garvey or his wife to live.

Garvey was too frightened to think that his wife would be killed, and he would be, too, if Carlisle wasn't stopped.

"I even took a serving of last night's supper myself. If it was deadly, then I wanted to die, too. I'd've killed my friends. Men who trusted me." Garvey's shoulders trembled, and he covered his face with both hands and wept.

Nick had never known a man stronger or with a better humor than Garvey Bates. To see him talk about serving poison, taking it himself, to see him weep and tremble. Royce Carlisle had brought a good man to this with a vicious threat.

But Nick now had a witness—a man who could bring Carlisle down if they got him in front of a judge and jury.

"We'll find her, Garvey. We'll protect her."

Garvey raised his head, agony in his eyes. "He meant it, Nick. I've never seen eyes like that. He's a man capable of murder, and he'd never feel one minute of regret."

"We'll be cautious. And we won't tackle him alone. We'll get help."

"Let me go with you. I'll make sure he knows I did what he asked. He said he'd have my wife ready to come home when I reported in. You can follow me to where he's holding her and arrest him."

"Garvey, I don't know." Jilly came to his side and rested both of her hands on the man's strong shoulders. "This is my trouble. Carlisle's angry because of me. We'd put you in danger along with your wife. We can't—"

"Mrs. Ryder, let me. Dangle me in front of him even if it puts me under his guns. After I face him, if I live, I'm going to turn myself over to the law. I should have come to you, but I was so afraid, I had to follow his instructions. I'll take the punishment I deserve, even if I hang. I'm guilty, and I'll stand up to it. But my wife—" Garvey's voice broke, and his eyes filled. "My Mabel is a good woman. Save her if you can."

TWENTY-FIVE

JILLY STRODE INTO THE HOUSE and didn't stop moving until she'd charged up to her room. She got her coat and hat, a black Stetson she'd acquired when she'd lived at Zane's ranch. She put on boots and tossed a few things into a satchel because she might be living on the trail and away from home for days. She didn't intend to come home until Carlisle was in prison or dead.

As she headed back downstairs, Nick met her on the steps. "I told everyone we're leaving. Michelle and Zane are already on the trail down the mountain. They sent a wire to Marshal Irving asking him to send help to El Robles Blanco, and to respond with a telegram to Hatcher's Creek. They're hoping they don't have to ride all the way to Sacramento to get someone to act as security for us. They'll meet us in El Robles Blanco when they can. Caleb, Laura, and Mama are staying here to care for the men."

It was only a slight modification of the plan they'd had before they'd spent time seeing to the men. Now, with information on the poison Garvey had used, and reassurance that there wasn't any more of it, and the household servants along with a few of the abler men to help, they could leave.

"Garvey is packed and saddling horses for the three of us. We leave in fifteen minutes." Nick jerked his chin in a take-charge kind of nod.

She nodded back. He ran on up, and she headed down.

By the time Jilly had fetched jerky and biscuits, Nick was packed and outside.

Jilly was only a few paces behind him, pulling on her coat. She saw Garvey on horseback, and he didn't look good. He wasn't as sick as some of the men, but he probably shouldn't be making this long, tiring ride. If they ever got that stupid train running, the ride down the mountain wouldn't be so long and tiring.

"We're not going to flat-out gallop." Nick's voice surprised Jilly. Very much a man taking charge. Surprised and annoyed her.

"We can't go that fast anyway on this winding, rattlesnake of a trail," Nick said. "Garvey, we need to hear what Carlisle expects you to do. Where are you supposed to meet him?"

"I'm to go home and wait there until he comes. He'll bring Mabel back with him and get my report on how it went."

Nick's jaw flexed as he listened. Garvey rode between them, Jilly on Garvey's right. Nick looked across the length of Garvey's broad chest. Jilly met his eyes.

"We have to tell him," Jilly said.

Nick nodded. Hooves clopped along on the steep trail. They wound to the left to ride along the face of the wooded mountainside, then the trail would curve to the right, and they'd ride downward again. Once in a while the trail was wider and better riding where the mountain wasn't so steep.

"Tell me what?" Garvey looked so sick, but Jilly wasn't sure if it was sick from poison or sick with fear. Some of both, no doubt.

"There is no way Carlisle can let you live, Garvey." Jilly watched as his pallid face, tinged with the unhealthy green of sickness, went bone white.

She shot out a hand to steady him.

"I suppose we could have waited until we got to lower ground," Nick muttered.

"I'm sorry. But if you weren't sick and scared half to death, you'd've figured it out yourself."

"Will he already . . . be done with Mabel?"

This time Nick's hand shot out. The two of them kept Garvey on horseback as they wound around another curve, this one steeper.

Jilly wondered if they should just let Garvey slump over the saddle horn and ride along unconscious.

"He can't let Mabel go free, either," Jilly said. "You are both witnesses to a crime, and Carlisle isn't a man who'd want any witnesses."

"But he mentioned the bomb that went off with the strikers," Garvey said. "He admitted he'd done it."

"And he can't let you walk free with that knowledge. He knew it when he told you. I suspect he wasn't truthful to his man about the bomb's power. He intended to kill the men who'd set it off. A good way to silence them."

"What are we going to do?" Garvey asked.

There was too long a silence while Jilly considered that

233

question carefully. Both men let her think, which she appreciated.

"I don't think he'll hurt Mabel until he's sure he got what he wanted," she said. "It would make sense for him to bring her back to you, then kill you both in your own home. Maybe the law would blame it on robbers or think you'd been attacked for personal reasons."

"Or," Nick said slowly, "he could keep her alive so he can send you back to the mountain to do more harm. We think we've gotten rid of every traitor hired by Edgar. And I'd say kidnapping your wife and threatening you is proof that there's no one in league with Edgar up there."

Garvey's chin lifted a bit. "You know, you're right. He said something . . ." Garvey rubbed his temple as if he had a headache. The combination of poison, terror, and trying to remember probably amounted to that.

Garvey finally shook his head. "I'll keep thinking, but something he said makes me wonder if you're not exactly right about him wanting more from me."

Jilly felt some of the tension she was carrying ease. "He'll come to your house without Mabel. Tell him you pretended your wrist was still hurting too much to work, and with everyone sick, you decided to go on home for a few more days."

"That sounds likely," Nick said. "Carlisle won't be done harassing you yet, Jilly."

Jilly nodded. "Garvey, he'll threaten to harm your wife if you don't do whatever evil thing he's thought up next. Tell him you know she's already been killed, and you won't do another thing for him. Refuse to help unless you can see that she's unharmed."

"Yes, that might work," Garvey said.

"He'll either go to get her or take you to see her. And we'll follow." Jilly patted Garvey on the shoulder. "He may refuse to cooperate. We'll stay close in case you need us to grab him."

Jilly could think of so much that might go wrong. "We're just plain guessing what's going to happen, and in truth, we have no idea how such an arrogant, powerful man will react to being pushed by a man he sees as a pawn in his nasty game."

"We'll stay close, Garvey." Nick frowned, clearly believing Jilly's list of worries. "We won't let Carlisle harm you. And we'll keep searching until we find Mabel. I promise."

Garvey nodded. "I believe you. I know you're being kind when I don't deserve—"

"Stop, Garvey." Jilly changed her pat on his shoulder to a viselike grip on his arm. "If someone took Nick, one of my sisters, or anyone I loved, there's not much I wouldn't do to save them. I hope I never have to make such a terrible choice as you were forced to make."

"He's going to kill her, Mrs. Ryder," Garvey said fervently. "I should have come to you before I did such a terrible thing. But I saw his eyes. I listened to his threats. My Mabel is going to die unless we stop him."

"So we'll stop him." Jilly's voice snapped, and Garvey fell silent.

"Let's not waste any more time with the guilt that's tearing you apart," she said. "I forgive you. The men up at the camp, if they find out the truth, will forgive you. Your job is safe, and if you want, Mabel can come up to the mountain and live there with you. We'll save her from Carlisle, and we'll make sure this doesn't happen again. And we'll see to it that Carlisle ends up in prison for what he's done, and for the men killed in that explosion and for the tampering he's done to my railroad. All of those things are crimes. The world will be a better place with Royce Carlisle in prison."

"Your color is better, Garvey," Nick said. "How are you feeling?"

"I'm holding up. I think the clean air cleared my head and settled my stomach some."

They reached a level stretch. The worst of the steep trail was past.

"Let's pick up the pace," Jilly said. "Holler if you think you're going to fall off the horse."

They still couldn't gallop flat out, but they managed a steady trot until they reached the bottom of the mountain, with miles to go before Hatcher's Creek, the nearest town. Then another hour on horseback to El Robles Blanco, where Garvey and Mabel lived.

They'd be all day getting to El Robles Blanco, and then they'd have to find Carlisle and Mabel.

Michelle and Zane would leave word for Jilly at the telegraph office in Hatcher's Creek, then they'd ride on to El Robles Blanco, hopefully to find help arriving on the train.

If all went as planned, by the time Jilly, Nick, and Garvey reached the Bateses' home, there'd be help there, at least Michelle and Zane, if not someone from the law.

TWENTY-SIX

NICK INSISTED GARVEY get off the horse and sit on something that wasn't trotting while he checked the telegraph office.

A message from Michelle said there'd been no response waiting from Marshal Irving, and she'd sent him a second wire to come to El Robles Blanco. She'd also wired another to Uncle Newt, the governor.

Jilly had run in to one of the diners and came out with a bowl of broth for Garvey. He ate slowly and kept the food in his belly. She handed Nick a sandwich with roast beef in it.

"Good thinking. I hadn't considered food."

She gave him a tight smile. "I've got trail food, and that would have worked for us, but not for Garvey. He might be steadier with something in his stomach." She pointed at a woman standing outside the nearest diner with her arms crossed. "She wants her bowl back."

"She doesn't look happy."

"I might've been a little, um, brusque with her. But I gave

her double the price of her sandwiches and a bowl of soup, plus she filled up our canteens."

"She should be smiling."

Garvey stopped spooning and drank the soup. Nick wolfed down his sandwich, then took the bowl to the woman at a jog.

"Thank you for the food. We're in an emergency situation. A life could be at stake."

Her frown eased. She took the bowl and went inside.

By the time Nick got back to Jilly, Garvey was climbing on his horse. Jilly was taking the last bite of her sandwich. Nick got a canteen and took a big drink, then gave Jilly one so she could wash down the food she'd eaten in gulps.

They were out of Hatcher's Creek at a gallop fifteen minutes after they rode in.

The sun was setting on the long summer day when they neared El Robles Blanco. It wasn't a big town, but large enough, and wooded enough they could slip into town. They headed first for the railroad station and found Michelle and Zane waiting for the train.

Michelle rushed over to them. "Marshal Irving and four other lawmen are arriving on the train, but it's running late. We are afraid to approach the sheriff in case Carlisle has a connection there. Carlisle might get a warning that we're coming. Zane will go with you to Garvey's house. Beyond that, I don't know how to begin to find Mabel."

"No," Zane said, "that's Michelle's plan, not mine. I'm not leaving her here alone. The station only has one man working here, and just like the sheriff, we don't feel like we can trust him. Michelle isn't safe here alone."

Jilly locked eyes with Michelle, thinking.

Nick waited patiently. He glanced at Zane and saw him doing the same. Obviously, they were both learning their wives very well by now.

Finally, Jilly said, "Garvey, give Michelle and Zane careful directions to your home so they can come later. We'll follow you now. If Carlisle acts as I expect him to, he'll be watching your house for some sign you've returned. Nick and I will stay back, keep hidden. We'll wait for him to make contact."

Garvey gave directions, and after a long look, he turned and headed away.

Nick knew once Jilly had heard the directions, she could get there without help. They waited as long as Jilly could stand, then took off after Garvey.

El Robles Blanco was a town hacked out of a dense forest of towering white oaks. It was easy to fade into the shadows and slip along behind Garvey.

The town was good-sized. The train had made it a success. The streets were well graveled. There were tidy lawns where houses sat but often a wooded stretch separated the buildings.

It was a quiet night. Only a few houses had lights in the windows. A dog barked in the distance, and Nick wondered if it heard Garvey, and if the dog would give them all away.

A perfect time for prayer as they moved along.

Jilly's hand caught his before he'd even begun praying about everything that could go wrong. She tapped his chin with one finger. In the near pitch-dark, Nick saw the barely visible outline of a house ahead. He heard the door open and close. A lantern cut through the darkness. The windows had curtains, but they were thin enough Nick could see the outline of Garvey's form.

Jilly tugged him into the woods, and together they slipped closer to Garvey's house.

Nick hoped it was right to get closer. Hoped and prayed.

ROYCE, SITTING IN A CHAIR in the corner of the room, lifted the gun when the lantern flared to life, and aimed at Garvey Bates's heart. "You did as I asked?"

Bates nearly jumped out of his boots. "Y-yes. I did it."

The big man's voice broke, and Carlisle took vicious satisfaction at bringing such a big man to heel. It reminded him of his father and brothers, who were now so far beneath him.

Royce had found the perfect tool to use against the Stileses. This big, powerful man was so softhearted and weak-minded, he'd do whatever he was told to protect his wife.

It was all Royce could do not to smile. He had plans for Jillian Stiles. Plans to break her just as he'd broken Garvey, plans that were just as viciously satisfying. Though now the woman had acquired a husband. Carlisle found it distasteful that she'd given herself to another man. He should have had her first. It was so unappealing he'd considered turning his attention elsewhere rather than have a woman who'd been used.

But that red hair. That fiery spirit. She'd gotten herself deep into his mind, and he couldn't give up now. He wouldn't. He'd add having another man before him to all her other punishments.

"Where's my Mabel?" Bates's first words marked him as a weakling.

"She's safe, but she remains in my hands until you've done one more job for me." Or however many jobs Carlisle needed. But one at a time.

"You've—you've k-killed her. I know it." Bates bent his head and wept.

Carlisle was so disgusted by the man he was tempted to shoot him just to rid the world of him.

He watched Bates's legs wobble, then give out. He bent over his knees, nearly to the floor, sobbing aloud.

"You've killed her." His voice rose to a shout. "Just finish me now. I've done as you asked, and I'll never believe a man as heartless as you kept her alive. I won't do another thing for you. End it!"

Bates was roaring by the end. Royce had to shut him up. Kill him, or let the fool see his old battle-ax of a wife. She'd been nothing but a pest. Given to scolding and complaining about being kidnapped. Crying when Royce slapped her mouth, then soon enough back to begging and complaining. Royce had been tempted to end her complaints with a bullet, too, but he'd wanted more from Bates. And for that, he was sorely afraid he'd regret it if he didn't keep Mrs. Bates alive.

"Shut up, and I'll take you to her."

"Y-you will?" Bates's hand covered his mouth, and the noise cut off, but Bates stayed as he was, his shoulders trembling. The sound was gone, but the tears went on.

"Pull yourself together, man. Get to your feet, and let's go." Royce was already considering all he needed to do with this change of plans. He'd walked over. Mabel was a fair distance away, but Royce didn't want the trouble of hiding a horse or buggy, and he didn't want to involve a driver. Royce had planned to simply be here waiting in the dark like a spider. He liked that image, liked the idea of Bates caught in his web, then later, Jillian caught. He enjoyed imagining it.

He'd planned to give Bates new orders, leave Bates in a trembling heap of fear, and slip away. Well, he'd managed the fear part, he thought as he studied Bates.

But it wasn't going to be so simple. Now he'd need to show Bates his wife. After Bates had seen her, Royce would have to move the woman. There was no other choice because once Bates knew where she was, he might bring the law into this to get her. The sheriff in El Robles Blanco wouldn't arrest Royce, he'd accepted the bribe with pathetic eagerness. But he might ruin the hold Royce had over Bates, and that would be an inconvenience.

Bates pulled himself together with what looked like his last ounce of strength, staggering as he gained his feet.

"Out the door. Go to the street, and turn to the right. We're going for a walk. Once you've seen I've kept the old nag alive, we'll discuss your duties."

Royce decided then and there he'd crack Bates over the head with his pistol, once they'd finished with this little meeting. The nagging wife might shut up when she saw Royce was willing to dispense pain. And Bates could lie unconscious while Royce moved his hostage.

They'd be long gone by the time Bates came around and headed back up the mountain with his new assignment.

Bates stepped outside. He almost fell against the post

holding up the small roof over the front stoop, then he trudged down two steps.

Bates's shoulders hunched, and he trembled again, then he moved on, a bit steadier now, a bit quicker. The man had finally realized he was going to see his wife, and he was eager.

Royce compared the hefty Mrs. Bates, her graying hair and double chin, with the lithe and beautiful Jillian Stiles.

Bates was a fool if he didn't know Royce couldn't let either of them live. But for now, he'd let them both keep on dreaming.

JILLY LEANED HER BACK on the house wall. She'd heard enough of Carlisle's ugly threats through a cracked window. Carlisle wanted Garvey alive to do more dirty work.

And Garvey had done it. Carlisle was leading them to Mabel.

It was so quiet she was almost afraid to breathe, let alone leave her hiding place. If Carlisle looked behind him at the wrong moment, could he see Jilly and Nick against the white wall of the house? She didn't think so, not in such deep shadows, but any movement might draw his eye.

She'd heard Carlisle say to turn right. Jilly didn't know this town, but Garvey had led them here from the north side, where the train station was, and Jilly had seen the businesses when they passed Main Street.

Now they would be walking east. Were they near the edge of town? Had Carlisle rented a house or bought one? Did he have Mabel out in the country? How could he keep from being discovered? In a small town, people noticed the comings and goings of others.

All Jilly could do was follow Carlisle as they'd planned.

Carlisle reached the street and tucked his right hand in his pocket. Jilly saw the outline of a pistol before Carlisle's hand vanished. Her stomach twisted as she thought how quickly this night's madness could turn deadly.

She noticed Garvey lagging until Carlisle was almost at his side.

It must have suited Carlisle to close the gap. Maybe he thought two men walking out together wouldn't draw much attention. But if one walked just a few paces behind, it might strike witnesses as odd and stay in their memory.

The two men passed a clump of the white oaks that had given El Robles Blanco its name. Just as Jilly was ready to take a step out from her hiding place, a shadow separated from the trees.

"You've got him?" A hulking man who made Garvey look small by comparison, also armed, stepped up to Carlisle's side.

Jilly froze. It made sense that Carlisle wasn't alone. Somehow, she'd decided he was. She and Nick had moved very carefully, keeping to the woods, slipping around in the darkest shadows. They hadn't been spotted by the watchman, it seemed, but they'd been very fortunate. Her heart pounded until she felt it in her ears. Knowing how close they'd come to running afoul of an armed man had her fighting to control her breathing.

Nick had a pistol in his holster, but she didn't want this to end in gunfire.

"Keep quiet, Rossiter." Carlisle's terse response marked him as the leader.

The other man fell silent and walked along on Garvey's far side, surrounding him until they were out of sight.

Nick tapped Jilly's arm, and with no more than that, the two of them walked swiftly across neatly scythed grass to those same trees, and Jilly peeked around a trunk.

Carlisle, Garvey, and Rossiter were visible in the distance, walking straight down the middle of the graveled street. She could hear the soft crunch of their feet and knew she and Nick didn't dare walk on it.

While Carlisle moved straight forward, Rossiter was more wary. He looked behind him and to both sides of the streets, scanning constantly.

A savvy man. Dangerous.

Even if they kept to the grass, moving silently along the wooded stretch, there was no possible way that Rossiter would miss being followed.

Jilly stepped back and let Nick have a turn looking. He stayed there, watching. To keep from tugging on his shirt and demanding a turn, Jilly ran through some of her favorite calculus equations. She was particularly fond of Euler's integrals. She could slide along adding to his beta and gamma functions and solve them like a puzzle.

Then she began rereading in her photographic memory some of her favorite sections of Legendre's *Eléments de géométrie.* That man could talk his way around polynomials like nobody's business.

Finally, just when she'd about exhausted her patience, even with someone as fascinating as Legendre, Nick reached back and tapped her arm, then slipped around the tree. Jilly, with no idea what had made him move, trusted him to judge the situation, and followed along. The street ahead was empty. Nick took to the grass alongside the graveled street for the sake of quiet without Jilly having to instruct him. Proud of her husband, she willingly fell in behind. There wasn't enough room for the two of them to walk side by side between the gravel and the trees around the houses along the street.

With little worry about being spotted by the neighbors this late, Jilly focused on moving silently and praying for wisdom for when they would have to make quick decisions about how to proceed.

They walked a fair distance, not surprising considering how long they'd hidden behind that tree. When Nick finally turned, he slipped behind another tree and peeked around, then he set out walking on the edge of the graveled street much faster than before.

Jilly saw why. Garvey and Carlisle were nowhere in sight.

Nick came to a drive off the street, probably an alley between houses. He crouched and studied the ground, then rose and moved on quickly. Jilly looked, too, but saw nothing. She couldn't read tracks much beyond following footprints left in new-fallen snow, and if Nick saw a trail, then his eyes were much sharper than hers.

Nick came to an intersecting street and stopped so suddenly Jilly walked right into him.

She controlled an *oof* when her breath was knocked out of her. Again, Nick reached back, but this time he patted her arm.

Then Nick pointed to his left. She saw Carlisle, Garvey, and Rossiter in the distance, turning once again to their right.

The chase—a very slow, silent chase—went on for another quarter of an hour. They left the town behind, and the street turned in to a narrow dirt road with trees growing close on both sides.

Carlisle was living out of town, less trouble with cries for help.

Jilly was at Nick's side when they saw Carlisle walk toward a structure she couldn't quite see tucked into the woods, but whatever it was, this road seemed to lead up to it and end.

There was a quiet rasp of metal, maybe a key turning in a lock, and a faint metallic squeak like hinges that hadn't been oiled in a long while. When Jilly looked again, a black rectangle was all that was visible. The men must have gone inside.

Jilly and Nick hurried toward what appeared to be a barn. Maybe they'd found Mabel at last. Now how to get her and Garvey out of there and put a stop to this?

In the silence, Jilly realized she'd have heard the train come, and she hadn't. What was delaying it?

Michelle and Zane would never find them. And no lawmen had come yet. Jilly and Nick were going to have to save the day alone.

It was a good thing Jilly liked being in charge.

TWENTY-SEVEN

NICK'S NERVES had gone ice cold when that man had appeared out of nowhere. Was there another sentry out here? Were they walking into a trap?

Fighting for silence and to remain unnoticed if someone was watching, he reached the small window to the side of the barn door just as a light flickered on inside.

Arrogant fool. Carlisle was so sure he was safe. So sure no one would dare to follow him or even suspect him that he just lit up a lantern so Nick and Jilly could look right in. From inside, darkness usually made windows reflect like mirrors. Carlisle wouldn't see them watching.

But watching wasn't enough. They had to get Mabel and Garvey out of this mess. And make sure Carlisle went to prison for it. Nick had hoped he could pick the right moment and get the drop on Carlisle and end this.

But that was when only Carlisle had a gun. An arrogant man who'd probably figured he could buy his way out of any trouble, even a kidnapping and confession of murder.

And he might be right.

At minimum, Nick could have put an end to this terrorizing of Garvey and Mabel. But that second gunman worried him much more. The man was alert. He'd kept his gun drawn, though he'd held it against his leg, pointed down so it wasn't visible. Now that they were inside the barn, he stepped back, well away from Garvey and Carlisle, to keep his eye on things. And his gun was once more up and pointed. Nick studied him, to recognize him when the night was over.

With Rossiter in the picture, if Nick drew a gun, he'd have to be ready to fire. He'd do it if he had to, but he was hoping he could end this without gunplay. Once lead started flying, anyone could get hit. Jilly, Garvey, Mabel . . . anyone. It made him sick to think of it.

A soft squeak drew Nick's attention to Carlisle, who swung a square door up. It was set in the floor, an opening to a cellar.

"Help!"

A woman's voice. This was how Carlisle kept her quiet, since even out of town someone could pass by.

"Mabel, my Mabel!" Garvey leaned forward so far Nick feared he'd fall in.

"Garvey, is that you?" The woman sounded frantic.

"It's both of us, old woman." Carlisle's voice cracked like a whip, and Mabel didn't speak again. Carlisle dropped the door shut with a hard slap.

"You said you wanted to be sure she was alive. Now you are."

"No!" Garvey came at Carlisle. "Let me see her. Let me talk to her."

Carlisle brandished his pistol, but Garvey kept coming. Nick turned to rush in, even into the teeth of gunfire.

Jilly caught him and sank claws into his arm. She hissed.

Nick looked at her, and she jerked her head toward the window.

Carlisle pulled something from inside of his coat and swung it hard, cracking it across the side of Garvey's head. It looked like a club or a blackjack, like a policeman would carry.

Awful, painful, but not fatal. Rossiter rushed to Carlisle's side and stood between him and Garvey, but Garvey was no longer a threat. He staggered back and fell to one knee, then sat down hard. But he didn't pass out.

"I don't want to kill you, Bates." Carlisle strutted out from behind his guard. "But I will. Make no mistake about it. Now let's go back to your house. I'll watch you through the night and see you off on the train in the morning. You'll take it to Placerville. I've got a dynamite charge, and I want that bridge blown to kingdom come."

Jilly hissed again. Louder. Rattlesnake loud. Carlisle didn't hear it, thank heavens.

Nick moved close enough his lips touched her ear. "Mabel first."

Jilly nodded, but Nick wasn't sure he could keep her from leaping on Carlisle when he came out the door.

Moving as quietly as possible, Nick dragged Jilly around the corner of the barn. The door squeaked open, and at that second, they heard the distant chugging of the incoming train.

The lawmen should be on it.

Nick ran a calming hand up and down Jilly's arm. He didn't want to tackle her. He leaned close and whispered, "Train."

She nodded. He had sharp eyes, but on this moonless night, he couldn't make out much. He *sensed* her nod in agreement.

If Michelle and Zane met the lawmen on that train, they'd head straight for Garvey's house. They'd get there near the same time as Carlisle, while Nick and Jilly saved Mabel. This could be over in just a few minutes.

The square of light cast on the ground through the window winked out.

Garvey, Carlisle, and Rossiter came out the door. Nick didn't look, but he heard the footsteps. One heavy and stumbling, Garvey; one light and lithe, Carlisle. A third set steady, stealthy, Rossiter.

Nick flinched thinking of that crack on the head with the cudgel. He'd like to lay that across Carlisle's head just once.

Nick waited until the footsteps faded in the night, then he hurried around the corner to see a padlock on the door.

No way in there. He went to the window. Worried about the squeaking, he waited again. Judging the men to be far enough away, he tried shoving the window up. It didn't move. He tried swinging it. He ran his hands along the sides, hoping for some sign of a hinge.

Jilly gave him a shove, which sent him stumbling. Once he was away from the window, something hit the glass. Mercifully, it was quieter than he'd feared.

The train was getting closer to the station, and hopefully any noises in the night would be chalked up to that.

He saw her hand wrapped in something. Her skirt, he

thought. She ran it around the edges of the window until all the jagged pieces of glass were knocked away.

The window had been four small panes, and Nick grabbed the slender wood that framed the glass and snapped it off. The window was small, but they'd fit through.

Jilly climbed in while Nick watched behind them, hoping the men were well out of earshot.

"I'm in."

Nick gave that dirt road one last look, then quickly swung himself into the barn. They rushed for the cellar door.

It had a sturdy metal hasp on it but no padlock. Nick threw the sliding hasp and grabbed the door to lift it.

"Mabel, it's Jilly Stiles. We've come to rescue you." Jilly stuck her head over the edge of the cellar door.

"It's Jilly Ryder," Nick reminded her.

"I know, but I wasn't sure if Mabel had heard of the wedding."

"Miss Stiles?" Mabel's voice wavered as if she was so full of hope and fear she'd lost control of it. "Is that really you?"

"Yes, it's me, Mabel. Are you all right? Did he harm you?"

"He was rough with me, and he had a man with him that shoved me too hard a few times. The skinny one is the boss. He cut my hand and wiped the blood on my dress, then he took the dress from me. I'm down here in my chemise. I'm freezing."

While Jilly tried to calm Mabel, Nick laid the door fully open on the barn floor.

"Can you get up?" Jilly knelt on the floor.

"No, there's no ladder. There was one when he made me

climb down, but he took it with him. Miss Stiles, he has Garvey. He's going to kill us both. I know it."

"We're intending to make sure that doesn't happen."

"We'll get you out," Nick said, "then we'll get Garvey and arrest Carlisle. We're going to make sure he never hurts anyone again."

Nick looked around the barn. It was cluttered with tools of many kinds. In the darkness, it took him a while to spot a wooden ladder that looked made for the cellar. He rushed to pick it up, conscious of the time passing.

"Stand back while I lower this." Nick only took a second to look down. He couldn't see anything. The barn was in pitch-darkness, the cellar worse if that was possible.

Nick slid the ladder down slowly, hoping not to hit the poor lady. She'd been through more than enough.

The moment the ladder base hit the cellar floor, Mabel was scrambling up with the speed of a woman escaping a death trap.

She emerged from the cellar and threw her arms around Nick's neck with a sob. She was a stout woman and on the short side.

Feeling compassion for her, standing here crying in her unmentionables, Nick simply wrapped his arms around her and picked her up.

"Let's get out of here." He carried her to the window.

When they were all outside, Jilly took off her coat and slipped it on Mabel, guiding her arms into the sleeves. The coat was long enough to be reasonably decent.

"Move as quietly as possible, Mabel." Jilly held Mabel's right arm and Nick had her left. The poor woman was trembling in the aftermath of this dreadful business. "But we are going to hurry even if that means a bit of noise. I want to stop Carlisle before he hurts Garvey. And if he does hear us coming, he might abandon Garvey and run."

Mabel calmed down enough to rush along at their sides.

They dashed down the dirt road, no men in sight.

They reached the corner where the road became gravel again.

Nick pressed them back, glanced around, and saw Rossiter coming around the corner.

Rossiter saw him and whipped his gun out as Nick dove under the gun and plowed the man backward, landing hard on the ground.

"Carlisle, run. Run!" Rossiter alerted his boss.

Nick slammed a fist into the man's roaring mouth. A flurry beside him was barely recognizable as Jilly threw all her weight onto the man's gun hand.

With Rossiter's hand pinned down, Nick fought with desperate fury. Jilly was grappling with an armed man, a man who operated with cool professionalism. Carlisle could afford the best of everything, why not the best guards, too?

Then another scrambling of activity. This one accompanied by shrieking. Sounded like Mabel. She'd cast her body across the man's legs and had them pinned to the ground while Jilly used all her weight to hold down the man's arm. Nick got what little was left of him.

A clatter drew Nick's attention for a split second. He saw Rossiter's gun go skittering across the road. Jilly had disarmed him.

With Nick's attention diverted, Rossiter gave an almost inhuman twist of his body, and Nick went flying headfirst. Whirling to face the man, Nick saw Jilly race for the gun and scoop it up.

Rossiter saw the gun leveling and turned tail and ran. Not toward Garvey's house, where he might stand with Carlisle and fight, but straight north. In seconds, he was swallowed up by a heavy stand of trees.

Mabel was sitting in her underthings, hidden mostly by Jilly's coat, right in the street.

Panting from the exertion, Nick said, "We go rescue Garvey."

Knowing the shouting would very likely have alerted Carlisle, they all ran. Nick supported Mabel, but the woman gave it her all and kept up well. Rescuing her husband seemed to give speed to her feet.

They reached the Bates's household and kept running. Nick crashed through the door to find Garvey in a heap on the floor, groaning.

Mabel cried out and rushed for her husband.

Nick and Jilly looked frantically around the small house for Carlisle. It had one story and just a few small rooms. Was Carlisle here? If so, he was armed.

Nick dashed for the settee, the only thing big enough to hide behind in the front room. There were curtains not drapes—no place to hide there.

Nick, gun drawn, went bursting through doors with Jilly right behind him.

A bedroom, a second bedroom, a third room with a nice table in it, then the kitchen. All the rooms were simple. No closets, no beds high enough off the floor to hide under, no wardrobes large enough for a man to hide in.

Finally assured it was safe, Nick hurried to Garvey's side to see Mabel struggling to roll her husband over. Nick helped, but Garvey was coming around and managed to push feebly against the floor and get onto his back.

"Is he shot? Where's a doctor in this town?"

"No, Nick," Jilly said. "I see no gunshot. It looks like Carlisle knocked him over the head and ran."

"Train," Garvey muttered, tossing his head. "Placerville spur. He had explosives for me to use. Said he'd do it himself."

"Jilly, get them out of here. Hide in the woods until it's safe. Then get him to a doctor. I'm going after Carlisle." Nick stood and sprinted out the door. He heard footsteps pounding behind him and skidded to a stop.

Jilly plowed into him just as he turned around.

"Mabel heard every word you said and already has Garvey on his feet."

Nick glanced past her to see the two hobbling toward the back door.

"She'll take care of Garvey. You're not going after Carlisle alone. He's too evil, too nasty. You're too honorable."

"He wants you, Jilly, so it's best if you stay away from him."

"He wants me to be a widow. He won't kill me. But you, he is eager to kill."

Nick felt himself flare with fury. "No, go with Mabel and Garvey."

Jilly dodged around him and ran for the train station.

Nick needed to go over those vows with her a little more carefully, but he didn't have time for that now. He had to catch her first. And he might as well face it, she was coming with him to stop Carlisle. And face his guns. And confiscate his explosives. Nick rushed after her, not to stop her, but to race her to the train.

CHAPTER
TWENTY-EIGHT

THEY HAD A LONG WAY TO RUN, and as they neared the station, Jilly saw the train begin to roll and picked up her speed.

Was Carlisle on it? Had Michelle met the lawmen? A frantic look around told her no one stood near the station on this dark night. If the lawmen had come, no doubt they were heading for Garvey's house and somehow, they'd missed each other in the dark.

Nick was a pace behind her as the caboose neared the end of the platform. She leapt to grab hold of the back end of the train and clambered aboard. Nick made a guttural sound, then landed right beside her. Jilly got to the door just as Nick clamped his hand on hers.

"No," he whispered, so close to her ear that even with the racket of the train she heard.

Nick jabbed a finger past her face, directing her attention inside the caboose. Two men were riding in there. One dressed like a conductor. The other must be the brakeman.

258

Nick dragged her to the side of the small window in the back door. "Those two will do their best to throw us off the train."

Both men were burly and severe looking and one had a nightstick on his belt.

She knew the brakeman had several jobs, mainly managing the brake, but it looked like he was also uniquely qualified to get rid of anyone who didn't have a ticket. The conductor might sell them one, but she wasn't sure of the rules for people who jumped on after the train was moving. And besides, she didn't want to talk to them when she was hunting for one of their passengers. The two men might object. But she couldn't proceed to hunt through the train without going through the caboose.

Then Nick's jabbing finger pointed up.

Jilly's eyes followed, and she saw the ladder to the train roof.

With a swallow of dread, she knew there was one way to get past the caboose unnoticed, and that was to climb.

Nick whispered again. "You first."

How could a man give orders, whisper, and sound sarcastic all in two words?

Her husband was a man of many skills.

Grimly unhappy about how she was going to spend the next few minutes but determined to stand between Nick and any horrible plans Carlisle had for him, Jilly took a firm grasp on the ladder and headed up.

The train was still moving slowly as it picked up speed out of the station. She crawled along the center of the train. Sturdy rails formed a ladder that lay flat on top of the caboose. No problem hanging on to a normal ladder, but the wind blew, and the car rocked as if it wanted to shake her off.

And that was at five miles an hour. They had to get off this roof before the train reached higher speeds.

The wind buffeted her. She felt the tight knot in her hair give way until her hair blinded her.

She was acutely aware of any noise she might make crawling, noise the brakeman and conductor might notice.

She clung to each ladder rung until she almost needed to pry her hand off to reach forward, but she forced herself on until she reached the far end and climbed down the ladder to the platform. Her knees shook, and she didn't dare speak for fear of stuttering convulsively.

Nick landed beside her light as a cat, the show-off. He took her arm, peeked into the caboose through the window, then turned to the next car and hustled her across the steel coupling. Once across, he reached past her, opened the door, and with the next step, they were inside with the door firmly closed behind them.

Glancing around, Jilly saw countless stacked crates. She fought her hair back to some semblance of control, twisting it into a rope and tying a knot in it.

Nick watched in stillness through the window until he saw whatever he was looking for. An enraged man coming after them, no doubt.

He left the window and took her hand. They threaded down the narrow aisle of the freight car. He slipped outside, tugging Jilly along. With a glance inside the next car, he pulled the door open and stepped in.

Horses. Jilly's stomach twisted at the narrow center lane.

Almost like they lined the horses up so it would be easy for them to kick any train jumpers coming through.

Nick headed down the aisle fast. The front of the car had grain bins full of oats. For one moment, they were away from the prying eyes of the brakeman and the steel-shod hooves of restless horses.

Nick peered through the window and leaned back. "The next one's a passenger car."

"Can you see if Carlisle is in there?"

Nick shook his head. "Not from here. I counted the cars when it was pulling out of the station."

Jilly hadn't taken the time, but now she tapped in to her photographic memory and said, "Eight cars."

"Yes, a small train. And probably fairly empty of passengers at this time of night. The back three cars are the caboose and freight and stock. The front two cars are the engine and the tender car with the wood and water. That leaves three passenger cars."

Jilly nodded. "If one of them is a sleeper car, it would be easy for Carlisle to hide in one of the berths with the curtains or even the door closed."

"And we'd have to look in every one of them, which will stir up the passengers. A screaming woman would bring the conductor fast."

"If it's a sleeper car, we have to assume Carlisle is in one of them. He'd want the privacy."

Nick nodded. "But he could be anywhere—if he even got on the train. And he's carrying some kind of bomb."

He reached for the door handle and hesitated. "I have an idea that makes it all a little easier. At least no one will be able to come at us from behind. And if there are explosives on the train, it might save lives."

Jilly furrowed her brow in the darkness.

NICK GRINNED, pulled her close to the train car, then dropped to his knees and reached under the car. He was a while finding what he was looking for. This car was a little different from the one he'd been on, but you weren't a brother-in-law to Michelle Stiles without knowing trains were constantly being improved.

He felt for the safety chain, and when the uneven rolling of the train eased the taut hitch, he pulled it loose. Then he shoved harder than he thought he should've had to, but finally the connecting latch gave, and the three train cars behind them detached on the level stretch of rails. The back cars shouldn't go careening backward, especially with the brakeman there to slow them.

He watched with a fond smile on his face as he left that burly brakeman and conductor farther behind with every turn of the train's wheels.

They'd put about a hundred yards between them, and Nick could feel the train speeding up.

With fewer cars to pull it was an easier job. But he didn't feel the engineer throwing the brakes or cutting down the steam. It'd happened just right. The train was already picking up speed, the slight lessening of the load it pulled seemed natural to the engine's chuffing energy.

Rising from the platform, Nick said, "It's only about fifteen miles to Placerville. If Carlisle is planning to blow up the bridge, he'll have to do something to reroute the train, or get off and walk to the bridge. We'll be going sixty miles an hour soon, so we could be in Placerville in ten minutes."

"Fifteen miles going sixty miles per hour is fifteen minutes."

His wife was a mathematics show-off.

"But we don't reach full speed for a while, and then we slow down, and we've been on this train for maybe ten minutes already. Did you calculate all of that?"

"I didn't, but I was hurrying."

"So ten minutes and a stop. We should be able to put an end to this at Placerville."

"But he's got the explosives. He might blow up the train if he can't blow up the bridge."

"You're right that he might do something desperate. He's not acting normally. Going to Garvey himself. Now intending to blow up the bridge himself. Up until now, Carlisle has hired his crimes done, and he even had that sentry on hand. Rossiter could have kidnapped Mabel and threatened Garvey. This is personal for Carlisle, Jilly. I think he's gone over the edge. I'm afraid if he can't have you, he'll be willing to kill you."

As the front cars separated farther from the back cars, Nick thought he heard a shout from far behind them, but he wasn't sure. It was a certainty that the engineer five cars ahead, inside a roaring engine, didn't hear it.

He twisted the door handle, and they stepped into the passenger car.

Twelve people sat in about twenty benches, all of them

looking drowsy. Jilly walked ahead of Nick because the center aisle was too narrow to walk side by side. They checked
everyone. No sign of a skinny man with death in his gaze
and a bomb in his hands. They kept moving, not wanting
to draw attention.

Nick wondered if the passengers, the men especially, were
noticing the beautiful redhead passing them. No one said
a word.

They left the first passenger car and stepped out onto the
connecting platform again. They did the same for the second
passenger car. Again, no one who could be Carlisle. And no
one seemed to notice them.

Once they were outside, Jilly asked, "Are you going to
detach them, too?"

Nick thought it through. Those folks might be willing to
fight Nick if they saw him as a train robber. On the other
hand, if something happened to Nick and Jilly was alone,
those men in the passenger cars might protect her. On the
third hand—and he was out of hands—Carlisle had explosives. Getting rid of these passengers might save their lives.

They were almost up to full speed. If he didn't separate
the passengers now, the engineer would definitely notice a
lessening of the weight of the train if he did it later. He had
to do it right now or never.

"Let's separate the passengers. The riders in the last car
will still be in danger if Carlisle sets off the explosives, but
at least these folks will be safe." Nick repeated his detaching
and was faster at it this time. He even had a little time to
spare to get the cars left behind without the engineer noticing and stopping.

He braced himself for the passengers to come out and start hollering. Could they get the attention of the engineer? They'd mostly been dozing.

He stood up and pulled Jilly close, then they watched while seconds ticked by. The train picked up speed with much less effort now.

Nothing from the passenger car. Nothing from the engineer.

They went around a wooded bend and lost sight of the cars they'd left behind.

"We did it." He hugged Jilly's waist.

"You did it, husband." She kissed him on the cheek.

He smiled at her. "Now comes the hard part."

"Unless Carlisle isn't on the train at all, and we're leaving train cars behind for absolutely no good reason."

"From what Garvey said, he's on this train. Let's go find him. I'd like to have a little talk with him."

"I would, too," Jilly agreed.

They stepped into a sleeper car. A much better hiding place.

The aisle on this car was to the left of the berths. The doorways were curtains.

"Five berths," Jilly whispered grimly. "Let's get started."

They went through methodically. The first two berths were empty.

The next berth had a man snoring loud enough it reminded Nick of the rumble of the two-man saws that took down trees. Nick glanced in quickly and saw a stranger, but he didn't figure Carlisle would be sleeping.

The next one was a couple, squeezed together in a tiny excuse for a bed.

The woman, nestled on the inside, opened her eyes and squeaked.

Jilly quickly poked her head in and whispered, "Excuse me. My mistake."

She dropped the curtain, gave Nick a wide-eyed look as they stood there waiting for the woman to raise an alarm.

Nothing.

One more.

They approached the last berth. Nick got his shoulder in front of Jilly so he'd be the one to look. Carlisle had to be in there, and they needed to stop him.

Nick drew his gun, reached for the curtain, and shoved it aside, whipping the gun so it aimed right into the berth.

TWENTY-NINE

A MAN SLAMMED his shoulder into Nick's gut. He came in under the gun, knocked Nick hard into the train wall, shoved his hand up, and the gun fired into the ceiling.

Now the woman screamed.

Nick had been focused on Carlisle, he'd forgotten Rossiter was also at large.

Well, they'd found him.

Nick slugged the man on the back with his gun.

Rossiter had him pinned to the train wall, and Nick's blow didn't even slow him down. He shifted so he had Nick's arm trapped, and the gun was useless. Then the man pounded a solid fist, again and again, into Nick's gut.

Jilly hit Rossiter like a small cyclone. She slammed a gun to his head.

Nick only now remembered her picking up Rossiter's gun when he'd tackled Nick out on the road.

Rossiter's grip weakened. Jilly smashed the gun twice

more. Nick got his arm free. He couldn't pull the trigger because the bullet might hit Jilly, so he twisted the gun, holding it by the barrel, and brought it around to the man's ear. Jilly got in another blow at the same instant, and together, they knocked Rossiter aside. Nick leapt to his feet, staggering as the train hit a rough patch on the rails.

Rossiter produced another gun. Nick dove at the man's feet. They crashed to the floor just as the woman who'd been awake pushed her curtain aside and rushed into the aisle.

Rossiter's gun went flying.

Nick's earlier gunshot had awakened the husband and the snoring man in the other berth. The jumble of bodies rushing toward him distracted Nick just long enough for Rossiter to escape his grasp, knock the gun from his hand, and run out the back of the car. Nick looked frantically for a gun, his or Rossiter's, but people were crowding into the aisle, and he had no time to search.

He ran after the escaping sentry, dodging all three riders.

JILLY TOOK A SINGLE STEP after Nick when the door behind her opened. A viselike hand gripped her arm and yanked her out of the front of the sleeper car so fast the passengers, watching Nick chase Rossiter, didn't seem to notice.

If they did, Jilly didn't see them because by the time they turned around, she was outside, shoved up against the train car.

Carlisle shoved his face to within an inch of hers. Even in the dark, his eyes glittered with satisfaction. "I have you now, Jillian."

Jilly jammed the gun muzzle in his belly so hard he drew in an inverted scream, then he knocked the gun aside. It went flying off the train.

With a laugh that said he wanted her to fight him, he pulled her forward, across the connecting platform to the tender car.

She screamed, and he slapped his hand over her mouth so fast she doubted Nick, wherever he was, heard it.

But what about the people in the sleeper car? Would anyone come?

"You do as I say, Jillian. If you fight me, you'll lose. And I'll enjoy making you lose."

He dragged her up and across the water tank, then down onto the woodpile and loomed over her. One hand crushing her wrist, the other covering her mouth. Carlisle was a small man, but he was surprisingly strong. Jilly had to wonder if madness fueled his strength.

The way he bent down over her . . . It was her nightmare come to life. Only much, much worse.

NICK JUMPED OUT onto the platform to see Rossiter scramble up the ladder to the roof of the sleeper car. Nick went up fast to see him racing away down the train, standing up. He reached the end, skidded to a stop, and turned.

The man roared and started straight for him. Nick knew this was it.

Rossiter, furious and a strong fighter, was planning to end this struggle right here and now. One of them was going to plunge over the side of the train to his death.

JILLY WASN'T GOING TO BE a cowering victim. She clawed Carlisle's ugly face, then kicked him hard enough he fell down on top of her.

Something in him, his eyes, his expression, seemed to snap.

Nick had said the man had gone mad, and she saw it was true.

He stumbled to his feet and turned her so her back pressed against his front. His hand still tight on her mouth.

Jilly knew if she stayed alive long enough, Nick would come.

If he stayed alive long enough.

Carlisle shoved her forward. The uneven stack of cordwood made walking impossible, but somehow they moved forward to the front end of the tender car. He dangled her over the edge, and for a second, she thought he intended to drop her to her death between the rushing cars. But he held on and let her mouth go so they could climb down the stacks of wood to the engine.

With her mouth free, Jilly screamed to wake the dead. Carlisle whipped a kerchief around her mouth and gagged her. But she'd made enough noise.

The engineer and the wood stoker turned just as Carlisle shoved her toward them.

These men would help her. And Nick would come.

They crossed the platform just as the engineer's eyes slid to Carlisle's. The man nodded and said, "We're almost there."

Then he and the stoker turned their backs on her.

It struck cold terror in her heart to realize Carlisle had come to these men first and paid them for their cooperation.

The engineer pulled a cord, and the whistle blew.

Placerville was dead ahead.

NICK HEARD THE SCREAM.

Jilly! He'd gone after Rossiter and forgotten Carlisle.

Before Rossiter could attack, Nick dropped over the back end of the car, caught the ladder, and scrambled down. He saw the same chaotic scrambling inside the sleeper car, but he had no choice. He yanked the door open and rushed through the crowded aisle. "Get in your berths. There's a man coming. Dangerous."

That just made them run amok.

He dodged and shoved them. Got through as the door he'd come in slammed open.

Jilly had been outside when she screamed. But what little was left of the train was all outside. Nick dropped to his knees and, as quickly as he could, detached the sleeper car.

He grabbed for the top of the tender car just as he heard the sleeper car door slam open. At a glance back, he saw Rossiter leap between the gradually separating cars. Then Rossiter was on his feet and up the back of the tender car. Rossiter tackled Nick from behind with the force of a charging bull.

Nick caught a glimpse of Jilly in the engine just as the whistle blew and he felt the brake go on.

Then Rossiter flipped him onto his back. The blow knocked Nick sideways, straight for the edge of the rolling car.

THE STOKER PULLED on the locomotive brake.

"Why isn't it slowing?" The engineer blasted the whistle again and again. It was the signal to the brakeman in the caboose to throw on the back brake, but the engineer didn't know the caboose had been left far behind. But without that brake they should still be able to stop. They were only pulling two cars.

Jilly kept still, with Carlisle's arm wrapped tightly around her neck, the kerchief gagging her. But she was paying attention. Waiting. Her moment would come when she could get away, fight back. Do something. If no one helped her, she'd help herself.

She'd finish Carlisle herself.

"The caboose is gone. Hit the brake harder." The engineer looked frantically out the window again, then shouted, "The track is switched to the new line. We've got to get this train stopped. The track ends right past the bridge."

"Keep going. We'll stop at the end of the line." Carlisle laughed a strange, high-pitched noise that wasn't the same as his cool, ruthless voice at all.

A man who'd gone over the edge. And now he seemed to want to go over the end of the train tracks.

Where were the explosives? Did Carlisle have sticks of dynamite? Did he have some form of bomb rigged to blow like it had the day of the strike?

The train slowed but still rushed on, around a curve that was almost too sharp to take at this speed. Holding her breath, Jilly felt the pull as the train strained to the limit of Newton's second law of motion.

Judging the slowly reducing speed of the train and the curve of the track, Jilly thought they'd make it around. But a train engine was a heavy thing. It could only take so much pressure on a turn.

For a moment, Jilly felt the train go light on its left side, as if it was getting ready to flip.

The engineer hollered and threw himself at the brake, adding his weight to the stoker's. Carlisle staggered backward under the pressure of the sharp turn, dragging Jilly with him. She stumbled, dropping to the floor, then whirled and kicked out at Carlisle's knees. The open back end of the engine was right behind him.

NICK CAUGHT THE EDGE of the tender car as the town of Placerville raced toward him. Rossiter landed right above him and slammed a fist on Nick's left hand.

Hollering, Nick lost his grip and struggled for a toehold.

The train was supposed to stop here. Then Nick could fall, but he wouldn't be badly hurt from this height on a stopped train.

But it wasn't slowing down as much as it should, and it was going around a curve that made Nick's body fly out from the side of the train. Overhead, Rossiter lost his footing and fell straight for Nick.

He caught hold of Nick's legs and clung, fighting for his life.

Nick got a solid grip on the side again, but Rossiter's massive weight was too much.

His grip was slipping. If he fell off, living or dying didn't matter because Jilly would be abandoned to Carlisle's mercy.

Rossiter clawed for Nick's belt and began crawling up,

using Nick's body as a ladder. Nick's legs, now free, were able to kick.

He knocked at Rossiter, letting go with one hand and swinging a fist sideways to beat at the man. Just as he thought they'd both drop from the train, the car shifted, and Nick grabbed hold of the side with both hands again.

Right beside the train, a post swung to dangle a water-spout. They weren't stopping, but the spout still came at them. Rossiter, intent on climbing, crashed into the spout and flew off the train.

Nick, his fingers so sore they were barely working, dragged himself up to the top of the pile of wood and rolled to face the engine just as Jilly dropped, twisted to face Carlisle, and kicked him hard enough he went staggering back. He'd fall off, too, then they'd stop this train and go arrest what was left of him.

Carlisle made a wild grab for the frame around the open window of the locomotive and saved himself, then he charged for Jilly and wrapped an arm around her neck just as Nick landed on the floor of the engine.

"Stay back, or I'll break her neck."

The train, much slower now, straightened. Nick expected the men to continue stopping the train. Instead, the engineer swept up a set of iron tongs. The stoker picked up his shovel. Both leered at him.

"Drive the train." Carlisle gave a hard nod of his head at the engineer, who lowered the tongs and turned to the controls.

"He's going to blow this train. He's going to kill us all." Jilly's voice was cut off when Carlisle tightened his grip on her neck.

Nick saw the engineer hesitate. How much money had Carlisle shoved into his hands when he'd climbed on this train? Enough apparently.

"He didn't tell you that part of his plan?" Nick asked.

"Shut up!" Carlisle's eyes blazed with an unholy fury. "Shut up, or I'll kill her."

"You're going to kill her anyway. You're going to blow up this train with all of us aboard." Nick shouted at the engineer and stoker, "Stop this train! However much money he gave you, it'll be worthless if you're dead. The tracks end right after the bridge, and it's right ahead."

Nick saw Jilly groping at something Nick couldn't see in the dark. Suddenly, she whipped up an iron bar and slammed it into the side of Carlisle's head.

Nick saw the bridge a few yards ahead. He grabbed Jilly, and together they leapt from the train. He saw the engineer and stoker jump from the other side. Jilly rolled, then jumped up and ran for the controls that worked her pivot bridge.

"I'll be back for you, Jillian," Carlisle roared. "You're mine!"

The train went onto the bridge, and Jilly yanked on the lever. The bridge began to turn.

Carlisle saw the bridge leave the other side of the riverbank and threw himself at the brake. It was too late. The engine went flying off the end of the tracks toward the river.

With the unbridled scream of a madman, Carlisle detonated his bomb, and the engine exploded in midair. It plunged, burning, into the river.

CHAPTER

THIRTY

NICK DRAGGED JILLY to the ground as shards of burning iron whizzed through the air.

They lay there, breathing hard, fighting for control of the fear and anger that had rampaged for the last hours.

Finally, Jilly poked him in the stomach. "It seems to be over. You're crushing me."

Nick lifted his head and smiled down at her in the starlight.

She smiled back. "We've got a mess to clean up."

"Men to pick up who've been scattered along the track." Nick rolled to the side and stood. He extended a hand to Jilly, and when she caught hold, he lifted her to her feet.

She slid an arm across his back, and they turned to look at the still-smoldering iron. "Passengers and train cars, dropped off here and there."

They just stood in each other's arms. Jilly felt the cool of the night wind. Listened to the silence after too long with the chugging train, the shouts and threats and screams.

A night bird cooed. Back to living its life after the noise and blaze had disrupted its world.

If a bird could get back to normal so quickly, so could she. "Let's see if we can find the engineer and stoker and take them back to Placerville."

"And find Rossiter. He smashed into a waterspout in town. I'm hoping none of them have run off."

Jilly kind of hoped they had. Let someone else sweep them up.

By the time they were back in town, they had the engineer limping along in front of them, holding up the stoker, who seemed to have at least a badly sprained ankle.

Nick had taken a moment to frisk them and found a thousand dollars divided between them. A small price considering they were being paid to cooperate with murder.

They'd protested they didn't know Carlisle's intent until he'd appeared in the engine with Jilly. By then they'd taken his bribe and were afraid to defy him.

Jilly intended to teach them the true meaning of fear.

They met a group of men riding horseback toward them. Rossiter had been found unconscious by the tracks, and with the train blasting through town, heading fast toward a track that led nowhere, they thought a rescue might be in order.

They were right.

Jilly explained from on horseback, with Nick riding behind her. They had the two train employees riding, too, heading for the doctor and jail.

As they reached town, Michelle, Zane, and a band of US Marshals came galloping into town to save the day. They reported a lot of disgruntled passengers would be arriving on foot from down the track within the hour.

Marshal Irving also broke the news that Edgar Beaumont's

body had been found in the San Francisco Bay. He had a bullet through his heart.

Jilly wondered if it could be true that their troubles were finally over. "Let's send a wire to Mama that we're unharmed, and Carlisle and Edgar are no longer going to be a problem. We'll tell her the details when we get there."

"There will be a train coming through later in the day," Michelle said. "There's a boardinghouse here in town. Until our ride arrives, let's try to get some rest."

The marshals dealt with the law, the prisoners, and the straggling passengers.

The foursome woke up the owner of the boardinghouse, who seemed disgruntled until they told him about the train, explosion, and arrests. Apparently, he was a man who liked to get the news more than he liked to sleep.

He had no one staying with him, and they were shown to two bedrooms. Michelle and Zane headed for one, while Jilly and Nick almost staggered, arm in arm, to the other.

They swung the door shut, and Nick pulled Jilly into his arms. Easy enough when she was pulling him into hers.

"It's over, isn't it?" Jilly asked. "Carlisle is dead? Edgar is dead?"

Nick rocked her. She didn't cry. Instead, she just felt peace. She felt the weight of her soul lifted and eased by God.

She felt love.

Together they slept, and it was the most peaceful night Jilly had known in far too long. But she hoped . . . no, she truly believed, it was the first of many.

EPILOGUE

JILLY ALWAYS CAME BACK to the mansion on Nob Hill. This time it was for dinner after a funeral. Edgar Beaumont was buried in a pauper's grave, far away from Liam Stiles. Mama didn't plan to buy the foul man a headstone.

They did have a short graveside service, conducted by Caleb. His sole focus was comforting Mama, helping her take the first steps to letting go of the guilt she bore for bringing Edgar into their family.

And now dinner on Nob Hill.

To begin a life without the plague of Edgar. Without the cruelty of Carlisle. Without any of the fears that haunted Jilly's dreams.

Mama presided over a solemn meal.

Afterward they retired to the sitting room. Mama said, "I don't know how to feel. I never wished him dead. I just wanted him out of my life."

Laura sat beside her, drawing her into a hug.

Caleb came to stand behind the settee and rested his hands on Mama's shoulders.

Zane sat in an overstuffed chair near the fireplace, which was unlit on the warm summer day, and pulled Michelle down onto his lap.

"Well, he's out now," Nick said quietly. He took Jilly by the hand and drew her to a matching chair facing Zane. He sat, but she dodged him just enough to sit on the arm of the chair.

"I've already informed Marshal Irving I intend to sue Carlisle's estate for the cost of all this misery," Jilly said. "The train company, of which he's part owner, intends to sue for the cost of the engine. He was a very rich man, and his estate is going to pay for all the damage he's done."

"And they found a long string of crimes Rossiter is wanted for, including setting off that bomb during the strike on our railroad spur." Michelle added, "Carlisle had kept a list, probably to keep Rossiter from betraying him. It's got enough evidence for Rossiter to hang."

"All the damage done by Carlisle's explosion on the train was to the engine and tender car. My bridge was unharmed," Jilly said. "It's still working perfectly. We'll be able to go back to building the train tracks tomorrow."

Nick slid an arm around her waist and yanked her down on his lap. "Let's wait a couple of days. My heart needs to quit pounding quite so hard."

She wrapped her arms around his neck and hugged him. "We'll wait."

"Which reminds me," Mama said, "I received a telegram from Old Tom before Edgar's service. The men are much better. No one's going to have any permanent harm from the poison. They can use a few more days to recover, too."

Nodding, Jilly hugged Nick harder. She noticed Michelle whispering to Zane, who smiled at her.

"I think we could all use some happy news," Michelle said. "We wanted to wait and give Laura a bit more time to be the focus of our attention, but we think it's right to share. We're expecting a baby."

A smile broke out on Mama's face. She stood and charged for Michelle to throw her arms around her. Michelle barely got to her feet in time to keep Mama from ending up in Zane's lap.

Laura was just a pace behind, with Jilly closing in fast.

NICK SMILED AT CALEB, then Zane.

The three of them eased around the room until they stood together. Nick noticed they were all smiling fondly at the group of women.

"Your turn, Nick," Zane said quietly.

"I can't wait." Then he frowned. "But maybe she should finish building the train track first."

"Babies come when God provides them." Caleb slapped him on the back. "And you'll find a way to slow Jilly down enough to take care of a baby. Although it might be that you'll take care of the baby while Jilly works."

Nick shrugged. "My ma had a new baby near every time I turned around. I can change a diaper and rock little ones to sleep. I'd be a good hand at caring for a baby."

The three of them studied the laughing, chattering women. The Stiles women.

The lumber baron's daughters and their brilliant mother.

Four women up to the task of taming a wild land and taming three men who didn't know they wanted to be tamed until it happened.

"I just hope I get a few years with our children before they get smarter than me," Nick said.

Zane and Caleb nodded, then started to laugh. Nick joined in, and the three of them entered the little knot of women. It wasn't a family of four. It was a family of seven and two on the way.

The lumber baron had built far more than a lumber dynasty. He'd built a family to be proud of, a family full of love, a family that was a model of devotion, and they were all together right here in the mansion on Nob Hill.

Read on for an excerpt
from *Forged in Love*,
the first of Mary Connealy's
next historical series, WYOMING SUNRISE,
available March 2023
wherever books are sold.

After being left for dead with no memory, Mariah Stover attempts to rebuild her life as she takes over her father's blacksmith business, but the townspeople meet her work with disdain. She and the new diner owner are drawn together by similar trials they face in the town, and when danger descends upon them, will they survive to build a life forged in love?

ONE

AUGUST 1870
PINE VALLEY, WYOMING
NEAR THE WIND RIVER MOUNTAINS

A BULLET SLAMMED into the side of the stagecoach carrying Mariah Stover, her pa, and her older brother.

"Robbers!" The driver's voice roared in the hot Wyoming summer as the crack of a whip lashed, driving the horses faster. "Everyone fight or die!"

Mariah heard the man riding shotgun on top of the stage land on his belly and open fire from the roof.

Bullets peppered the coach.

Mariah sat between Pa and Theo, facing the horses. Pa, a Civil War veteran, snapped his Spencer repeating rifle into his hand and fired out the window in a steady, rolling blast.

Theo threw himself to the opposite seat, occupied by two men who looked terrified. He aimed, fired, and fired again with his Colt pistol. Pa's rifle echoed the pistol in a steady volley of gunfire.

Mariah dug for the pistol in her satchel and checked the load. She looked out the window to her right. No one there.

Her pa and brother were tough men used to Western ways, who knew civilization was often left behind at the town's edge.

You just had to hope the uncivilized wouldn't follow you right into town.

You protected yourself, or you died. The stagecoach driver had it right.

Pa fired out his window, and Theo used the window beside the two others. Both men looked more city than country, and if either of them had a weapon, he didn't produce it. They just slid aside for Theo.

Mariah had a six-shooter. When Pa paused from firing his Spencer, the one he'd gotten in the war when he'd been a sharpshooter, Mariah shouted, "Lean forward while you reload."

Pa did so without looking or speaking, focusing completely on his rifle and trusting her to be tough, competent, and ready.

Mariah watched out the window and saw four men riding ever closer, blasting away. One of them went down, likely from the gunfire of the man on the roof.

She aimed and fired, aimed and fired, and kept going, trying to get the most out of her flying lead.

They were miles from town. No way to get help before these gunmen finished their fight, died trying, or were driven off.

"Get back," Pa hollered.

Mariah needed to reload anyway, so she gave way to Pa's superior marksmanship.

A cry from overhead ended the gunfire from the shotgun rider. Mariah saw him plummet from the top of the stage. As the three remaining outlaws rode past him, two of them fired into his body.

Pa growled in disgust at the vicious killers. He opened fire again. Mariah had her gun ready to go when she saw someone coming up beside the window on her side. She whipped her head around in time to see the rider empty his pistol into the city boys until they were riddled with bullets.

Her hair came loose from its knot on the back of her head and blinded her for just a moment as she cried out in horror. Then she glared at the skinny blond man. An ugly scar cut across his left cheek and through both his upper and lower lips. She pressed her body against the door and leveled her gun just as she heard a snap from under the belly of the stagecoach. An axle giving way.

She opened fire on the gunman as the stage skidded sideways. Crimson bloomed on his left arm. He brought his gun up with a wicked smile that revealed one of his front teeth was missing right in line with the scar. Their eyes met. He aimed.

The stagecoach tilted wickedly toward Mariah's side and slammed into a boulder alongside the road. The gunman fell back to avoid the boulder. The stage hit so hard the door flung open, and Mariah fell out. She felt the weight of the stage smother her.

More guns fired. Pa's Spencer fell silent, then Theo's Colt stopped blasting.

A bullet hit her in the side. White fire bloomed in her belly as the stagecoach settled hard on her.

The world went dark.

MARIAH'S EYES FLICKERED OPEN from where she was caged by . . . by something. Voices sounded from outside. She tried to cry out for help, but the weight on her chest was so heavy she couldn't draw a breath to manage it.

"They're all dead—just like always."

"What about the woman?" Whoever said that sounded on edge. "First woman we've ever killed. I don't like it. And the Stovers. What were they doing on this stage?"

"Like it or not, she's dead. Crushed under the stage, and I got a bullet in her just to be sure."

Mariah stopped trying to call for help.

"I'll get the strongbox."

A bullet blast made her flinch, which hurt everywhere.

A third voice asked, "Is there a good haul?"

"No, only a couple hundred. When we stripped the bodies, we got a couple hundred more."

"I thought this stage had a payroll on it for Fort Bridger?"

"We got bad information, or they pulled a switch, sent the money by another route."

"Maybe they know there's a leak. Maybe he needs to die. I don't like talking outside our group."

"He don't know why I was asking. He don't know nothin'."

"He'll put it together when he hears about this robbery."

"The horses broke the traces and got away, too. We're too

close to town. We've gotta clear out. When those horses go storming into town, a rescue party will come a-running."

"You sure everyone's dead?"

"You helped kill them, same as me."

"The Stovers were good folks. This is a bad business."

The stage was pressed to Mariah's face so she saw the dark wood and nothing else. She couldn't move her arms or legs, could barely draw a breath. Her head was pinned and aching. The pain was dizzying, and it came from every part of her.

Her belly was the worst, but her chest felt like it'd been smashed out of shape. Her vision blurred as she fought for each shallow breath. Her whole body was crushed.

Finally, she heard horses galloping back the way the stagecoach had come.

As much as those men terrified her, being left alone was almost worse. Tears slid from the corners of her eyes as she thought of Pa and Theo.

Thought how it felt like she was already in a coffin.

CLINT ROBERTS WAS LOITERING outside his diner, hoping to catch Mariah's attention, when he saw the stagecoach team charge into town. The stage he'd been watching for wasn't behind it. The thundering hooves and wildly out-of-control speed told of panicked horses. He could think nothing but the worst. "Sheriff, get out here!"

Clint sprinted for his horse, penned up in the corral behind the blacksmith shop. He'd already lost one family. It would kill him to lose another one. The Stovers certainly didn't count him as family, but he'd begun to count them.

He didn't ride in from his homestead every day—it was an easy walk. But today he'd hoped Mariah and her family would be back, and he'd wanted an excuse to stop in, get his horse, and say hello.

The sheriff burst out of the jailhouse, saw the stage horses, and raced for his own mount tied to the hitching post. Willie Minton, the town deputy, was only a pace behind. Other men were coming, too. They all knew the stage was in trouble. And the trouble might be ugly.

Clint was galloping before he reached the edge of town. The stage had been late, so he hoped that meant they'd been close to town.

Mariah. Mariah. Please, God, let her be all right.

He'd been waiting until he felt established before he approached her, or, better to admit, before he approached her flinty-eyed father. Maybe even better to admit, he'd been waiting until his heart healed enough to risk sharing it with someone again. As he galloped up the trail, he was sick to think he'd left it until too late.

Had he failed Mariah just as he'd failed his family?

TWO

MARIAH WASN'T SURE if she'd passed out or was just so dazed and under so much pressure from the stage that time meant little to her. She startled when she heard a voice.

"That's John and Theo." A voice she knew well.

"It's got to be the Deadeye Gang." Another familiar voice. Sheriff Joe Mast. A man she trusted. She tried to cry out, but she barely managed a wheeze. No one heard.

"Everyone's dead. Most robbers wear masks when they hold up a stage, take everything of value, and ride off without killing anyone," the sheriff went on, sounding furious and grief stricken. "John and Theo were tough men. If they couldn't hold off those men with Sculler on the roof fighting, no one can. The stage line should have outriders."

"They did for a while, but no one's struck around here for a year." Mariah recognized Willy Minton's voice. "We thought they'd moved on. Who ever heard of outlaws taking a year between robberies?"

"Where's Mariah?" That first voice again. Clint Roberts,

who owned the only diner in town. But he wouldn't normally ride with the sheriff. "I know Mariah rode out with her father. They were going to a funeral down in Laramie."

There were sounds of movement. Men striding all around.

"You don't think they'd take her, do you?" the sheriff asked.

Mariah wheezed. It was the only noise she could make, and it sounded about like a gust of wind.

"They've never done such a thing before," Deputy Minton said. "But have they ever killed a woman before?"

"Not too many women out here." The sheriff strode off to Mariah's left. "I've never heard of a woman being on a stage that got robbed by this bunch."

"Have they ever found such a beautiful woman as Mariah?" Clint thought she was beautiful. Not many did, as she worked alongside her pa and brother in the blacksmith shop and tended toward trousers, bulky leather aprons, and soot.

"Look down here," Clint's voice sharpened. "That's a corner of her skirt."

Footsteps pounded toward her. She wheezed again. This time, with them close and paying attention, it was enough.

"She's still alive," Clint said. "Sheriff, hitch the horses to the stage so we can lift it. I'll only need a few inches. Just enough to drag her out."

He crouched low and looked under the stage while there were more sounds of activity. "Mariah, we'll get this off you and get you to the doctor. Hang on."

Hang on? She didn't have much else to do.

She wanted to ask about Pa and Theo, but she knew enough and couldn't get a word out in any case.

CLINT DREW HER OUT, his hands under her arms. Once Mariah was clear of the stage, he shouted to the men riding with him, "I've got her."

The stage dropped back to the ground with a crack.

He knelt beside her, checking for broken bones.

"You're bleeding." He was scared to death of what harm had been done.

"I hurt all over."

"I'm taking you to town." He slid his arms under her and lifted, knowing it hurt. Hating it.

The sheriff was at his side.

"I'll get her to the doctor," Clint said.

"Go on. We'll be along when we're able." The sheriff gave Mariah a worried look and didn't mention bringing in the bodies.

The bodies. Mariah's family. Clint wanted to blame himself for that, too. He knew this trail was dangerous. The stagecoach robberies had seemed to stop, but he could have ridden along. He could have gone out to meet the stage. One more gun. The sound of an incoming rider. It might've been enough to save everyone.

With the sheriff's help, Clint swung up onto his horse and kicked the little black mustang into a gallop. He didn't have the will to go slowly, even if it spared Mariah pain. She would hurt whether he went slow or fast.

He looked down to apologize and realized she had fainted. Kicking the horse to go faster, he hoped it was only a faint.

Please, God. Please let her be all right.

DOC PRESTON TOOK ONE LOOK and went into action. "Get her in the back."

"Mariah." The doctor spoke quietly, grief already in his voice as Clint laid her down. "John and Theo were with her."

"Yes, both dead. Mariah was pinned under the stage and left for dead. Heaven knows what injuries she has from the weight of the stage."

The doctor focused on the worst bleeding. He got a wicked knife out and slit the front of her dress to reveal an ugly bullet furrow cutting along her belly just below her navel.

The doctor took a pad of bandages and pressed them to Mariah's stomach. "Hold this down hard while I get a needle and thread."

As the two of them worked together, Clint told all he knew about the stage. They'd been at it awhile when Nell came charging in, with eyes only for Mariah. "Let me help."

Sheriff Mast was a few minutes behind. He looked from Mariah to the doctor to Nell and, finally, to Clint. Gravely, he said, "I need to be alone with the doctor for a few minutes. Doc, can you spare these two?"

"Uh, well, yes."

"I'm not leaving her." Nell set her jaw as firm as granite.

"Neither am I," Clint said.

"Um . . . Nell, I guess you can stay. But, Clint, please go on out. Let us talk in private. It's a matter of the crime. I'm not ready to talk to you about it yet."

Clint glared at the sheriff, and for a minute, he wrestled with leaving. He wanted to tell the sheriff he wasn't man enough to make him leave, but something in the sheriff's expression convinced him this wasn't a request made lightly.

Clint jerked his chin down in a nod. "I left things undone at Le Grand. I'll be right across the street."

He stalked out. Leaving her felt like tearing his own skin.

THE SHERIFF STEPPED INTO THE KITCHEN of Le Grand as Clint hung up the last of his pots.

Clint had left the back door unlocked, hoping he'd get news about Mariah and wanting to make it easy for anyone to get to him.

What he saw in Sheriff Mast's eyes twisted his gut. "What's wrong?"

The sheriff lifted both his hands as if to stop Clint from speaking. Or to push away the words that had to be spoken.

"I'm sorry, Clint." The sheriff stared at the floor, unable, it seemed, to meet Clint's eyes. "Mariah didn't make it."

Sheriff Mast turned his back to face the door connecting the kitchen to the dining room. Clint thought he was leaving, and he leapt forward to grab the man's arm.

But the sheriff wasn't going anywhere. He just stood and stared at the floor.

"She wasn't that bad. What happened?"

"Doc thinks maybe a broken rib punctured her lung or her heart. Maybe a head injury. He isn't sure."

"No." Clint pushed past the sheriff and ran for the doctor's office.

"Clint, wait! No, come back here."

But Clint ran on, sprinting through his dining room and out onto the street.

Mariah. Mariah. Please, God. It can't be.

As he ran, he saw the undertaker, Jim Burke, outside the mortuary, building a box. He had a big stack of wood for all the coffins he needed to make.

Including Mariah's. No. No. No.

He was vaguely aware of children playing in the school-yard and Pete Wainwright, Pine Valley's mayor, standing outside his general store.

He slammed through the door to the doctor's office. Doc Preston came out of the back room and firmly clicked the door shut behind him.

"Clint, go on home. You can't be in here."

"She wasn't hurt that bad. Are . . . are you sure?" How could a doctor not be sure? Stupid question, but Clint had to ask. "Let me see her."

"No, Clint. Nell's with her, and she doesn't want any company. Go on."

"I will not *go on*," Clint shouted. "What happened?"

The sheriff rushed in.

Clint turned and saw through the open door that Jim Burke had quit building, and Pete Wainwright had taken the wooden steps down to the street.

"Come away, Clint," the sheriff said.

"I will not leave here without seeing her. I won't." His voice rose with every word. "I can't." He felt the burn of tears in his eyes. He refused to let them fall. He hadn't cried since his family had died with him nowhere near to help them.

Nell came out of the back room. She shut the door just as firmly as Doc Preston had.

She stood silently. Clint's chest heaved as he watched her.

Nell was Mariah's friend. If Nell said he could see her, then he'd be allowed in with no fuss.

"I'm going to see her. I'll knock you out of the way if I have to, Doc. Nell, you can't stop me."

She didn't respond. She looked at the sheriff, who'd come up beside Clint. Clint braced himself to fight.

"We have to tell him," Nell said quietly. "I didn't know you had feelings for her, Clint."

"Don't try and stop me, Nell." He repeated, ignoring her comment about his feelings.

The doctor looked at the sheriff.

"I'll have your word that what we tell you goes no further than this room," Sheriff Mast said with intensity. "Then you'll leave and mourn Mariah fully and publicly."

Clint swiped his wrist across his eyes. "What are you talking about?"

"Come into the back." Nell opened the door and let Clint in. To see Mariah unconscious but breathing steadily. Not dead.

Grief faded, replaced by elation. And fury. Clint boiled over. "What—"

Soft hands gripped his arm, drawing him back from the mad ramblings of his mind. He looked down into Nell's blue eyes. Kind eyes. Not the eyes of a woman who wanted to hurt someone.

"We're saying she died."

Clint waited for more, but Nell held his gaze as if allowing him to take in her single sentence for an extended time.

And then he knew why. "So the Deadeye Gang won't come and kill her."

"She's marked for death," Nell said. "We talked it over, and we think she should be declared dead. We'll bury an empty coffin, then we'll spirit her out of town and send her far away. I'm afraid that's her only hope."

He was going to lose her. But better to lose a living woman than a dead one.

One was a victory and the other terrible defeat. For Mariah, there was no choice. For Clint . . . he ended up with a broken heart either way.

"Thank you for telling me." Clint touched Nell's hand. He knew loss wasn't new to her. Nell was a widow who'd left her old life behind for the frontier.

"I didn't do it because you were causing a scene and possibly drawing a crowd who'd find out the truth," Nell said.

"Then why?"

"Because hiding her is going to be hard and dangerous. I offered to hide her in the rooms over my shop until she's well enough to travel. But if there's any suspicion that she's not dead, my place is the next place they'd search after her own house. But they might not think to hunt through the rooms over the diner."

Clint had lived above the diner for a while, but now he had cabin on his homestead. He could easily use those rooms to hide Mariah.

And stand guard much more discreetly. As he fully intended to do.

ABOUT *the* AUTHOR

Mary Connealy writes romantic comedies about cowboys. She's the author of the BROTHERS IN ARMS, BRIDES OF HOPE MOUNTAIN, HIGH SIERRA SWEETHEARTS, KINCAID BRIDES, TROUBLE IN TEXAS, WILD AT HEART, and CIMARRON LEGACY series, as well as several other acclaimed series. Mary has been nominated for a Christy Award, was a finalist for a RITA Award, and is a two-time winner of the Carol Award. She lives on a ranch in eastern Nebraska with her very own romantic cowboy hero. They have four grown daughters— Joslyn, married to Matt; Wendy; Shelly, married to Aaron; and Katy, married to Max—and six precious grandchildren. Learn more about Mary and her books at

maryconnealy.com
facebook.com/maryconnealy
seekerville.blogspot.com
petticoatsandpistols.com

Sign Up for Mary's Newsletter

Keep up to date with Mary's latest news on book releases and events by signing up for her email list at maryconnealy.com.

More from Mary Connealy

Michelle Stiles has stayed one step ahead of her stepfather and his devious plans by hiding out at Zane Hart's ranch. Zane has his own problems, having discovered a gold mine on his property that would risk a gold rush if he were to harvest it. But soon danger finds both of them, and they realize their troubles have only just begun.

Inventions of the Heart • THE LUMBER BARON'S DAUGHTERS #2

◊ BETHANYHOUSE

You May Also Like . . .

After learning their stepfather plans to marry them off, Laura Stiles and her sisters escape to find better matches and claim their father's lumber dynasty. Laura sees potential in the local minister of the poor town they settle in, but when secrets buried in his past and the land surface, it will take all they have to keep trouble at bay.

The Element of Love by Mary Connealy
THE LUMBER BARON'S DAUGHTERS #1
maryconnealy.com

Assigned by the Pinkertons to spy on a suspicious ranch owner, Molly Garner hires on as his housekeeper, closely followed by Wyatt Hunt, who refuses to let her risk it alone. But when danger arises, Wyatt must band together with his problematic brothers to face all the troubles of life and love that suddenly surround them.

Love on the Range by Mary Connealy
BROTHERS IN ARMS #3
maryconnealy.com

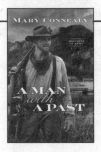

Falcon Hunt awakens without a past—or at least he doesn't recall one. When he makes a new start by claiming an inheritance, it cuts out frontierswoman Cheyenne from her ranch. Soon it's clear someone is gunning for him and his brothers, and as his affection for Cheyenne grows, he must piece together his past if they're to have any chance at a future.

A Man with a Past by Mary Connealy
BROTHERS IN ARMS #2
maryconnealy.com

⬧ BETHANYHOUSE

More from Bethany House

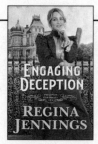

Olive Kentworth takes on an architect project with her male cousin posing as the builder and uses her job as a nanny to hide her involvement. Little does she know that her charges' father is famous architect and competitor Maxfield Scott. As the architectural one-upmanship heats up, will Olive and Maxfield miss out on building something for their future?

Engaging Deception by Regina Jennings
THE JOPLIN CHRONICLES #3
reginajennings.com

Ivy McQuaid has been saving up for a home of her own with the winnings from the cowhand competitions she sneaks into—but everything changes when a man from her past returns. Undercover Pinkerton agent Jericho Bliss is on the hunt for a war criminal, but when Ivy becomes involved in his dangerous life, his worst fears come true.

Falling for the Cowgirl by Jody Hedlund
COLORADO COWBOYS #4
jodyhedlund.com

Charlotte Durand sets out on an expedition in search of a skilled artisan who can repair a treasured chalice—but her hike becomes much more daunting when a treacherous snowstorm sets in. When Damien Levette finds Charlotte stranded, they must work together to survive the peril of the mountains against all odds.

A Daughter's Courage by Misty M. Beller
BRIDES OF LAURENT #3
mistymbeller.com

BETHANYHOUSE